Love You
Mucci
Grandma
Sylvia

Breeze...the Mermaid

by

Sylvia Fraley

with

Ronald B. Walkshorse

authorHOUSE®

AuthorHouse™
1663 Liberty Drive, Suite 200
Bloomington, IN 47403
www.authorhouse.com
Phone: 1-800-839-8640

© 2008 Sylvia Fraley. All rights reserved.

No part of this book may be reproduced, stored in a retrieval system, or transmitted by any means without the written permission of the author.

First published by AuthorHouse 7/22/2008

ISBN: 978-1-4343-7379-3 (sc)

Library of Congress Control Number: 2008902379

Printed in the United States of America
Bloomington, Indiana

This book is printed on acid-free paper.

Writing contributions, cover art and illustrations
by Ronald B. Walkshorse

Chapter 1

Morning finds Breeze, an unusually beautiful and adventurous young mermaid, washed up on the rocky shore by the cove she loved so much. Her mother, Oceana, and her father, Neptune, had been searching for her all night…and now, there she was, lying limp and looking lifeless among the rocks.

Oceana was beside herself with grief. Neptune was showing his usual grumbly "I told you so" attitude. Leaving Oceana in the water at the ocean's edge, he pulled himself over to where Breeze was. YES! She was still alive! What a relief! Carefully, Neptune pulled Breeze back into the water, dressed her wounded tail with a healing poultice, took her up in his strong arms and started swimming towards home…grumbling all the way. Oceana swam close behind adding more and more salt to the ocean with her tears. That's how the ocean got so salty—tears from sensitive sea creatures. It didn't take long before they were back in their cave home.

No sooner had they entered it than Oceana let out a loud squeal. Breeze opened her eyes slightly for just a few seconds, smiled at her mother and let out a little sigh…then closed her eyes and went into a deep sleep. Immediately, Oceana threw her arms around her and hugged her dearly. In anger, she turned toward Neptune. "YOU DID THIS…YOU WITH YOUR SECRET KNOWLEDGE ON HOW TO REPLACE OUR BEAUTIFUL TAILS WITH HUMAN LEGS!" She flipped her tail at him angrily, wrapping it around his waist. Shaking her finger at him she added, "YOU CAUSED THIS!"

Neptune had to agree. He had learned from the ancients just how to become human and had passed this along to his mischievous, daring daughter, so he had little to say. In his younger days, he too had been mischievous and adventurous. He had been on board pirate ships and fancy ships with people sitting all around eating and drinking. Yes! He had tasted of the excitement…and these were the kind of stories he had passed down to Breeze, explaining every detail to her as best as he could. So, Neptune just smiled, swished his tail around Oceana, and gave her a big kiss.

Thinking back to when Breeze was little…

Neptune had to laugh as he remembered the first time Breeze learned how to substitute legs for her beautiful tail. She was still really small. Actually it was right after one of his lessons on how to get people legs….The one where she said "I got it! I got it! I can do it!" Breeze just disappeared for the whole morning. He winked at Oceana as he went on…. "Here's how the story goes…." Neptune laughed again.

"I don't believe I've heard about this!" Oceana frowned. "Why didn't you tell me about this before? She was very young and could have been killed being away like that!"

"Breeze never told you about this?"

"NO! Why did she tell you and not me?"

"Guess I'm just easier to get along with." Neptune smirked. "Listen! Here's what happened. You know Breeze has always been fascinated about how the humans live and how it feels to walk on two legs.

"Yes! She's ALWAYS been that way. Still is! Don't know why either. It's such a beautiful place here in the ocean. It's so peaceful."

"She snuck away that day...." Neptune continued. "After one of those leg lessons I gave....Swam straight to that big, beautiful, cloud-like ship that always used to be in the harbor. Just happened THAT was the day that the cloud-ship floated out of the harbor. It didn't bother Breeze that it was moving."

Neptune, feeling proud that HE was the one she had told the story, to stretched to his full length, stuck out his chest, and smiled. "Breeze told me this story several times. She swam around the big, cloud-like ship a few times getting up the nerve to go up into it. Then she conjured up her land legs and climbed up the ladder that reached into the sea. No one was there so she wandered down the deck. Here's how the story goes...."

The owner of the cloud-ship and his lady came out on the deck to wait for their breakfast. The lady took one look at Breeze standing there with no clothes on and started screaming. The master of the cloud-ship shook his fist at Breeze and yelled, "WHO ARE YOU?

WHAT ARE YOU DOING ON MY YACHT?" He pushed his chair back so fast and so hard that it fell clattering on the deck, then he started running towards her. Still yelling, he continued, "WHERE ARE YOUR CLOTHES? HOW'D YOU GET ON HERE?"

All this yelling and the man running straight at Breeze scared her. She was still just a very young little mermaid. Not thinking clearly, she started running around the deck....ran screaming with that high-pitched voice of hers down the stairs and into the galley followed by the ship's owner...who was still yelling.

"HEY! LITTLE GIRL! COME BACK HERE! YOU KNOW YOU DON'T BELONG ON THIS SHIP! STOP HER! SOMEONE PLEASE STOP HER! STOP THAT NAKED LITTLE GIRL!"

Three chefs were in the galley at that time making breakfast. They were all so totally shocked by what they saw when Breeze came running into their kitchen that they started yelling. "HEY! STOP! YOU CAN'T COME IN HERE! THIS IS THE SHIP'S KITCHEN! YOU'RE NOT ALLOWED IN HERE!" Two of the chefs also began running after Breeze, trying to catch her.

"I DON'T KNOW WHO SHE IS!" yelled the flustered yacht owner, "but she's a stowaway. Probably ran away from her parents. We have to turn back to shore. I'm going to let one of you take her to the police station. We'll let the law handle this! The little brat belongs back with her folks. Just look at her!"

In her haste to get away Breeze bumped into a very large man wearing a big white hat. The flustered chef was doing his best to stay calm while he stood in front of a big black gas stove trying to cook. He was determined to finish what he was doing in spite of all that was going on. She caused him to spill breakfast all over the floor and down the front of his apron.

Two other men, also wearing big white hats, were running close behind Breeze trying hard to catch her. They were just about to reach out and grab her when the first man slipped on the 'breakfast' that was splattered all over the floor...onto the counter...in the burners of the stove and down the cupboard fronts. The other man reached out to catch himself and caused the whole stand full of pots and pans to come clattering down on top of them. There they both were sitting in the midst of all those pots and pans on the food that had just been spilt on the floor...shaking their fists and yelling angry, obscene words.

There was so much confusion that when Breeze quickly turned around she pushed the cook who had the food spilled all over him really hard...pushed him to the side, knocking him into the stove's gas burners, which caught his sleeve on fire. She managed to run right past him and the surprised man who had started chasing her when she first came on the ship...ran straight back up the stairs and to the railing. She shocked the man who was hot on her heels when she quickly turned around and came to an abrupt stop...looked right into his eyes...gave a great big smile...jumped over the railing and back into the sea. Immediately she conjured her tail back and watched all the people running here and there around the deck throwing all the floatable objects they could find into the ocean for her to grab onto.

Neptune gave a very small know-it-all type grin and did a flip in the water. "Don't really think she'll do THAT again."

"NO? You can never tell about that one!" Oceana looked at her sleeping daughter. "I sure would like to know what she got into this time. Her tail is really messed up. She's YOUR daughter! YOU filled her head with all the adventures YOU took. Now she's trying to be just like YOU. I would never even THINK of doing anything like that!"

"That's because YOUR mother and father were both soft, passive, uninteresting and non-adventurous and would live in the same cave all their life. Neither of them would have the courage to venture any farther than the food that they see in front of their face." Neptune stretched himself out and puffed himself up as big as he could. Then he continued.... "Why, take ME, for example. I'm a true SEA WARRIOR...have changed the course of whole fleets of ships...basked on uncharted tropic islands—"

Oceana cut his sentence short. "Never took me to any of those nice places."

"That's because you'd be scared."

"I would not!" she said, flipping her tail at him again....TRY ME! When Breeze gets better....You just TRY ME! I want to go somewhere exciting too!"

"OK...OK! But...don't say I didn't warn you!" With that, Neptune took her in his strong arms, pressed his lips against hers, and gave her soft, sexy kisses as they slowly glided down to the deep parts of the ocean... down to where they could be alone with their love.

It was several hours later that Oceana popped her head back into the cave to see how Breeze was doing. Breeze was still asleep. Now she was getting worried and started crying again.

"What's this? You crying again?" Neptune exclaimed as he popped his head up through the water. "I THOUGHT this water was getting saltier. See how you are, Oceana! I take you down for the love adventure of your life and you pay me back by filling this cave with your salty tears. What's the matter now?" Neptune grabbed Oceana and gave her a big hug. "Why...I'll just take you down there again....I'll just...."

"You don't understand!" Oceana whimpered. "She's still asleep. Just look at her, tail all bruised up like that and...and..." She looked at Neptune and started yelling. "INSTEAD OF BEING WORRIED ABOUT YOUR MISCHIEVOUS...NON-THINKING DAUGHTER... YOU'RE...YOU'RE BEING YOUR USUAL MALE SELF...AND THINKING ABOUT...WELL...YOUR SELFISH PLEASURES!" She flipped around and swam to the other side of the cave. "You...You're only thinking about...making more babies so I can't EVER do anything FUN!" With that Oceana smacked the water really hard several times with her tail, making a terrible, loud sound that echoed back and forth along the walls. Taking a deep breath to calm down a bit, she continued, "Remember the time you sent Breeze to get some pearls from those oysters so you could surprise me with them?"

"Ah...yes!" Neptune said as he flashed a big smile and put his arms around her again. "Oceana! My darling...I asked for those because I love you."

"Humph! Just look at all the trouble THAT caused. What did you say to her to make her do what she did?"

Chapter 2

Neptune went on to tell the story...
Early in the evening he found Breeze in one of her favorite places...on a big rock in a cute little cove watching a beautiful sunset. "Breeze, my sweet little fancy-finned daughter how would you like to do your big daddy a little favor? Be fun for you too."

Breeze took her eyes off the sunset and flipped her tail around to the other side of the rock. Looking up out of the corner of her eye, she flashed a sly grin. "What do you want me to do for you this time, my Father?"

"Oceana and I have been together for a long time. I just want to give her something special that she wouldn't get for herself. Would you go to where the oysters live and see if you can find a few pearls for her?"

That's all it took for Breeze to be gone. She flipped up her tail and dove into the ocean. "I'll just get my friend Galley to come along," she yelled back. Galley was her best friend, about the same age—half grown.

She went to where she knew her friend was…in the middle of a family of sea lions giving them a merry chase and causing trouble. When Galley heard about going to the oyster bed she thought it would be GREAT….So, first thing the next morning they were on their way.

The oyster bed was a couple hours' swim away in an area that was not really suited for mermaids….It was kind of a dull place with somewhat of a mushy, muddy bottom and no pretty things. On their way there the two mermaids found themselves nibbling on all the different kinds of seaweeds and even put a few cute little sea horses in their hair.

"These things are hard to open!" Galley said as she managed to get into her first oyster. Finding no pearl inside, she asked, "What are we supposed to do…Open them all? There are thousands of oysters here. I can only eat a few, and you can eat some too but…what if we go through these and find NO PEARLS?…Then what?"

"I don't know!" Breeze answered as she munched on an oyster. "I didn't think it would be this hard to find a pearl. Maybe these aren't the right kind of oysters."

"Is there another kind?" Galley asked. "I sure don't feel like doing THIS all day!"

"Me either!" exclaimed Breeze. "Tell you what! I know of a place where the people have lots of oysters… in cages. I think they keep them for pets or something. Maybe we should go there and see if THOSE oysters have pearls in them."

"Sounds like a good idea." Galley was totally disgusted with what they'd done so far that day and was open to almost any suggestion. "Is it very far?"

"No! Let's go!"

A couple hours later found them in the middle of lots of cages filled full of oysters. Breeze broke open the first cage she came to and started picking through the oysters. Opening one of them, she shouted. "HEY! THESE ARE JUST TOO SMALL! WE CAN'T DO ANYTHING WITH THESE!" She carelessly left the lid open and bumped against the cage, spilling its contents onto the ocean floor. She then swam over to the cages on the opposite side and announced, "I'll try some of these!"

After breaking open several cages and cracking open some of the oysters in them Galley shouted, "I don't think this is a good idea at all! THEY'RE ALL JUST TOO TINY!"

"THERE'S ANOTHER BUNCH OF CAGES WAY OVER THERE!" Breeze yelled. "Let's try some of them!"

It takes seven to eight years to make pearls in oysters, and Breeze just happened to come across the ones that were going to be harvested that day. She opened several cage doors and started pulling out oysters. The first one she cracked open had a big pearl in it. She pulled it out of the oyster and held it high in the air, shouting out with delight, "LOOKIE! LOOKIE, OVER HERE! LOOKIE WHAT I FOUND! COME OVER HERE, GALLEY!"

The two of them quickly broke open all the cages and were in the middle of opening more oysters. "WOW!" screamed Breeze. "HERE THEY ARE! ALL OF THESE HAVE GREAT BIG PEARLS IN THEM!" She held out her hand to show Galley.

"YEAH!" Galley yelled back. "LOOK WHAT I'VE FOUND!"

"HEY…YOU THERE! STOP! THIEF! WHAT DO YOU THINK YOU'RE DOING? GET OUT OF THERE! STOP WHERE YOU ARE! STOP WHAT YOU'RE DOING! STOP RIGHT NOW!" Several men came running out of the little building and down the wooden walk towards Breeze and Galley, yelling, "GET OUT OF THERE! HEY, BILL! GRAB YOUR GUN AND GET OUT HERE…FAST!" Just then a human came running out of the building carrying a big black stick. The human doing the yelling snatched it out of his hand and yelled, "GIMME THAT GUN! I'LL FIX 'UM! FIX 'UM GOOD!"

Breeze looked at Galley, and Galley looked at Breeze. Immediately they slunk under the water and were gone, leaving dozens of cages overturned. Most of the oysters were dumped on the ocean floor and, in their haste to get away from the screaming, the pearls they had worked so hard for were also dumped into the sea.

"Did you save any of those pearls?" Galley asked.

"NO! I was too scared!" answered Breeze. "What do we do now? My father has sent me to do one simple thing…gathering a few pearls…and I can't even do that!" Then Breeze had another idea. "Hey, Galley! You know…I can change my tail for legs….So…come with me to where the people go. I saw pearls there! Lots of them! I'll just reach in and grab them."

"Let's GO then!" Galley was all excited. "Maybe there'll even be enough that so I could have some."

"Yeah! Of course you can have some." Breeze gave out a cheerful little laugh. "Just come on….Follow me… I'll show you!"

Late afternoon found the two of them in front of a stone wall looking at people walking in and out of fancy boxes. There they were, right in front of their eyes….Just what Breeze had been talking about….Lots of pretty, shiny, differently colored stones and PEARLS sitting right there in the open for everyone to see and take.

"LOOK!" Breeze was excited. "This ought to be a lot easier than cracking open those silly oyster shells."

"Yeah!" Galley agreed. "And a LOT better than being chased and yelled at….But…how are you going to get them? They're way up there on land and we're down here in the water."

Breeze glanced at Galley, gave her a smile and said, "Don't you remember? I know how to change my tail into legs like those people have. I'll just walk up there and GET those pearls…and a lot of other pretty things too!"

"Well! Hey… Breeze! If YOU can get legs…why can't I get legs, too? Then we'll both be able to have some fun."

"I can't teach you that!" Breeze frowned. "At least I don't THINK I can. Maybe we'll try later when we're not doing this."

"OH, OK! Later is OK. I'm kind of scared to do that anyway. I'll wait here. You can throw the stuff down to me, and I'll catch it all for you."

Breeze conjured up her land legs and began climbing the ladder up to where the people were. She pulled herself up onto dry land and was about to walk over to where the pearls were when...

All the humans seemed to stop what they were doing. Many of them started screaming and pointing their fingers. Some of the big humans were pulling the little humans into those funny looking boxes they stayed in. All the humans seemed to be rushing to get away from Breeze.

Breeze stood up, looked around, and had quickly began walking toward where the pearls were when she heard yelling.

"STOP! YOU THERE! STOP! YOU CAN'T JUST WALK AROUND HERE WITHOUT ANY CLOTHES ON! WHAT'S THE MATTER WITH YOU?" Several people with dark clothes on starting running towards her.

Breeze ran to where the pearls were, reached out to grab them, and hit something with her hand. "OOOH! OW!" she yelled. Realizing she couldn't reach in and just grab what she wanted, she quickly turned around, ran through the people with the dark clothes and jumped back into the ocean.

"What happened?" Galley asked.

Gaining her pretty tail as she jumped back into the water, Breeze answered, "This was WORSE than either of the other places we've been. We need to get away from here!"

Galley agreed. "OK! Now what? We still don't have any pearls!"

"I don't know!" Breeze was upset. She knew Neptune would be upset and angry that she had not carried out his wishes, and she really didn't want to go back there and tell him. After thinking about it for a while, she suggested they head over to the sunken ship and just enjoy the rest of the day there.

Galley was all for that. "GREAT!" She exclaimed. "I thought all this was going to be FUN! NOTHING has been fun today! I'm almost sorry I came with you, but the ship should make up for it. Maybe you could teach me to get legs...like you do."

"Really beautiful here!" Breeze said as she stopped to rest on some rocks. "Did you see those huge clams we just swam over? Wonder if THEY have any pearls in them."

"Silly!" Galley smirked. "Everyone KNOWS pearls only come from oysters or something like that. I'm not sure something that huge would have a pearl.....But let's go see anyway!"

Turning back, they saw that a huge fish had just been caught in one of the big clams. "I'm not dealing with this!" exclaimed Galley. "We could get killed trying to get something out of one of those! We could get eaten!"

"I know! I know! We have to use our heads. Let's watch them for a while and see just how they act. Maybe we can figure out a way to look inside them."

There were several of the giant clams sitting around with their shells gaping wide open...just waiting to catch something. The mermaids swam over them again, making sure they didn't get too close, then sat down on a rock that was jutting out over the area and watched.

"There's NO WAY we can do this!" Galley complained. "I think I'll just go home! YOU can do this all by yourself!"

Not wanting to be alone during this, Breeze pleaded with Galley to please stay. She thought for a minute then said, "What if something happens to me doing this? No one will know! You don't have to do anything, Galley.... Just watch...and...maybe...afterwards, I'll try to teach you how to get legs."

That did it. "OK!" Galley said.

What the two inquisitive mermaids didn't know was....These giant clams were guardians of very special pearls. Breeze and Galley were treading on a sacred area that had been set aside by Neptune, Breeze's father.... And these clams were the protectors of very special giant pearls. Not only that but the pearls were part of the treasures of Atlantis, and the giant clams were placed in that specific area solely for the purpose of guarding those treasures.

"I think I know what we can do." Breeze smiled as she came up with a suggestion. "I've noticed that the clam's shells close around anything and everything that touches them. This leaves no way to look inside or get inside without being trapped. You CAN help me here, Galley. We're going to the pirate ship and bring back something really big...something real strong that will hold those clams open so we can see inside. We'll just drop them in there from above."

"OH, WHAT A NEAT IDEA!" Galley exclaimed. "I CAN'T WAIT! LET'S GO!"

"OK! OK! Just a minute! I want to watch just a little longer to make sure this'll work."

They sat there on the rocks till the light started to fade from day to night, munching on seaweed and other goodies they'd picked along the way. Finally when there was almost no light left Breeze said, "Think it would be a good idea if we just went to the pirate ship now... spend the night there and come back here first thing in the morning when we can see better. We can search the ship at first light and see what we can find that would be strong enough to prop those shells open."

"OK! Sounds good!" Galley agreed. "I'm getting kind of tired anyway. It's been a long, hard day."

The two of them swam off towards the ship. When they finally did arrive there it was very dark, so they just went to sleep for the night.

Next morning they found neat stuff—or so they thought—to prop the clams open with. After picking up several sticks that had white, seaweed-like stuff wrapped around them, they swam off to the clams.

Galley was the first to drop one of the sticks into the clam. She dropped it long-ways instead of crossways, and the clam just closed over it and spit it out.

Breeze was more careful. She dropped hers just the right way, but the clam was stronger then the stick and it broke into lots of little pieces. "This is not going to work!" exclaimed Breeze. "We have to go back to the ship. There HAS to be something stronger there that we can use."

Back to the ship they went. They swam over to where there were several big, long, black rocks with holes running down the middle of them. It took a lot of effort but they finally managed to get two of them off what they were sitting on. Cradling them in their arms, they headed back towards the giant clams.

This time Breeze was the first to drop her long rock. It landed just perfectly. The clam tried to close its shell but the rock managed to keep it propped open. Breeze swam down close and looked inside. There, to her surprise was the biggest, most beautiful pearl she'd ever seen. It was as big as her head. "WE'VE GOT TO GET THIS OUT!" Breeze shouted. "GOT ANY IDEAS?"

Galley was hovering above the clam with her mouth open, still holding her big, long rock. "Just a minute!" she said. "Let me drop mine into this clam....See what's in here." Sure enough, there was another pearl of equal size and beauty. "OH, MY! WE'VE JUST GOT TO GET THESE!" she yelled.

There was nothing in that ocean that would reach into the clam's shells and bring the pearls out. Neither girl dared to put her hands in there for fear the shell would close and she would be stuck in there. The only thing to do was to leave the giant clams as they were with their shells propped open and go back to the pirate ship to see what else they could find.

"How about this?" Galley shouted, holding up a long stick with a hook on the end.

"That's GREAT!" Breeze said, all excited. "Are there any more of these, or is that the only one?"

"Yes! There are lots of these....Right over here!" Galley showed her where they were.

"Let's get a couple more of those long black rocks, too, so we can prop more clams open."

"OK!"

Off they went with their arms full...back to where the clams were. Each mermaid cradled one long black rock with a hole running through it in her arms and several long sticks with a hook at the end. The sticks were tightly clenched in their hands. Each also picked out another giant clam to drop their long stone into, and soon there were four clams sitting there with their shells spread wide open.

Breeze was the first to try the hook stick. It worked really well. Out rolled the biggest, most beautiful pearl she'd ever seen. "WOW! LOOK AT THIS, GALLEY! HOW MANY OF THESE DO YOU THINK WE CAN CARRY BACK?"

"I don't know! Maybe two…one in each arm. They're too big! I can't believe they're so big! Didn't know pearls could grow so big."

"Neither did I"

They managed to get all four pearls out of the clams. Of course, they couldn't, nor did they want to, take the long black stones out of the clams. So…the clams were left with their shells gaping wide open.

With each arm full of a huge pearl, the mermaids decided to head for home. They chose to swim through a different area than they'd ever been before just to have a change in scenery. Still filled with the excitement of their pearl adventure, they couldn't stop talking about how they had faced danger and conquered the clams.

All of a sudden something unusual caught their eyes and they stopped swimming abruptly. Both mermaids did a double take, and their mouths hung wide open. There…up against a huge rock…half hidden in the seaweed was the largest, most magnificent giant clam they'd ever seen…or even ever heard about. Approaching closer, they noticed the clam's tongue was sticking out. Resting on that tongue was the most prized pearl of all. It was the size of all the other pearls put together. There it sat! On the tongue of that big, overgrown giant of a clam…the most gorgeous pearl of them all…a perfectly shaped, deep-toned BLACK PEARL!

Chapter 3

"OH...MY...YES! Galley, I've just got to get this for my father. He'll be so pleased." She approached closer to the giant clam. "We can hide the pearls we already have over here." She chose a spot under a layer of rock that looked like it was protected. "Let's go back to the ship and get some more long black stones."

"OK!" Galley answered excitedly. The ship wasn't that far back, and she loved all the adventure. "I'd like to take a longer look at that ship too...if it's OK with you. I just love sunken ships. They're full of so much interesting stuff!"

While Galley was busy playing with the toys on the ship, Breeze was busy taking apart the biggest long black rock she could find. After all, THIS was a REALLY HUGE CLAM. "Want to help me with this?" Breeze asked. "This rock is really large. I'm having a hard time getting it loose."

Galley helped her but had little interest in doing it. As soon as the long rock was free, she went swimming back through the ship. This was a bit irritating to Breeze. She was ready to go. Now she had to wait for Galley. She waited for a long time.

"OK!" Galley announced. "I'm back! I'm ready to go now! Let's get that big old clam propped open." She made no attempt to help Breeze carry the big, long, black rock nor did she make an attempt to keep up with Breeze.

Breeze soon noticed she was lagging way behind. Turning her head to see why, she asked. "What's keeping you, Galley? Why are you being so slow? Aren't you excited about what we found?"

"Well, yes!" came the reply, but there was no excitement in Galley's voice. Just before reaching the giant clam Galley stopped for a second and put something down on the ocean floor…then went to help Breeze with the big rock.

They took great care to place the long rock just so, to make sure it kept the clam's mouth open. To their surprise…the clam was just too big and too strong. The mermaids hovered above it in the water as they watched the huge, strong giant clam shell slam together hard against the long rock. It slammed shut with such an awesome force that it bent the rock into an unrecognizable shape, and then spat it out.

"THIS IS UNREAL!" exclaimed Galley. "We can't do this one! It's too big for us!"

Changing the subject, Breeze squinted her eyes and looked questioningly at Galley. "What was that thing you took from the ship? I saw something in your hand!"

"Oh...Nothing!" Galley slowly swam over toward the prize she'd found. Picking it up off the ocean floor, she held it close, not wanting Breeze to see or take it.

"Let me see that!"

"NO! I found this, and it's mine!"

Breeze chased Galley around the area several times trying to get a closer glimpse. Round and round they swam, mostly over the top of where the giant clam lay with its tongue stuck out.

The clam, now secure in the thought that they couldn't take its prize, watched all that was taking place and just shrugged it off. After a few minutes the clam began to be tired of all the commotion and closed its eyes to get back to the nap that had so rudely been interrupted earlier by the two arguing mermaids. Its tongue rolled in and out a few times showing off the big black pearl...purposely tempting the mermaids.

Finally, Breeze caught Galley. She was able to get her hands on the object Galley was clutching so close. "LET ME SEE THAT!" she yelled.

"NO!" Galley yelled back, trying to twist away.

Breeze tried hard to pull the object away from her. The object was very beautiful and shiny...reflecting the rays of the sunshine that were filtering through the salt water from above. It was brilliant silver in color, and there was a strange symbol etched in its surface...the symbol 'P'. Galley was not about to let go without a fight. "THIS IS MINE! I FOUND IT! AND I'LL KEEP IT!" she yelled.

The two mermaids became angrier and angrier, struggling to posses the unusual shiny silver ball. The yelling was uncomfortable to the clam. He kept his eyes closed hoping it would all just go away….But it didn't.

"GIMME IT!" Breeze yelled.

"NO…IT'S MINE…I FOUND IT.…I…I FOUND THIS, AND IT'S MINE!"

"OH, YEAH!" Breeze screamed. "YOU WOULDN'T EVEN BE HERE IF IT WEREN'T FOR ME! GIMME THAT!" Breeze was getting louder and louder and angrier and angrier.

Both mermaids had lost their tempers. They also lost sight of the real reason they were there. The pulling and tugging and yelling continued for some time.

The giant clam was beginning to really get upset. They were NOT leaving. They were getting louder and louder and churning up the water, which made his nap impossible.

All of a sudden, their struggles were stopped… abruptly! The beautiful silver ball they both had wanted so badly broke apart, and they were each holding a piece of it. They glared at each other with their mouths open.

"OH! OH, NO! NOW LOOK, BREEZE! JUST LOOK WHAT YOU'VE DONE!" Galley was holding the big part that now had dark colored stuff oozing out of it. She couldn't stand it that her prize was broken with its contents spilling out.

Breeze was holding the smaller part of the ball. She immediately realized it was some sort of a container… that the twisting and turning for possession of the pretty ball has caused it to open. She was angry that Galley blamed her for breaking it. "IF YOU WEREN'T TRYING TO STEAL THIS…IF YOU WEREN'T

TRYING KEEP IT ALL TO YOURSELF...THIS WOULD NOT HAVE HAPPENED! I THINK IT'S YOUR FAULT, GALLEY! WE'RE SUPPOSE TO SHARE...REMEMBER?"

Both mermaids were stunned and surprised that the ball would come apart so easily. They watched silently as dark, powdery stuff oozed out slowly from the larger piece of the ball that Galley was still holding. The stuff was scattering widely as it filtered its way through the water, and the container was emptying fast. It wasn't long before almost all of its entire contents had fallen down upon and into the open mouth of the giant clam. The two mermaids forgot their arguing and looked at each other for a second, each silently wondering what that strange stuff was. They swam down closer to the clam hoping to find some of the powdery stuff on the ocean floor so they could examine it.

They swam too close! Soon, they found they had an unusual burning taste in their mouth...almost as if it were hot lava from one of the volcanoes nearby. Their eyes started burning too...kind of like the time they weren't looking where they were going and swam right through a bunch of jellyfish. Next, their noses started burning, and they began to sneeze. They sneezed...and they sneezed. They sneezed so hard that bubbles came out of their noses. Now they were scared. Really scared! Nothing like this had ever happened to them before.

All of a sudden, a horrible, loud sound came from deep inside the giant clam...like the rumbling of an erupting volcano. "AAAAAHHHHH...CHOOOOOOOO!" A giant bubble rose from the monster-sized clam, engulfing them both. For a short time, they were tossed to and fro…spinning around and around and upside down. This made them dizzy and sort of seasick. As the bubble burst; they tried to stabilize themselves by grabbing onto one another.

Finally catching their balance, the two trembling mermaids looked down at the still sneezing clam and found the sand on the ocean floor was even being churned up by its sneezes. Their eyes and nose were slowly getting back to normal. They stayed right where they were for the moment, hovering above the clam till the water calmed down and the sand settled.

To their delight, they noticed the giant clam had sneezed so hard it blew the huge black pearl a good distance away. The clam's foot was reaching out to try and retrieve it but the mermaids were faster. They swiftly swam down to where the beautiful black pearl rested.

"OH…NO, YOU DON'T!" yelled Breeze. "THIS PRIZE IS MINE!" She reached down to pick it up, but it was too heavy….Even in the water…the black pearl was just too heavy.

Galley was right there to help. "How are we going to get THIS home?" she asked.

"I don't know," Breeze said as she looked up. "I don't want to leave those other pearls here either. We found them, and we need to take them all home."

"Well! Just how do you think we're going to get ALL of these back?" Galley asked. "The two of us are having a hard time trying to lift this one."

"I'm not leaving any of these!" Breeze announced, flipping her tail. Then she muttered. "I'm taking ALL of these! There's just got to be a way."

"Look behind you, Breeze! That clam is making its way over here. Better think of something! FAST!"

Breeze swam behind the big black pearl and started rolling it in the sand. She rolled it to where the other pearls were. "I'm going back to the ship! Watch the pearls! Maybe there'll be something there that will help."

"You've got to be kidding!" Galley smirked. "There's nothing in that ship that would help you! I know! I've been through the whole ship!"

"Are YOU SURE? Oh! Then I...I don't know! I just don't KNOW!" Breeze started to cry. "I just have to get these to my father." She swam above the scene and looked down again. The giant clam had changed directions and was on its way towards ALL the pearls. "GALLEY!" she screamed. "YOU'VE JUST GOT TO HELP ME!"

"OK! OK!" Galley slowly swam toward the pearls with a big frown on her face. She knew they couldn't carry all those pearls and was no longer happy about being involved in her friend's escapades. "JUST WHAT DO YOU WANT ME TO DO?"

Breeze was beginning to get angry with Galley's attitude again. She was almost ready to say something to her that she shouldn't when a frisky dolphin dove down in front of them...almost hitting her tail. All of a sudden several more dolphins showed up. They had become curious about what was going on and wanted to join in the fun. Breeze was quick to take advantage of the situation. Picking up one of the white pearls, she tossed it in front of the first dolphin. Of course, the dolphin thought she was playing and took off with the pearl. One after the other Galley and Breeze tossed the white pearls up, and the dolphins pushed them through the water with their noses. The last dolphin spied the big black pearl that was still sitting there all by itself. With a quick sweep of its nose, the huge pearl was taken along with the others.

In order to make sure they went in the right direction, Breeze swam ahead, grabbed the pearl off the nose of the first dolphin, and swam off with it…in the direction of Neptune and home. She and Galley kept stealing the pearls from those dolphins until they were almost home. Then, one by one they snatched all the white pearls, placed them together in the sand, and managed to make the other dolphin drop the huge black one right on top of them.

All this 'fun' had taken several hours. All the pearls were now safe and close to home. With big smiles on their faces, Breeze and Galley went to get Neptune. They led him to where the treasured pearls were… presented him with the huge white pearls and bragged about how they got them. Then they showed him the big, beautiful, black one. They just knew he would be so pleased.

Neptune, however, was not pleased. He was furious! Slapping his tail on the ocean bottom, he yelled, "DO YOU KNOW WHAT YOU TWO HAVE JUST DONE?" His eyes glared at them as if they were on fire. Then he continued, "THOSE ARE SPECIAL TREASURES…NOT TO BE DISTURBED! TREASURES FROM ATLANTIS!" His angry words got louder than ever. "YOU HAVE TO PUT THEM BACK! RIGHT NOW…RIGHT BACK WHERE YOU

FOUND THEM! JUST EXACTLY LIKE THE WAY YOU FOUND THEM!" Neptune stopped yelling for a minute. With a questioning look, his eyes glared first at his daughter then at Galley. In a very calm voice, he asked, "How did you two ever manage to get these pearls away from those giant clams...especially that big black one? THAT clam was the biggest and toughest of them all?"

With a slight grin on her face and meekness in her voice, Breeze began to tell their story. Galley was sort of hiding behind her not wanting to feel any more of Neptune's wrath. When it came to the part about the big, shiny black pearl, they noticed Neptune was listening intently and the frown was gone from his face. When Breeze started telling about the dolphins, she noticed a slight grin on his face. The more of that was told, the bigger his grin got. After all was said, the mermaids remained perfectly still...awaiting their punishment.

Neptune was silent for a long time...glaring at them with stern eyes; then he reached out his long, strong arms, put them around the two young mermaids, and gathered them close.

By this time, both Breeze and Galley were shaking... not knowing what type of punishment was going to be dealt out.

All of a sudden, Neptune opened his mouth wide and started laughing. He roared with laughter. "You two little, half-grown mermaids did what hundreds of other big, strong sea creatures failed to do. Those clams were all bigger and stronger and tougher then any in the ocean. Stronger and tougher then the two of you...But YOU TWO little ones managed to get those pearls."

He laughed his hearty laugh again, louder than ever. "Wish I'd been there to see! I'll see to it they are all put back!" Neptune then bent down, hovered over Breeze and Galley, and spoke in a really loud, commanding voice. "NEVER...EVER...TELL YOUR STORY!... NOT TO ANYONE! THIS STORY IS TO BE OUR SECRET! DO YOU HEAR ME?" He put his hand on his daughter's shoulder and smiled widely. "We don't want anyone else to know this can be done...especially by two half-grown, mischievous mermaids."

"Neptune...DARLING!" Oceana said as she laid her head on his big, strong shoulder. "What ever did happen to those big beautiful pearls? Hmmm? What happened to that great big black pearl? You never showed any of them to me, and you never told me what happened to them. In fact...if I remember right...I didn't get any pearls at all."

It was getting close to dark by the time Neptune finished his story. Oceana noticed Breeze's tail swishing slowly back and forth. Her head left Neptune's shoulder and in an instant she was beside her beloved mermaid daughter. "Are you OK?"

Breeze opened first one eye then the other...looked at her mother and smiled. In a meek little voice she answered. "Of course! Of course I'm OK. What makes you think I'm not OK?" Breeze slowly sat up and was about to explain where she'd been.... "I've just—"

"YOU ARE NOT OK!" Neptune roared as he broke into their conversation. "I'LL TELL YOU WHY YOU ARE NOT OK! You've worried your mother here to where she was crying! Just LOOK at yourself! LOOK AT YOUR BEAUTIFUL TAIL! Just HOW are you going to explain THAT?" He shook his fist at her. "I NEVER WANT TO SEE YOU LOOKING LIKE THIS AGAIN! All the things I've taught you. DO YOU KNOW...THAT OUT OF ALL MY CHILDREN... YOU'RE THE ONE THAT'S ALWAYS GETTING INTO TROUBLE? YOU ARE ALWAYS GETTING INTO THINGS YOU SHOULDN'T! What'd you do this time...Get on one of those big black ships?...Or just follow underneath it where you couldn't be seen? THAT'S IT! THAT'S IT, ISN'T IT, LITTLE ONE?... And YOU got caught in the big metal propeller. Didn't you?" By this time, Neptune was hovering over her glaring down at her...with his fists still clenched. "Why...I ought to teach you a lesson. Think I'll—"

Oceana could stand no more. She snuggled up to Neptune and put her arms around his neck...gave him a kiss and curled her tail around him. "Maybe..." she whispered as she kissed his cheek again. "Just maybe... she's learned her lesson this time. Just look at her!"

"Get up, Breeze!" Neptune commanded. "Go get yourself something to eat...and...and...DO SOMETHING WITH THAT...THAT TAIL! No self respecting mermaid should look like that!"

Breeze wasted no time leaving. She didn't want to hear anymore.

Neptune grabbed Oceana around the waist and pulled her down to the dark depths of the ocean where they could be alone.

Breeze was thinking about what she'd done...and would be a lot more careful doing next time. *Yes!* She thought, remembering her last exciting adventure.... *There WILL be a next time.*

Chapter 4

Breeze remembered leaving the area where they all dwelt in search of something different to do. She was tired of the same old thing and decided to investigate one of those fancy big ships with all the humans on it. She also remembered the time she visited the cloud ship and all the trouble THAT caused. Now, she thought, she was bigger and could handle herself a lot better. Upon reaching the ship, she conjured up her legs and started climbing up the big round pieces of metal that went into the water at one end and up to the ship on the other. From the water they looked like they went right into the ship....Good way in! After a long climb however, she found herself standing in the last little link...with the side of the ship towering in front of her and the ocean...a long way down behind her. She couldn't go any farther. The links dead-ended right there at the ship. There was no way to get into that ship so she just turned around and stood there for a second. She wasn't about to climb back down all those little metal circles so she took a deep breath, pushed herself

Breeze...the Mermaid

off and dove back into the ocean. Breeze managed to conjure her tail back while she sailed through the air.

Although Breeze was frustrated at her first attempt, she just knew there had to be a way to get into that ship. She wanted so badly just to see what it would be like to be a human for a little while so she swam around and around the ship. There just was no way in. She even swam all over underneath the ship. There was just no way in.

Just when she was about to give up, here come her dolphin friends, five of them. They thought Breeze was playing with the ship, and they all wanted to join in. First one then another started nudging her. One of them even swam under her lifting her up on its back. Breeze was all for the fun. She figured she couldn't get on the ship so she'd just play around it...maybe catch site of some of the humans that were standing around on top of it.

Dolphins swimming near the ship always brought lots of attention from the passengers on board. One little boy caught sight of Breeze in the water and started pointing his finger, yelling, "LOOK! I SEE SOMEONE IN THE WATER! LOOK! OUT THERE! SOMEONE'S FALLEN OVER! SOMEONE'S IN THE WATER! HEY, EVERYBODY! SOMEONE'S DOWN THERE! SOMEONE'S DOWN THERE...IN THE WATER, AND THE BIG FISH ARE ABOUT TO GET HER!"

All of a sudden everyone swarmed to that edge of the ship. Loud sirens sounded, and all the ship's engines stopped. Breeze saw several human figures holding their arms out causing the people to go away from the ship's railing so she couldn't see them. Then a little boat was lowered down towards the water with two humans in it. When it finally reached the water, a white circular thing was tossed towards Breeze. She ducked so as not to be hit with it. The humans in the little boat started shouting at her, and she was afraid.

"GRAB ON! GRAB ON! PUT IT OVER YOUR HEAD SO WE CAN PULL YOU ONTO THE BOAT!" They were both shouting really loud, and their hands were waving at her to come over to them.

Breeze hesitated for a minute then swam over to the boat…totally ignoring the white rescue rings and float devices.

She stayed about four feet away for a few minutes, not sure what she should do. Breeze wanted so much to see what was on that ship. She did notice, as she got closer, their voices seemed to calm down a bit and they both started reaching for her.

Finally Breeze's curiosity got the best of her. She conjured up her people legs and swam close to the boat. The arms that had been reaching out for her were now touching her…were holding her under her arms and were pulling her onto the little boat.

The two men in the lifeboat were ship's officers sent to rescue a passenger they thought had fallen overboard. One was younger, and this was his first trip as an officer. The other was older and had been in his position for a long time. Neither of them expected—nor were they prepared for—a beautiful, young, voluptuous maiden with very long hair…and NO CLOTHES ON! The fact that she had no clothes on took them by surprise. Both quickly sat back in the ship with their mouths open…And….Yes! They were staring at Breeze. Each was quick to grab one of the blankets that were placed there for rescue purposes.

Breeze didn't realize she was supposed to be wearing clothes. She knew nothing about clothes…So she just sat there wearing only her beautiful long hair and a big, sexy smile. Finally, the older man got up enough courage to introduce himself, placed the blanket around her shoulders and asked. "Are you okay? What happened? How long have you been in the water? WHERE ARE YOUR CLOTHES?"

Breeze didn't understand the man's language. The blanket was hot and scratchy, and she wanted no part of it. She looked up at the man, gave him a sweet smile, took the blanket off her shoulders, and quickly tossed it back into the boat.

The man reached down, picked up the blanket, and asked, "Miss! What happened to your clothes? Can you tell me who you are?

No answer.

"You'll have to keep this blanket wrapped around you till we get you back on board ship and into your room. Which room are you in?" Again he placed the blanket on Breeze's shoulders.

No answer! Breeze was unsure what to do, so she just sat there flashing that big, sweet, innocent-looking smile. This time she tossed the blanket over the side of the little boat and into the water.

The younger officer pressed his lips together and said, "Let me try!" He picked up another blanket, scooted over to where Breeze was sitting, and said, "Miss, I don't know how you come to be without your clothes. You seem to be in good condition for being in the water so long." As gently as he could, he placed the blanket back on her shoulders and, in a very soft voice, said, "I wish you would say something. Tell us who you are and how you wound up in the water. You know...there are people up there that are concerned about you, but you can't just..." He shook his head. "You can't just have NO clothes on. What happened to your clothes?"

No answer.

"There are women and little children up there, and you need to keep this blanket around you." The man still had his arms on Breeze's shoulders...loosely holding the blanket there.

Breeze looked directly into the young man's eyes and put her hands on the edges of the blanket in an attempt to take it off again.

The young man kept his hands on Breeze's shoulders to make sure that blanket stayed right where he'd put it....He looked back into her eyes and said, "Miss! I don't know what happened to your voice or how you fell overboard but...YOU HAVE TO WEAR THIS BLANKET!" His hands stayed firmly on her shoulders to make sure the blanket stayed around them.

Breeze made two more attempts to take the blanket off but finally realized that she was supposed to wear it in order to go onto the big ship. So...she relaxed and left it around her shoulders.

"That's better!" The young man sighed, taking his hands off her shoulders. He made a motion for the boat to be pulled up to the deck. Then he asked again, "How did you fall overboard?"

Still no answer.

Licking his lips in frustration, the young man tried his best to remain calm and again asked. "How did you fall overboard?"

Breeze gave him her sweet smile...but no answer.

"Miss! What is your name?"

Still no answer.

Turning to his senior partner he said, "Something just doesn't seem right here. Maybe she hit her head when she fell overboard or something. I think we need to take her to the nurse's station."

The crowd was still standing next to the railing when the boat reached its little docking area. The men stepped out and both of them offered Breeze their hand to help her get out of the little boat. Breeze didn't take hold of either of their hands. She just stood up, held onto the blanket with one hand and jumped out of the boat... jumped right through the ship's officers waiting hands. The crowd began cheering because she was okay. To Breeze, they were just making all kinds of loud noises that she just didn't care to hear, so she ran right past their hands, right through the crowd, and into one of the ship's corridors.

The two ship's officers who were on the little boat quickly ran after her and were soon joined by several others...all yelling! The young officer who had wrapped the blanket around her last shouted. "COME BACK, MISS! WE NEED TO KNOW YOUR NAME! We're not going to hurt you." Then he realized what was happening...realized that with the loud yelling and so many people running after her, the girl might just be frightened....So he turned around and tried to stop the others. "I think she may be frightened. She may have lost her memory out there in the water so long. I don't know what happened to her clothes, but she had none on when we rescued her. Maybe if only one of us was to slowly follow after her, it will be easier. She may just be afraid because there are so many of us running after her." The others agreed, and the young ship's officer continued on his way….This time he followed instead of trying to catch up.

Breeze noticed the yelling had stopped and so had most of the people who were after her. She slowed down to a fast walk. Soon, she came into a really big area where there were lots of humans. Looking from one side to the other, she noticed every one of them looked different. They were all different colors. They even had things on their feet that made noise. The closest she'd ever been to a human before was when the nice man on the little boat made her keep that itchy thing around her.

Still clutching the 'itchy thing' he'd put around her, Breeze looked all around the area. She noticed there were lots of different interesting things. She chose to go look at the area that had those silly, colorful things humans put on. She called them "people colors" for want of a better word. Reaching out to take one of them, she felt something hard against her fingertips. Remembering how her hand hurt when she reached for pearls some years ago, she immediately pulled her hand back. Just at that moment a human walked through an opening. Breeze turned and walked in through that same opening and started putting her hands on all the fine pieces of clothing. Of course, she was STILL clutching that itchy blanket the nice man gave her.

Looking across the room, she saw two humans pulling the pretty colored things over their heads. *So!* She thought. *That's how they all look so different. They WEAR these things....*Like she wore sea horses and sea shells in her hair. Breeze found a very colorful, sparkly dress, pulled it off the hanger, dropped her blanket, and slipped it on over her head.

It only took a few minutes for the lady in the store to see what was happening. When she did, she noticed a blanket lying on the floor and Breeze standing there putting on clothes...one after the other...all on top of each other. The lady dropped what she was doing and hurried over from the other side of the store to stop what was happening.

At that same time, also noticing what was happening, the young ship's officer walked into the store to get Breeze. He was quick to act. "Ma'am, I'll pay for whatever she has. She's just had an accident and is not herself today." He took Breeze by the arm ever so gently and gave the lady his credit card. "Could we have a bag for some of these?" he asked.

Breeze, of course didn't understand. She wanted to keep wearing ALL the clothes she'd picked out and was reluctant to take any of them off.

The young man was very persuasive. He helped her off with all but the first dress she'd put on and put them all in a bag. This he handed to Breeze with a smile and again asked, "What is your name? Mine is Alex."

Breeze just looked at him, smiled, and took the bag full of clothes.

Alex took her arm and ushered her out of the store. He thought he would be able to walk her down to the nurse's station, but Breeze had other ideas.

She walked with him a little ways, looked through an open door, and noticed lots of people eating weird things. Breeze wanted to know just WHAT they were eating. Pulling away from Alex, she ran into the big room and started picking things up off people's plates and stuffing them into her mouth.

Alex was shocked. "Hey! You can't do that!" At that point, he realized there was something REALLY different about this girl. He reached out to take hold of Breeze's arm.

Breeze, thinking he was stealing her food, let out a very loud, high-pitched screech. She jumped onto the table that was right in front of her and ran right down the middle of it, stepping on the dishes and knocking over glasses filled with drinks. Food and drink were splattered everywhere. Breeze didn't stop with just that one table. She saw a door on the other side of the room. In her hurry to get away, she ran right toward that door and jumped from one table to the other, right down the middle of all them…leaving a wide path of splattered food and drink.

At this point, the whole ship's crew had been alerted by the dining area personnel that there was a crazy woman on board. Ship's officers were everywhere. Alex had reached out and tried his best to catch Breeze when she first jumped on the table, but she was just too fast.

Breeze knew she couldn't stay on the ship any longer. Too much trouble! She dropped the bag with all her pretty clothes in it and ran for the railing. The dress she was wearing was long and it got in her way, so she stopped for a moment, pulled it over her head, and left it hanging on the ship's railing.

That was the moment Alex needed. He reached out and grabbed for Breeze, catching her by her hair just as she jumped overboard. This action pulled him overboard with her.

Breeze, of course, conjured back her beautiful tail on the way down to the water. Because of the size of the ship and the distance down to the water they both went a long ways down under the water. This was no problem for Breeze. She was home! But for Alex...it was a problem. Realizing the nice man had followed her and gone down underwater with her; she grabbed hold of him and quickly pulled him to the surface. She took one look at him and realized he was in trouble. His body was limp, and his eyes were shut.

She could hear lots of yelling from the ship and could also see a little boat being lowered into the water. Breeze looked hard at Alex. He had been the only one on the whole ship who was nice to her….So…she gave him the kind of kiss only a mermaid could give…a great big…long kiss. It was the kiss of life for Alex, forcing the air he needed into his lungs and reviving him.

Alex couldn't believe what had just happened….He took one look at Breeze…took one look at her tail as she splashed it on the surface, and said, "You're a…A…A MERMAID!"

Breeze had never kissed a human before. She liked kissing Alex. She liked it very much! So…just as the men reached out to pull Alex into the boat, she pulled him aside, put his head between her hands, and gave him another great big, long kiss. To her surprise, he kissed her back! Her heart started pounding. She smiled at him, gave him a big close hug, made sure he was close to the boat, and swam some distance away to watch them pull him on board. Breeze knew then….She'd never forget that last long kiss.

Looking up, she saw the big ship almost upon her. In her haste to get away and with her mind on the wonderful kiss she'd just had, Breeze didn't pay attention to which way the ship was headed and swam right past its big propellers. Her beautiful tail got all skinned up. Her body was thrown around and around, and she barely managed to escape with her life. Safe, but exhausted, she passed out and was washed onto the shore....This is where Oceana and Neptune found her several days ago.

Neptune had been silent the whole time Breeze told her story. When it came to the part where she kissed the human...for the second time...this bothered him and made him angry. "Don't you know what happens when you kiss humans?"

"No!" Breeze looked up questioningly. "What?"

"You could kiss him ONCE to bring him back to life. That's okay! BUT...TWICE!" Neptune yelled. "TWICE! WHY DID YOU KISS HIM...TWICE?"

Breeze meekly asked, "What's wrong with that? I liked kissing him!"

"YOU LIKED KISSING HIM?" roared Neptune. "YOU LIKED KISSING THAT HUMAN?"

Gathering up all the courage she had, she said, "Yes...Yes...I DID! I liked it! And I'll never forget that kiss either. It was a GREAT kiss!"

Neptune put his hand on Breeze's shoulder. "That's part of the problem, Breeze. Kiss them once, and you'll be able to go on to many others...not looking back. Kiss them twice and you are asking for heartache because you'll never see him again. Besides, Breeze, he's a human! A man thing! Not at all what I want for your future! I'd like to choose your future!" Neptune smiled...."Now, go away and get better before I get angry again about you messing with humans. I really can't stand looking at your tail...especially now that I know what happened to it.....Just go away for a while!"

Chapter 5

Breeze hung around the home area for a week or so till her tail got presentable. Each day she got more and more restless and bored. She spent her days watching the other mermaids her age. They all seemed to be doing just fine. Kind of like Oceana…homebodies… not interested in any adventure. No! She was not just satisfied to meander around doing less than nothing. This was NOT Breeze!

One sunny morning she decided she'd hung around doing nothing long enough. She kissed her mother, Oceana, good bye….She said she needed something different to look at and to do and took off to her favorite big rock to watch the sunset and dream. The rock was huge! It protruded out into the ocean a long way and was covered with barnacles and little, colorful sea creatures. Each wave that crashed against the rock created a fine spray that fell gently over her body. With the mist in her face, Breeze sat there a long time watching the sunset and envying the apparent freedom of the flocks of seagulls that flew by. Yes! She wanted to be just like them…going wherever she wanted to go…whenever she wanted to go.

Breeze remembered the words of her father, Neptune. "He's a human…A man thing!…Not at all what I want for your future. I'd like to choose your future!" *Choose my future! Choose my future? NO!* This was NOT what she wanted! She did not want her father—or anyone else—to choose her future. She sat there in the mist for quite some time remembering how angry he had been when she told him she'd kissed that human for the second time. *Humph!* She thought…*I'd kiss him again if he were here! I'd kiss him the THIRD time if he were here! And the FOURTH!* Throwing caution to the wind, she dove into the ocean and headed for land.

This time, she was going to the big city. She knew a little about human ways from the big ship adventure… enough to know she couldn't be around humans without wearing something. They'd all be yelling and screaming, and she hated that sound. She'd just take something to wear from the first human she saw.…It would be easy! She swam towards land where the people were.…She swam a long ways to an area she had never been to before. The town was an old sea-faring town that had a huge fish cannery in it.

Breeze was swimming close to the surface of the water when she neared shore. She saw lots of lines with bits of fish attached to them hanging from wood sticks. She knew only too well what these were. Some of her friends had been caught on the ends of things like these, and then the humans cut them into little pieces. Immediately, she commenced grabbing each line and chewing on it…breaking the hooks off and letting them fall down onto the bottom of the ocean floor. After that good deed was done and all the lines were left without hooks, she was ready to continue her journey. First thing she heard when she stuck her head out of the water were unhappy, yelling voices.

Humans are just awful, she thought. *All they do is yell and scream.* At that very instant she saw the humans tossing their lines back into the sea again...with pieces of fish on the ends of them. Not satisfied with what she had previously done—just chewing the ends of the lines off—she started yanking the poles out of their hands and letting them fly into the ocean one by one. The yelling got louder and louder. Breeze didn't want to show herself to these yelling humans because she didn't want to be chased again. She stayed there for a few minutes, safe under the water and watched them. There they were...running down the steps. Some of those silly humans were even falling over each other in the water trying to get those silly fish-killing sticks. No! Breeze definitely didn't want to go on the land here.

She swam further up the coast. She swam for a long ways and finally saw another interesting spot. Lots of humans were there. Breeze conjured up her land legs and went on shore. Not wanting to be seen until she found the things humans wore, she snuck into the building. Yes! There, hanging on the wall, were lots of things to wear. Breeze didn't like the feel of what she was putting on but, if it kept the humans from yelling at her, she would wear them. There was a big, long, white thing that hung clear down to her knees. She put that on. Next she slipped something on over her legs that looked like black whale skin. She peeked around the corner and noticed everyone was wearing those, so she was happy with that. Next she noticed all the humans in the building were wearing long, black things that went over their shoulders...so she put those on too. Now, for her feet! *Oh my!* Breeze looked at the people's feet. They were wearing big, huge, black things on them, and right on the floor in front of her were two of them.

*Those black things look just awful...*Breeze thought as she put them on. *How do humans walk in these?* The black boots she'd found were way too big....So were the plastic over-alls that she had pulled up. They almost reached her chin. The long, skinny things she'd put over her shoulders so she would look like everyone else were really uncomfortable, and the long over-jacket took some doing to get it on. She finally managed to struggle into it and sort of tuck it into the sides of those coveralls leaving the back just hanging there. Now! Now she was really ready to meet with humans. She was wearing exactly what they wore so she knew they wouldn't yell at her.

Breeze carefully took a couple steps toward the area they were in and almost fell down. "This is awful!" she muttered to herself. "How do humans walk in these things?" Just inside the door she looked up. On the other side of the door and over her head a huge fish was attached to the wall. This made Breeze mad because she knew someone had killed it and stuck it there. Then she really looked around. What a scary place! She saw fishnets...hooks...harpoons...little nets with sticks on them and thousands of fish moving across the room on long, flat narrow things. "Oh! This is awful!" Breeze let out a high-pitched, shrill scream and started to run....

But her huge boots got in the way, and she tripped on them. She bellowed out another shrill, high-pitched scream as her hands caught onto one of those moving fish trays. She did manage not to tumble clear down to the floor, but this caught the attention of all the workers. They immediately looked in her direction and yelled, "WHAT ARE YOU DOING IN HERE?" Then they really looked at her and burst out laughing. All their fingers were pointed her way.

Breeze had never heard human laughter before. It was not as bad as the yelling and much like her own... but she didn't like it either so she tried to run. This time she stumbled into one of the workers, who caught her.

"Whoa there!" he said. "Who are you, little lady... and...what are you doing in here dressed like that?"

Breeze looked him in the eye and jerked away, trying to leave. This time, she stumbled over the boots of the guy who was holding her. She fell all the way to the floor and let out another long, loud, high-pitched screech. "No one can walk in these!" she yelled. And she took them off one by one, tossing them across the room and into the moving fish trays.

The workers who were within reaching distance tried to grab her again, but without the clumsy boots on, Breeze was faster than they were. She jumped onto the closest fish tray, scattering fish everywhere. In their effort to catch her workers were tripping and slipping on the fish that had been scattered on the floor. When they reached for the moving trays to keep from falling, more fish went onto the floor. Breeze was jumping from one fish tray to the other, knocking large numbers of fish off each tray she touched. She thought the humans looked funny slipping around all over the floor....She started laughing and pointing her finger. This really made the men mad.

Breeze couldn't stand seeing her fish friends lying in piles on those trays and began gathering them up as fast as she could, throwing them out of the window and back into the sea where they belonged. She jumped from one tray to the other, picking up fish and throwing them out the window. Her haste to return them to the sea caused most of what fish were left on the trays to fall onto the already wet, slippery floor.

The workers were trying their best to catch their intruder but were having nothing but trouble. Breeze was fast, and it didn't take her long to pretty much clear out the first trays. The men wanted this girl out of their place. Bad! But they couldn't catch her. Frustration was setting in. The harder they tried to catch Breeze, the worse things seemed to get. They were continuously slipping and tripping on the fish that had landed on the floor, falling over one another and getting injured in their scrambles. Their yelling got louder and louder. Numerous efforts were made to catch Breeze, with no results. The workers were becoming more and more furious by the second. Their place of work had been trashed. Most of the fish that were left were lying all over the floor. Only a few remained in the moving trays. Their clothes were all covered with slippery fish slime, and NO ONE COULD CATCH BREEZE!

Their yelling got so intense Breeze couldn't stand it any longer. All this commotion upset her terribly, and she just wanted out of there. Before she left, she made sure to pull down all of the nets, hooks and harpoons from off the walls…flinging them over her head and backwards to land where they may. One by one she took off the pieces of clothes she had put on and threw them at the workmen.

As Breeze dove through the window to make her escape into the ocean she muttered, "What's the matter with those humans anyway? Can't they see fish belong in the water? Not lying on cold trays dying?" What a scary place that was! Definitely the wrong place for a mermaid like herself.

By now, Breeze was pretty sure all humans could do was yell. She headed toward the open sea to think about what she just went through….Maybe she should meet up with some friends to play with. The only thing she seemed to be able to think about was all those beautiful big fish, just lying there, helpless with those awful humans standing over them cutting them to pieces. The more she thought about it…the sicker and madder she got. Maybe she'd just go back there often…when no one was there and free all the fish that were caught that day.

No dolphins were in the area! No fish! No turtles! Nothing was there! *How strange*, she thought. Her wish was to dive down for the deeper part of the ocean so she could find something interesting and maybe fun to do. "OH! Oh, NO!" Breeze let out one of her harsh, shrill screeches. She could not believe what she was seeing. Humans had taken over the ocean floor. Cages were everywhere filled with her big crab friends. There they all were…in little round cages, yelling at her…begging for her to let them out.

Breeze swooped down to the cages below only to find out most of those crabs had been in there for several days with no food. Anger stirred up in her. It took her a while to discover how to let them out. There were lots of crabs in each of those little cages. Emptying the first one took no time at all. She went to the next cage…and the next…and the next. One by one they were opened. Now, she was happy watching them scurry around looking for food. "EEeeeeeeea!" She shouted with happiness. It had taken a long time, but most of the cages were now empty and lying there wide open. The ocean floor looked like a living carpet of big crabs.

Only three cages left….Then ALL the crabs would be able to go home. She looked over all she had accomplished and was very proud of herself for saving so many lives. As she went to reach for one of the last cages that were still full, she noticed it had moved. All three of the remaining cages had moved…and were still moving. Looking up through the water, she saw that a man in a big boat was pulling them in. This just couldn't happen! There were still crabs in those cages! Breeze hurried as fast as she could and managed to unloose crabs from two more cages. The last cage was still full of helpless crabs, and it was on its way up to the boat. Humans were pulling it up.

This just couldn't happen! Breeze grabbed hold of the cage, turned and tried swimming away with it. The cage was still on its way up to the boat. She worked as fast as she could. Just as the cage left the water and she was about to be pulled onto the boat with it, she managed to open it and turn it over. She shouted with glee as she watched the happy crabs fall, splashing back into the sea.

The humans in the boat caught a brief glimpse of Breeze shaking the cage, and heard her shout as she let the crabs fall back into the ocean. They had been tugging on that cage for a long time with all their might trying to pull it up. When the load was suddenly gone out of it and Breeze let go…it flew onto the deck with a force, causing them to fall backwards. Some of the fishermen landed clear on the other side of the deck and against the railing. One of them almost fell out of the boat. Of course…they began yelling. Each of them had seen Breeze. They knew what they'd seen….At least they thought they did.

Breeze took one glimpse at their angry, surprised faces as they fell backwards. Immediately she dropped down deep into the water and swam towards the ocean floor. She did not want to listen to any more yelling.

The humans scrambled over each other to get back to the side of the boat where the crab cage had been to make sure they saw what they thought they saw…a mermaid!….But Breeze was gone.

The rest of the pods were slowly pulled into boat and found to be empty also. The angry humans were never really sure exactly what they saw on the other end of that crab pod…or who it was that emptied their crab pods. Whatever it was or whoever it was….They shook their fist toward the sea and vowed it would either be caught or killed.

Chapter 6

Breeze hovered over the crabs, watching them for a long time...till the boat with yelling people floated away. She decided she'd go farther onto the land because the people she'd met so far both on the land and on the sea were very loud and awful to be around...except, of course the one she'd kissed. She would always remember that one with special thoughts.

Staying far enough away from the shore that no one would notice her, Breeze passed the awful place where they cut up her fish friends. She again delighted in chewing off the ends of all the lines that had bits of fish on them as she passed through the wood posts. She wanted to see something new and different so she continued swimming down the coast. Soon five mischievous dolphins joined her for some fun. She conjured up her legs, ran up onto the beach and stole a big round ball from one of those small humans that was playing with it near the water. Breeze noticed that even the little humans yelled at her. This time, she ignored them. That ball was tossed back and forth and enjoyed for quite some time...till they got tired of playing and it was left floating out at sea.

Breeze swam further along the coast, always looking towards the land to see if something interesting might be there that she could explore. Yes! There hanging in the air on some lines next to a big wooden building were lots of things to wear. She thanked all the dolphins for the fun she'd had and swam towards shore...followed by...all of the dolphins. When they saw her conjure up her legs they all wanted land legs too. Breeze told them it was a special gift that only choice mermaids get to have. She said goodbye to them again and waded onto the shore.

THIS IS GREAT! she thought as she began pulling things off the lines. First she yanked a huge red T-shirt off and put it on. Next she found something really neat that felt like skin and was the color of the sky. She stepped into it, one leg at a time, pulled it over her legs and up to her waist. With a smile on her face she was now ready to see what was inside the buildings. By this time, she had been in several of the people's places and knew where the doors were, so she walked straight up towards one of them.

Unusual sounds filled her ears, and she stopped for a moment. They were coming from the other side of the building, and of course Breeze's curiosity took over. She walked to the other side of the building. Locked in a big cage, she saw lots of big, plump birds. Some were red, some were white, and a few were black and white. Listening really closely, she discovered they were all upset about being in the big cage and wanted out. Breeze, always wanting to help, found the place where the cage opened. She opened it real wide and smiled. "There you go! Is that better?"

All the chickens were happy and let her know it. They started cackling as loud as they could. One of them even sat down in front of her and gave her a funny looking white thing that looked somewhat like a clam. She thanked the chicken and picked it up. Now, clams have a seam around them where they can be opened. This had no seam. Breeze tried real hard to open it but she couldn't. When she had trouble with clams, she'd usually just hit them on a rock several times and then they'd be easier to open, so she tried it with this new thing. SPLAT! All over her face and everything she had on. "That's not very nice!" she said, looking right at the chicken. "You should have told me how to open this!"

The chicken that laid the egg in front of her looked up and said, "Those are our children! The people eat them before they are born. They eat lots of them. I thought you knew."

"Oh, my! That's terrible!" Breeze said, frowning. "Doesn't that bother all of you?"

"No! Not really," said the chicken. "None of us have ever seen one of these become a baby, and we get free food and water and a place to stay that's away from things that can get us. It's a good trade."

"I don't think so!" Breeze commented. "You need to be free! Just like me!" With that statement she ran around to the other side of the building, and a wonderful smell came into her nose. She followed that smell. She just had to find out what was causing it. There it sat! In the window...big and round with liquids oozing out of the top and sides. The top looked a lot like dirt. She bent over and put her nose right down next to it…almost touching it. "Oh! Yum!" she whispered. Breeze reached out and picked it up. "What a find!" She'd never smelled anything like this before. Lifting the pie up to her face, Breeze opened her mouth as wide as she could…put her head right down into the pie, and took as big a bite as she could…right out of the middle of it. Pie was all over her face, in her hair, and on her hands. The taste was like pure sunshine, like nothing she'd ever tasted before, and she just had to have more. Turning the pie a bit sideways she took another huge bite. This time bits of the apples and a lot of the juice ran down her chin and onto her already stained shirt. Breeze ate over half of that pie before setting it back in the window where she found it.

Now, not only were the remnants of the egg she'd broken all over her face, in her long hair, and down the front of her red shirt, they were also joined by the juice and small pieces of apple pie. Her tummy was full and she was ready to go through the door and see what was inside when three big black crows swooped down past her head.

They began chattering loudly as they sat on and beside the pie, eating away at it as fast as they could. Pretty soon there was apple pie all over the windowsill, and juice was running down the inside and outside of the wall. The pie pan had been knocked onto the ground, and what little remained of the pie was scattered on the dirt. The crows' chatter got louder and louder as they swooped down to the ground to eat what was left of it.

Breeze was surprised she understood what the crows were saying. She understood all the earth creatures she'd met so far...same as those in the ocean. The birds seemed to be afraid of something called a broom and were on constant lookout for it. Not knowing what a broom was, Breeze excused herself and started walking towards the door. She was about to put her hand on it when one of the crows swooped down and warned her that the broom was in there and could come out any minute...that the bigger building was more interesting and had wonderful things in it.

It didn't matter to Breeze which building she went into first. The building they pointed to was open, and she could just walk right in...so she did. Once inside, she turned around to thank her friends and found out just what the broom was. Coming out of the door she would have just gone in through was a really big human with a very loud, shrill voice. The human was swinging something that looked like a stick with a bushy tail, smacking the ground, the house, and the tree standing next to it. The broom seemed to be trying really hard to hit the crows. Their loud chatter had the sound of fear in it, and they kept repeating over and over..."WATCH OUT! THE BROOM! THE BROOM!" She was really glad the crows had warned her. This human was screaming too! Just like all the other humans she'd seen...except for the one she'd kissed. For a brief moment, Breeze wondered if she'd ever see that human again.

All kinds of different animals were inside the barn, and they all started making loud noises when she entered. Each creature wanted to be let out of their little pens. Breeze didn't know the names of these creatures because she'd never seen any of them before. There were several horses locked in little areas. She let them out first and admired their beauty as she watched them run away. There were a couple pens with little spotted dogs locked up in them. They sounded kind of like the seals she played with on occasion, so she let them loose also. They went running after the horses, making loud, harsh sounds. Next she saw a cat and her kittens all curled up on some dead grass. The cat seemed friendly and asked her to share its bowl of milk.

Breeze had never tasted anything like this before and drank it all really fast. The cat introduced herself as Tabby and told her there was a lot more milk in the house but she'd have to go get it…said it was in a big, tall, white box. Tabby brushed up against her legs and started purring….Then she said she'd show her where the milk was if she'd get her some and bring it to the barn for her and her kittens. Breeze wanted to go into the house anyway and this was as good a time as any…. So there they both went…Tabby the cat in the lead.

Breeze was happy to see no human and no broom so in the door she went. Tabby ran right to the refrigerator, and Breeze pulled on the handle to open it. There in front was a big pitcher full of milk. She also saw other things that she'd never seen before and took the box of strawberries because they were pretty and red. With the refrigerator door still wide open they turned and walked out the door, leaving it open as well.

Back at the barn, she sat the milk on the ground, sat down on the ground beside it and started eating the big, juicy red strawberries. "This is GREAT! We don't have anything like this where I come from!" she exclaimed.

Tabby the cat was getting impatient. "Just pour that milk into the bowl, will you? We're hungry here!"

Breeze smiled, picked up the pitcher of milk, and poured it really fast. Before she could stop, half the bottle was spilled on the ground and running under where she sat.

Tabby looked up at her and asked, "Where did YOU come from?"...and went back to drinking the milk.

Breeze took turns drinking milk from the pitcher and eating strawberries. She finished the strawberries and threw the box aside. Putting the milk pitcher up to her mouth, she was just about ready to empty it when...

"BREEZE!" Neptune's stern, loud voice seemed to cut through the air like a knife. "WHAT ARE YOU DOING HERE?" He roared, "DIDN'T I TELL YOU TO STAY AWAY FROM THE HUMANS?" The ground almost shook from his angry, commanding voice. There he was, standing behind his daughter with his hands on his hips, looking down into her eyes with a stern frown on his face. He took her by the arm and pulled her to her feet....He took one look at her and laughed. "LOOK AT YOU!" He laughed some more...loud and long. "YOU'RE GOING HOME...MISS MERMAID! HOW DARE YOU DISOBEY ME!"

Breeze was shocked that she'd been found. The minute she stood up she knew she was in no condition to hear what she was hearing. Somehow the milk...or maybe it was the milk mixed with the strawberries... but she was suddenly very dizzy. She was sick to her stomach and felt like the whole world was going round and round. Trying not to let Neptune see how she felt, she said nothing…just looked at him with her eyes wide open.

Neptune's angry words and his loud laughter could be heard from inside the farm house. Out came the big human with almost as loud a voice as Neptune's. "WHO'S OUT THERE? YOU BEEN IN MY HOUSE? I KNOW YOU WERE IN MY HOUSE! YOU LEFT MY REFRIGERATOR DOOR WIDE OPEN! YOU!" There was a brief pause as the big woman looked around. She saw Neptune holding onto his daughter's arm. "HEY, YOU THERE! WHO ARE YOU? NEVER SAW YOU BEFORE! WHAT ARE YOU DOING IN MY BARN? GET OFF MY PROPERTY!" The woman started marching toward the barn….And, yes! She was swinging the broom…SCREAMING. Her eye glanced toward the apple trees and noticed the horses happily picking the fruit off them. Instead of eating the whole apple, they let it fall out of their mouths and onto the ground then reached up to get another. The chickens were busy picking up the scraps from under their feet. "OH! EEEEEE! NOOOOOOOOOO! YOU DID THIS! EEEEEEEEEEEEE." The big, bucksome woman immediately turned around, ran back into the house, and came out with the big stick under her arm. The stick was pointed directly at Neptune.

Loud, harsh sounds came from the big stick hitting the ground and trees as the big human walked swiftly toward the barn. The horses and chickens ran in different directions. The cat hid her kittens and the crows…well, the crows just continued sitting in the trees, enjoying themselves and making lots of chattering noise while they watched.

Neptune knew just what that stick was and pulled Breeze inside the barn. "YOU'VE CAUSED ALL THE TROUBLE YOU'RE GOING TO!" he roared. Pointing to the back of the barn, he added, "SEE THAT DOOR? MARCH! INTO THE OCEAN WITH YOU! NOW!"

Breeze knew him only too well...knew she'd better obey. She was already in trouble, so she did just like he asked....But she was in no condition to march. It was all she could do to stagger to the back of the barn and out the door. She was afraid she'd fall down from being so dizzy.

Neptune, angry as he was, could see Breeze was in trouble. "You're DRUNK!" he grumbled. "DRUNK! ON MILK!" He wanted his daughter to learn a lesson, but he didn't want her dead, so he picked her up, tossed her under one arm and swiftly carried her like a bag of feed to the edge of the sea. "DON'T EVER DO THIS AGAIN! WHAT'S THE MATTER WITH YOU ANYWAY?" Neptune asked. "YOU DIDN'T DRINK A LOT OF THAT MILK...DID YOU?"

Still, Breeze said nothing. She just looked into Neptune's eyes as he set her back on the ground and gave him a shy little grin.

"YOU DID, DIDN'T YOU? Didn't I ever tell you how cow's milk reacts on us? MAKES US DRUNK! THAT'S WHAT IT DOES! AND WHEN YOU'RE DRUNK YOU HAVE NO CONTROL....SO DON'T DRINK IT ANY MORE! NOW, GET IN THAT WATER! GET THOSE AWFUL, FILTHY CLOTHES OFF, AND LET'S GO HOME. THE FRESH OCEAN WATER SHOULD PULL YOU OUT OF YOUR SILLY DRUNKENNESS!" Neptune grumbled. "Drunk daughter! Can't believe I have a DRUNK MERMAID DAUGHTER!"

"NOW, MY DISOBEDIENT, FANCY FINNED MERMAID!" he continued. "YOU'RE GOING BACK HOME...WITH ME!" His eyes glaring at her as he roared another command. "YOU KNOW, YOU DISOBEYED ME! LOOK AT YOU! YOU'RE DRUNK! DRUNK! YOU'RE FILTHY WITH FOOD ALL OVER YOU... AND YOU'RE DRUNK!" He put his big hands on her shoulders and shook her hard. "DON'T EVER DO THIS AGAIN! DON'T THINK I'LL LET YOU OUT OF MY SIGHT FOR A WHILE, BREEZE. DID YOU THINK HOW OCEANA WOULD FEEL IF SHE KNEW WHAT YOU WERE DOING?"

Breeze said nothing. It was all she could do to stay on her feet. The whole world seemed to be going round and round. "No," came her soft little answer.

"BREEZE!" Neptune turned around and looked her in the eye. "ARE YOU GOING TO DO THIS AGAIN? DID YOU LEARN YOUR LESSON? WHAT'S WRONG WITH YOU? YOU KNOW BETTER! You look sick, Breeze! Do you know how I found out you were here?"

"No."

"The crabs told me...some of the ones you let loose. GOOD JOB! I'm not angry about the crabs you let loose....But YOU HAD NO BUSINESS GETTING INTO PEOPLE'S LIVES. DON'T EVER DO IT AGAIN!"

Breeze...the Mermaid

As soon as Breeze touched the cool ocean water she felt fine. Her tail was back, and she was no longer dizzy. She told Neptune about the lines with pieces of fish on the ends of them and how she'd chewed the ends off. She also told about the awful place where the humans were cutting up their fish friends and about how many cages she opened and all the crabs she let loose.

On their way home, as they swam under the wood poles, Neptune delighted in helping his daughter with the fishing lines....But instead of breaking the lines he pulled the human's fishing poles right out of their hands and threw them as far as he could into the water. Together, they swam away from the area and spent some time watching and enjoying themselves as the humans scurried after their poles and lines.

Chapter 7

For several seasons…under the watchful eye of her father, Neptune, Breeze was the perfect mermaid. She didn't venture very far from home nor did she get into any trouble. She did everything she was told and even seemed to be friendly with some of the young males in the group. She'd swim with them and do things with them but never really got too close to any of them.

One day she came before Neptune and Oceana, gathered up all the courage she could and made an announcement. "I've done all you wanted! I've tried to be like the other mermaids and find happiness here, but I'm just not like them. I love adventure! I love going places and seeing new things. I don't just want to spend the rest of my life doing exactly what everyone else does. I love you both…but I would like to leave for a while and find out what other things are like."

Neptune did as he usually did when boasting….He stretched out and puffed himself up as big as he could. He looked at Oceana and said, "You need to remember, I am a SEA WARRIOR! I've changed the course of whole fleets of ships! I've navigated uncharted waters! I've made unnumbered conquests and established the laws of the sea! I've basked on uncharted tropical islands! I've—"

Oceana smiled at him gently as she interrupted. "We know these things, my sweet husband, but we're talking about Breeze. She wants to leave again."

Neptune took a deep breath and continued, "I've been the leader of many, and my daughter Breeze here has my blood in her. Even though she's done things she shouldn't have done, she needs to remain true to herself. I have taught her much since her last escapade on the land...even some of their language. She knows now not to interfere in any way with humans on the land and what they do." He turned his head toward Breeze, gazed sternly into her eyes, and continued, "You do know these things now, don't you? In the sea, it is a different story. When a human is giving trouble to your friends in the sea we do have dominion."

Breeze held her head up high and answered, "You have taught me much, and I will remember all those things." She put her arms around Oceana and gave her a kiss. Then she put her arms around Neptune and gave him a great big kiss. "I'll not forget all the wonderful things you've taught me. You know I just have to see all the new and exciting things that are out there." With that statement she flipped around and was gone.

Usually when Breeze decided to go on an adventure she'd contact Galley or one of her other friends. This time she was all alone. Not even the dolphins were there. Her first thoughts were to go to where she had been when she kissed Alex. Then she thought she'd go to where all the ships stayed, but she'd been there before and gotten into trouble. She knew a lot more now, and things would be different. Her next thoughts were to find some clothes somewhere, maybe lying on the beach or something and just go for a walk between all those big buildings. Yes! That's what she'd do….Walk through all the buildings.

Breeze swam up to where all the boats were kept and decided to swim around each one just to see what they were all like. The harbor was pretty good sized, and this took a while. Most of the boats were the kind that caught fish…the kind she hated. These she looked at with disgust and pulled everything hanging off them into the water as she swam by. This left fishing nets floating here and there through the harbor like they'd been in some kind of storm.

When she was almost to the shore, Breeze noticed a great big boat sitting all by itself away from the others. She swam towards it to look it over. As she got closer, she noticed the ship looked familiar. Breeze stopped abruptly, remembering her last encounter with it. This was the very same boat she'd caused such a ruckus on…. The same boat from which she'd pulled Alex overboard when he took hold of her hair. She just HAD to take a closer look at this boat. Maybe Alex was on it. If she wore the same kind of clothes the humans did, maybe no one would notice her walking through the ship. Yes! She decided that was what she was going to do.

Walking through town could wait until later…or would it? Breeze looked longingly at the ship. She knew better than to try climbing up that rope—didn't work before! There was no way into the ship that way.

Breeze...the Mermaid

She couldn't just walk up there either, not without the clothes! All of a sudden, she had a brilliant idea. She swam back to where all the smaller boats were and chose just the right one to climb on board. She'd make sure there were no people on it or on any of the boats near it.

Breeze even swam around the boat to make sure no one was there....Then she conjured up her legs and climbed on board. She opened the little door, went inside, and started pulling people clothes out of drawers. Perfect! She'd seen the humans wearing these little two-piece strips of clothing and tried them on. She also pulled out one of those long, flowing pieces of clothes that was hanging behind a door. This would get her onto that ship. She put it on too and admired herself for a long time in the mirror that hung on the door. With a smile, she dove back into the sea to swim to the ship.

WHOA! Swimming with land legs was not easy! This was a new experience for her. The long, colorful, flowing piece of clothes that she'd put on over her bikini was slowing her down, so she pulled it off and let it fall to the ocean floor. That was better, but trying to swim with land legs was still...just no good...Too awkward...Very slow and hard to do. She couldn't use her tail because she had that silly piece of cloth on. Breeze pulled that off too. She put her arm through one of the big holes in the stringy piece of clothes, conjured back her tail, and took off to the ship. That was much better!

As she neared the ship, she noticed no one was on it. Thinking the humans must all be inside; she swam around the ship once, then conjured up her land legs, put her legs into the smaller holes of that little piece of cloth and swam to the shore.

There were two walkways to get on the ship, and they were both closed off so she couldn't enter. She stood there, dripping wet for a few minutes. A human walked out onto the deck and asked what she was doing there. His voice seemed nice enough, so she answered, "Alex? Want Alex!"

The man walked down the walkway toward her, mumbled something, looked in the direction where all the buildings were, and pointed his finger that way. Breeze turned around and headed for the buildings. She knew what that pointed finger meant, and she wanted to see inside them all anyway. Really, she was hoping to find Alex so she could get another kiss.

It was evening, and the sun was well on its way down. Breeze went into the first building she came to. There were lots of people there wearing long, flowing pieces of clothes like the one she had dropped to the ocean floor. She felt out of place and ran out of the door and into the ocean to look for the colorful piece of clothes she'd dropped. She knew it wouldn't be hard to find because it was the color of the sunset.

The moon was coming up by the time she found it. Not wanting to swim with it on, Breeze waited until she got out of the water, then she put it on. Several humans were standing around watching, and she noticed they all gave her frowning looks and pointed their fingers. Not to be stopped from what she wanted to do, Breeze ignored their looks and gestures and again headed for the building with all the humans.

This time when she walked inside, she was sure she would fit right in. Still, everyone looked at her with frowning and questioning faces. One human came up to her and asked. "You're all wet! What happened?"

Breeze understood the "all wet" part but not the "what happened" part...so she didn't know how to answer and just stood there smiling. The human took her hand and led her through long, narrow halls to a smaller room with lots of clothes hanging on hooks. She pulled one off and handed it to Breeze. Breeze understood that she wanted her to put it on. She had trouble trying to get it on over the long wet piece of clothes she already had on, so she took that off and left it lying on the floor. This left her wearing only the itty-bitty bikini underneath. Actually the long, dry piece of clothes felt much better than the wet one.

With a big smile on her face, she walked out the door and started walking down between the walls. A bright red box with a funny looking long arm on it caught her attention, and she just had to see what it was. Walking up to it, she noticed something big and red inside, but there was that barrier again that she could see through but not put her hand through. Breeze put her hand on the red part of the long arm instead and pulled it down as hard as she could.

BEEP!...BEEP!...BEEP!...BEEP!...BEEP!...All of a sudden water started coming from the ceiling. The box opened wide, and she could pull out the big red thing. It was very heavy, and she didn't know what it was. BEEP!...BEEP!...BEEP!...BEEP!...BEEP!... Humans started yelling and screaming! BEEP!... BEEP!...BEEP!...BEEP!...The sound was terribly loud and was hurting her ears. She'd never heard anything that sounded so awful.

Just then, the door opened to where all the humans were and she saw them running towards the door that went to the outside. Water was coming down from the ceiling on them. Everyone and everything was dripping wet, and the humans acted very frightened. BEEP!...BEEP!...BEEP!...BEEP!...Breeze just stood there holding the big red thing. Water was coming down from the ceiling onto her also, and that pretty long piece of clothes the human had given her was now dripping with water and getting very heavy. BEEP!...BEEP!...BEEP!...BEEP!...That awful sound was hurting her ears.

She was about to drop the big red thing and take off running when one of the humans grabbed her by the arm and took the red thing away. "OUTSIDE!" he shouted as he looked her in the eye. "OUTSIDE!" The man pulled on her and forced her to go with him. "COME ON!"

By the time they got outside, Breeze's head hurt from the noises. All the humans seemed to be upset and unhappy. She didn't want any part of what was going on so she just did the only thing she knew to do. She ran for the sea to get away from the loud noise and the yelling and screaming people. The man that had pulled her outside was running after her. Just as he was about to catch her she dove down deep into the water and into safety.

Chapter 8

Finally at a depth where she felt comfortable, Breeze flipped around to take a look back at where she'd entered the water. That long piece of cloth was really slowing her down, so she took it off and let it sink into the ocean. She was about to take that itty-bitty piece of cloth that she'd pulled over her people legs off too when she REALLY looked up. Big, bright lights on huge poles illuminated the whole area. Immediately, she swam upwards! She swam to just below the surface where the people still couldn't see her. "YES! YES!" Breeze couldn't believe her eyes. There he was! There was Alex…standing there staring down into the water. Her heart skipped a beat! Her mind was made up. She would swim up to the surface, jump onto the land, and give him a great big kiss.

Just then, two humans jumped into the water really close to where she was with funny round things on their backs, masks over their faces, and something huge over each of their feet. They were headed straight for her.

They thought she'd jumped into the water because of fright and now they were chasing her in the water.

This would never do. She couldn't go up out of the water now. That kiss would have to wait! Breeze didn't know they were there to rescue her. She thought they were chasing her because she'd done something wrong. As much as she wanted that kiss…it would have to wait. She flipped around and dove for the deeper water…took off that string thing that was on her people legs, and let it float away behind her…also took off the string top. Immediately she conjured her beautiful tail back. Now she could really swim…And leave those funny looking humans behind.

The divers were surprised to see a bikini suit bottom and top floating toward them. Before they could move out of the way, the bikini top had floated right onto one of the diver's masks, hooking itself over the nose part and around the diver's ear. As the diver tried to pull the mask off, the strap was loosened slightly and the bikini top was quickly working its way underneath. This made it hard for the diver to see. He tried hard to take it off…but by this time the skimpy bikini top was hooked pretty well. A thin, narrow piece of the material had woven itself in and around his diving mask and managed to get underneath one of the sides. The harder he pulled on it…the more it went under the goggles, lifting one side up somewhat. This was making it more and more uncomfortable. The more he tried to get it loose the more it became attached to the goggles. Out of desperation, the diver took off his mask to free the item, but he couldn't see what he was doing and just wrapped it around a couple times more.

His companion became aware of the situation and came to help. He immediately saw what the problem was, took the mask out of his friend's hands and untangled the little bikini top from it.

By this time, Breeze had become aware they were not following her anymore and turned around for a closer look. She didn't want to be seen but she did want to see what they were doing…in HER territory.…So she watched.…She watched them search the sea bottom. It never entered her mind that they were searching for her…searching for her body. After watching for a short time, she decided she'd have some fun. She'd let them see her tail…only her tail.

Because the bikini bottom had also floated into their midst, the divers thought maybe she'd been attacked by sharks or something. All they knew was…a girl, frightened by fire alarms, had jumped into the sea. Now they were looking for her body because they presumed she was dead.

Breeze covered her head with seaweed and swam out of the darkness as fast as she could, turning in a quick circle so they could just see her tail flashing. It was a beautiful tail unlike anything else in the sea, and she wanted to see their reaction. She made several passes around…just to make sure.

The divers saw her tail all right—saw her whole body from the seaweed on down. Breeze was so camouflaged they couldn't tell what she was…only that they'd never seen or heard about anything that looked like that. Now they were worried and frightened. THAT was the sea creature that did harm to the pretty girl who had jumped into the water. They called up to the surface for backup. It didn't take very long for backup to come…with spear guns.

Breeze knew what spear guns were. She'd seen them kill her fish friends before. To keep the divers busy, she circled around and got above them….Then she headed out to sea as fast as she could go. She didn't go very far. Alex was on that shore, and she wanted to kiss him one more time. Trouble was…she didn't have any people clothes. She'd just discarded them. Alex knew she was a mermaid anyway so she didn't bother going on any of the little boats to find something else to wear. Breeze just circled around and headed for where she last saw

Alex standing. YES! He was still there...standing with a huge crowd of people.

Breeze wasted no time. She reached up, grabbed onto him, and pulled him into the water. Looking at the surprised expression on Alex's face, she realized how he must feel...realized he must be in shock over the incident. Who wouldn't be after being pulled into the water by a mermaid? She quickly put one arm around him, much like someone would if they were rescuing a drowning person, and headed for the nearest small boat.

By the time Alex realized what had happened; he'd not only received a mermaid's sweet kiss but had been pulled to a small shelf on one of the little boats that were docked in the harbor. He managed to break loose from Breeze's grip long enough to pull himself up onto that little shelf.

With one energetic push of her tail, Breeze flopped up on the shelf too...almost landing in Alex's lap. She again put her arms around him and gave him a big kiss, looked into his eyes, gave him a big smile, pressed her body close against his...gave him another great big smile...and another long, passionate kiss.

For a brief moment Alex tried to resist, but that was only for a VERY brief moment. Breeze was a very well-endowed, beautiful young mermaid with nothing on...but a tail. He remembered the last encounter with her...on the boat....He remembered their kiss from when he first realized she was a mermaid. This just wasn't happening! It was almost like in a dream. Her kiss was wonderful...like none other he'd ever experienced...

almost hypnotizing. Of course he kissed her back. What guy wouldn't?

Breeze could hear yelling and screaming from the humans. She did not know that the divers had seen her pull Alex into the water and were on their way to the boat. All she knew was…in spite of how much she wanted to stay…she couldn't. So she pulled back a little bit, put her hands on the still surprised Alex's shoulders, and looked into his eyes. Breeze gave him another big smile and softly whispered his name. "Alex!" Again she pressed her body close to his and gave him a very long, very passionate kiss. Then she pulled back, put one hand on his cheek, softly whispered his name again, and dove back into the sea.

By this time the divers were at the boat and saw what was happening. They tried to grab Breeze, but she was too fast for them. She reached out, quickly slipped their masks off and threw them as far out into the ocean as she could. Then she flipped them with her tail, which knocked both of them backwards, out of balance, and several yards away from the boat. The divers with the spear gun were close behind and saw what had just happened….But Breeze was too fast for them too. She left the area before they could even take aim.

Alex didn't want the mermaid hurt. He'd really enjoyed those kisses, and she'd done no harm. He'd had a hard time getting her out of his mind when she'd kissed him before, after pulling him off the cruise ship. Now, he was really going to have a hard time. No human had ever kissed him like she did. It was about time he boarded the cruise ship to help get ready for another dream vacation. This time they would be gone for two weeks. He knew what he'd be dreaming about. He'd be dreaming about that beautiful mermaid and those kisses.

The divers Breeze had smacked with her tail came back to the boat and asked Alex if he had a way to shore. Of course, he didn't! One of the divers radioed ashore for a small boat to pick him up. The other began to make fun of him about what happened with Breeze. "We saw that! We saw that…That…WAS THAT A REAL MERMAID? It was, wasn't it? Did you really kiss that…THAT FISH?"

Alex didn't like what he was hearing. He was glad Breeze had hit them with her tail. Right at that moment he wished he could do the same. The little boat arrived, and he lost no time getting into it…He told the guy in the boat to leave right away, that the divers were not coming along…that they had something else to do. This left both divers stranded without their mask.

Not wanting to answer any questions, Alex went straight to the cruise ship. He'd almost missed the cruise because of Breeze's impulsive actions. He changed his clothes, went out on the lowest deck, and put his hands on the railing. As he gazed over towards the fast disappearing shore line, he was hoping to see Breeze… but he didn't. That ocean would never look the same to him again.

Breeze wasn't about to give up that easily. She just knew Alex would be in town, and she wanted to find him….And that's where she decided to go…into town again. She loved those last kisses and wanted more. Right now she was on her way to another boat for more people clothes. This time she picked one of the bigger boats. Swimming around it a couple times, she didn't see anyone there so she climbed up the ladder and went on board.

Oh! This was not like the other boats she'd been on. It had a box on it but the only clothes there were the kind those humans wore in that awful building were they were killing the fish. This boat smelled like dead fish too. She wanted no part of anything on this boat….She turned around and dove back into the ocean.

By this time, most of the lights that had been on in the buildings were turned off, leaving only the ones on big poles still lit. The moon was shining, really big and bright, and Breeze suddenly felt tired. Retracing in her mind all she'd been through that day, she decided she'd just go to sleep for a while and take her chances going through the town and maybe finding Alex again tomorrow….Maybe she'd go on that big ship where she had originally met Alex. She knew better now how to act and felt that this time she could pass herself off as human and no one would know.

Chapter 9

The sun was shining brightly when Breeze woke up the next morning. She could see its pretty reflections and the shadows it cast through the water and was anxious to be on her way back into town. Clothes! She HAD to have something to wear. After past experiences she knew the humans would never accept her as she was...without any human clothes on. Thinking back, she remembered that humans didn't like their clothes wet either. *That* she really didn't understand at all because wet was the very best way to be...especially for a mermaid. She decided to sneak aboard the big cruise ship. It had a walkway leading up into it. First, she would just swim to the nearest little boat, borrow a couple of those itty-bitty pieces of cloth to wear then, swim over to the big ship, put them on and walk onto it. No one seemed to mind those itty-bitty pieces of cloth being wet. Silly humans!

Breeze was sure she could find more pieces of clothes once she was on the ship....So up to the surface she swam. She had come to the surface between several small boats, chose the pretty red one, conjured up her human legs and climbed on board. She knew right where to look for human clothes…found just the right itsy-bitsy red bikini and put the top on. Swimming with land legs just wasn't her style so she put her head through one of the holes of the itsy-bitsy bottom and dove back into the ocean.

Since she was in the middle of several smaller boats and couldn't see anything but those boats, she pointed herself in the general direction where the cruise ship was and swam underneath what boats were in her way. Rising to the surface, she looked toward where the cruise ship was. Her mouth dropped wide open. The cruise ship was gone! Breeze looked all around but didn't see it anywhere. In the worst way…she wanted to be on that ship. If only she could speak human language, she could get someone to take her to the ship. The secret lay in those buildings. Yes! She was going to town again. She was going to learn human talk. If she learned human talk and knew more about their ways, she could get someone to take her to that big ship.

Breeze thought about what she was going to do for a long time and finally decided not to go on the shore right in the town. She swam down the beach a ways with the bikini bottoms still hanging around her neck, trailing back through her beautiful, long, thick hair. After a short time, she stopped at a place where she thought she was alone.

She could see at a distance there was a big building that looked empty and no one was around. Conjuring up her land legs, she pulled the bikini bottom off her head, slid her legs into it and wore it like it should be worn. Still no one was around, so she walked right up to the door and tried to open it. It would not open. Breeze decided to walk around the building hoping to find a way in. Through the big windows, she could see lots of tables inside but no people. There were lots of pictures on the walls. She walked around the side of the building...then started walking along the back. One of the windows was wide open. It wasn't as big as the other windows and was a lot higher up. The opening was long and narrow...just big enough for her to get through, but it was too high to climb into.

Humans don't have it so nice after all, she thought. At home...in the ocean...all she would have to do was swim up there and float through that window. But here! On land...It took a lot of work to do anything. Swimming was even harder with land legs. *Humans really have it rough!* She thought. *They can't even walk around unless their body is covered with something. How silly!* She looked back up at the window and decided to walk the rest of the way around the building. Maybe there was a better way in. There wasn't! Everything else was shut tight.

There were several benches sitting around here and there, and Breeze lost no time getting one of them. She also noticed that things were heavier on land than they were in the sea. She tugged and pulled at that bench until it was sitting just below the window. Standing on it, Breeze could almost see in the window but not quite. She put her hands on the window's edge to pull her self up and noticed something was in the way. It moved but not very much. Thinking she'd just move it aside like a piece of seaweed, Breeze hit it really hard. Her hand went right through, and it seemed to hurt, even bled a little…but she had to get inside. This did not stop her from doing what she wanted to do. She continued to pull herself up, pushed the stuff in the window out of the way and…finally managed to get her head through the opening.

Inside she could see several small areas sectioned off with small containers of water in them. *How strange,* she thought. *What possible use could humans have with these funny looking containers of water?* It wouldn't even be easy to drink out of one of them. By now, she had managed to pull herself up enough to get one leg in the opening. The rest of the way would be easy. Looking down again, she decided she'd scoot over to where she could grab onto one of the walls that were sticking up and going nowhere and let herself down to the floor. She just had a feeling NOT to step in any of those containers of water. The wall was too far down so she just grabbed at the bottom of the window opening, let her human legs swing down, and let go.

Her right foot did land in one of those small containers of water. Breeze started to lose her balance so to steady herself she grabbed on to the shiny little handle that was hooked to the container of water. All of a sudden she heard an odd noise. The water around her foot started going round and round while more water was pouring into the container. This scared Breeze, and she lost no time pulling her foot out. She almost fell down in her haste to get out of that silly little boxed-in area.

Without thinking, Breeze reached out to stop her fall. Immediately, her hands hit the edge of the sink bowl and she grabbed on. Water began to come out of a small shiny pipe and it was splattering all over her hands. This scared her too. She sucked in a deep breath and lifted up her head. For a few brief seconds the reflection in the big mirror also frightened her. It didn't take long for her to realize she was looking at herself. She stood up tall, took her hands out of the sink and began to make faces at herself in the mirror. This went on for some time until she heard people voices coming from outside the door.

Right now, Breeze wanted to observe, not mingle. She wanted to learn all she could about the humans and what made them scream and yell so much. Trying to act like she belonged where she was, Breeze opened the door. There was a long, passage way with lots of doors on both sides of it. No one was there. Human voices mingling with beautiful new sounds were coming from the other side of the door across from hers. Those sounds were almost like the whales make. Breeze just had to look. Slowly, she opened the door.

There were several humans in the room but no one screamed when they saw her. One of them, a young girl about her age stood up and walked toward her. She said some words that Breeze didn't understand…took Breeze's hand and led her to where they both sat down. "My name is Sandy," she said.

Breeze lit up with a great big smile. She understood Sandy. A couple of her friends were named Sandy, so she said, "Breeze!"

Sandy smiled and put her fingers in front of her mouth indicating not to talk.

Breeze understood what the fingers in front of the mouth meant. She got that at home from Oceana. They both sat there together until the music stopped.

"Do you sing...Or play an instrument?" Sandy asked.

Breeze just looked at her with questioning eyes.

Sandy asked again. "Do you sing...Or play an instrument?"

Breeze felt bad. She knew Sandy was trying to be friends but she did NOT understand what she was saying. She'd never been taught about instruments or human singing so she pointed to herself and said, "Breeze!"

Sandy knew now that Breeze didn't speak the same language. With both hands, she took hold of the front of her blouse and shook it. "Clothes!" She shook her blouse again and slowly asked. "Where...are...your...clothes?"

Breeze understood the word clothes real well. That's the word everyone used when they had yelled at her. She gave a great big smile, pulled at the front of her little bikini top, and happily repeated, "Clothes!"

Oh, boy! Sandy thought. *She really doesn't understand!* Sandy stood up, took Breeze's hand, and led her to a picture of a farmhouse with animals....She pointed to the picture and asked, "Where do you live? Where...is...your...house?"

Breeze just shook her head back and forth and pointed to the house and the animals, naming off the ones she knew as she ponted to them. Then she gazed around the room and saw a picture of the ocean and a big ocean liner....She walked over to it, pointed to the ocean and, with a big smile, said. "Home!"

Sandy now thought Breeze was from another country and had missed her cruise ship. Breeze seemed nice enough. She had an extra bedroom in the apartment she was renting so she'd just ask Breeze if she wanted to stay with her until she found what ship she'd been on... then she could go home safely. Sandy again pointed to the picture of the farmhouse and asked, "Want to come home with me?" She took Breeze by the hand and started to walk towards the door.

Breeze was hesitant, but went along for the walk. She was just happy someone was being her friend instead of yelling at her....so she went along.

Sandy led Breeze to her car, opened the passenger door and said, "Get in! We can go to my place for a while...get something to eat, and I'll see if I can find something for you to wear." She pointed to Breeze's bikini. "You can't just go around in...IN...THAT!"

Breeze had never been in a car before so she just stood there looking into the open door.

Now, Sandy knew something was REALLY different about this girl. She didn't know the language and didn't seem to understand about getting into her car. Again Sandy said, "Breeze! This is my car." She pointed to herself and said, "Sandy," then she pointed to her car and said, "Car"...then she got in and sat down...then she stepped back out of the car and pointed to the seat. "Breeze! Sit down."

Breeze looked at her, smiled and said, "CAR".... Then she said, "SIT DOWN," and she sat down in the car.

Sandy shut the door, which startled Breeze.

Now she felt like she was being held captive in that little box with windows that Sandy called a car.

Sandy walked around the front of her car, opened the driver's door, and sat down.

Breeze felt much better. She was now not alone in the little car-box.

Sandy turned to Breeze. "You ready? Have to buckle your seat belt, you know."

Of course, Breeze didn't understand a word Sandy said. So Sandy reached over, pulled the belt across and around her and fastened it.

Fear was beginning to take the place of the happiness Breeze felt from being befriended. She did not understand, nor did she like being tied into her seat. Then Sandy started the engine. It wasn't very loud, but it confirmed that fact that she really shouldn't be there…sitting in a seat all tied up. All of a sudden the whole car-box started moving. Breeze's eyes got very big. She sucked in a deep breath, stiffened up her body, and grabbed onto the door handle with her right hand. Her left hand was clenched into a tight fist. Yes! She was afraid! In the ocean, she could cope with most anything. Here on land, everything was new and different….And LOUD…And scary! The car-box was moving all right, and it was moving faster and faster. Trees and buildings were rushing by so fast she couldn't even see their details.

Other car-boxes were moving too…moving right towards them. Each time another car-box headed straight for them, Breeze thought for sure they were going to hit head-on. Her breathing became more rapid and got louder and louder as they drove. She sucked in her breath each time another one headed towards them. To her, this was one of the worst experiences she'd ever had in her life. She felt like screaming...but she didn't! She didn't want Sandy to know she was afraid.

Suddenly, an awful sound started coming into her ears. It reminded her of when she pulled the handle in that building and all the humans ran. The sound got louder and louder. Finally, Breeze let loose of the door handle and covered both ears with her hands. Two huge, red car-boxes were coming, and they were headed straight for them with bright red lights flashing. Breeze could take no more! Between the awful sounds and those two huge red boxes speeding towards her, she couldn't hold her screams in any longer. She let loose with one loud, shrill, scream after the other.

It had taken Sandy a few minutes before she became aware that Breeze just might not have ridden in a car before. When Breeze started screaming, she knew. She pulled over to the side of the road to let the fire trucks go by, then turned to Breeze and asked, "Are you doing OK?"

Breeze knew Sandy had asked her a question. Sandy didn't seem to be afraid at all. She didn't even seem to mind those awful, loud noises and the big, red boxes that had just passed them. Being the strong daughter of Neptune, she decided she wasn't going to show her terror. She was just going to sit there and pretend everything was OK. If Sandy could do this...she could do it too.

Her screams and the frightened look on her face had already given her away. Sandy sat there on the side of the road for a short time after the fire trucks passed. In calm, reassuring words she tried to explain what was happening.

Breeze didn't understand Sandy's words, but she felt her calmness and managed a smile.

Sandy, of course didn't understand why Breeze was so frightened. She started to pull back out into the street but had second thoughts, turned to Breeze, and said calmly. "Breeze, my house isn't far away. I'm going to pull back out on the road, OK?" She looked at Breeze intently and shook her head up and down.

Breeze understood the head shake and the OK. She smiled and repeated the OK.

Sandy lived on the top floor in an apartment complex overlooking the ocean. She dearly loved the water, especially the ocean. Her father owned the cannery down the road that Breeze had had so much trouble with. She'd always hated how the fish were treated and didn't have much to do with her father because of it. All her life she'd dreamed about being able to swim with the fish and really breathe underwater...just like the fish.

When they arrived at her apartment building, Sandy went around to the other side of the car and opened Breeze's door. Pointing to the top floor she said, "This is where I live, Breeze. I spend most of my free time either in or by the ocean. My apartment window looks out over the ocean. You'll like it...I think."

Of course, Breeze only understood a few words of what Sandy was saying but she seemed pretty happy saying it...so Breeze follower her into the elevator. The sensation of the elevator made her suck in her breath.

Again, she noticed that Sandy wasn't afraid, so she pretended not to be either.

Entering the apartment, Breeze had another pleasant surprise. There were lots of pictures on the walls...of the ocean, sunsets over the ocean, ships, a big whale, and even one of a mermaid swimming through seaweed. There were also a couple see-through boxes that had different kinds of fish in them. Breeze went right up to one of the tanks with fish. The tanked fish knew instantly what she was and told her they were unhappy in that small area...said they got well taken care of, fed good and all that, but they just wanted to be free to go where they wanted.

"I like the ocean a lot," Sandy said, as she opened the draperies that hung over her sliding door. Pushing the door wide open, she added, "Come on out here on the deck with me, Breeze."

Breeze was reluctant to leave the fish tank but as soon as the drapes were opened and she saw the view she was on her way there. She'd never been so high up in a building before. She'd been on that cruise ship...with everyone chasing her. That was really high up. She remembered diving into the ocean from there...long way down. This was on land! Completely different! Breeze marveled that they could make people boxes so big. She stood there on the deck and listened while Sandy pointed out different things. Breeze, of course, didn't understand much of what she was saying.

"You hungry?" Sandy asked.

Breeze just looked at her.

Sandy took her by the hand, led her to the refrigerator, opened it, pointed to her mouth, and said. "Hungry?"

Breeze understood that. She also saw the bottle of milk sitting in there and remembered how she felt after drinking it. She saw eggs sitting on the door and remembered one of them splattering all over her clothes.

Sandy pulled the milk out, reached into the cupboard for two glasses, and started filling one of them.

Breeze put her hand out and grabbed the empty glass. "NO!"

Sandy raised her eyebrows when she heard Breeze make such a bold statement, poured her a glass of water, sliced up a tomato, and opened a can of beef stew. With each item, she said the name of it and had Breeze repeat it.

After they ate Sandy left the room. When she came back she was wearing two little itsy-bitsy pieces of clothes similar to what Breeze was wearing, carrying two big pieces of cloth and some odd looking things. "Let's go!" she said.

Breeze followed her out the door and into the elevator…then out of the building and across the beach to the water.

One by one Sandy spread the towels out. She put on her diving mask and picked up her snorkel. She pointed to the extra mask and snorkel she'd laid on the towel for Breeze and said, "Go ahead! Put them on and let's go for a swim."

Breeze just stood there.

Sandy picked up the extra snorkel and mask and started walking toward the water…with Breeze following. She handed them to Breeze again, pointed to her own face and said, "It's OK, Breeze...Put them on, and let's go for a swim."

Breeze took the objects out of Sandy's hand. By this time, they had reached the water, and Sandy lost no time diving into the ocean for her swim. Breeze didn't want to be bothered with all that silly stuff. She dropped it all on the beach, including her bikini bottom, dove into the water, and conjured up her tail.

Sandy lost no time searching the ocean floor. She hoped to find some neat shells or some other special thing and had a small bag that she'd attached to her side just to carry them in. She was so busy looking at the sand and what she might find there she was oblivious to what Breeze was doing. The beaches where she lived didn't have big waves so she never stayed really close to the shore. A bit further out than she dared to go, she saw something fairly large sticking out of the sand. It wasn't THAT far out, so she decided to go for it and started snorkeling her way over there.

POW! All of a sudden something collided with her, knocking the snorkel out of her mouth and the mask up onto her forehead. Sandy was frightened half out of her wits. She stuck the snorkel back into her mouth and adjusted her mask. It was a dolphin! She noticed there were several dolphins swimming around her. One swam straight towards her and pushed her with its nose for quite some distance out towards the sea. She'd never known dolphins to act like this before and became more and more frightened. Sandy was a very good swimmer, but dealing with dolphins like this was something else. Lifting her head out of the water, she saw they had pushed her a great distance from shore;

she was becoming very worried. One dolphin swam under her, raised her up out of the water, and then sent her tumbling in the air.

Breeze saw what was happening. She was used to playing like this with the dolphins, but Sandy seemed to be upset…didn't seem to be enjoying herself at all…. Maybe she was even in trouble. She decided to swim over to her and motioned to the dolphins for them to stop playing for a while.

By this time, Sandy was way out in the ocean and getting tired. She looked back at the shore way off in the distance and started swimming towards it. Many times, she'd snorkeled in this ocean and NEVER had an experience like this.

Breeze swam up beside her, with a big smile on her face. The dolphins were swimming close by her side. When she looked at Sandy's face she could tell she was worried.

"WE'RE TOO FAR OUT!" Sandy screamed. "THEY PUSHED ME!" Sandy looked questioningly at Breeze, who didn't seem to be worried at all. In fact, she noticed that the dolphins seemed to be staying right along side her.

"HOME!" Breeze said. She lifted up her arm, gave a great big smile, pointed to the water, and again said "HOME!" She then pushed the dolphin next to her to the side, sank down under the water, and came up fast doing a big flip in the air.

Sandy gasped! She couldn't believe what she was seeing.

When Breeze shot out of the water her whole body was visible. She still had her bikini top on, but her legs were gone. From the waist down her body graduated into a long, beautiful tail. While in the midst of her flip Breeze once more happily shouted. "HOME!" Back in the water, she looked over at Sandy and realized she must be shocked at the fact that she was a mermaid and not another human.

Breeze swam over to where Sandy was, smiled again, and said, "OK?"

Sandy was still in shock! Not believing what she was seeing...but there it was. Breeze was a mermaid, and there SHE was...way, way out in the ocean where she didn't belong. At this point, she didn't know what to do. She was getting more and more tired by the minute, and land was a very long distance away, a very, very long distance away. "I have to get back to the shore," she said, almost in tears.

Breeze knew the word shore, and it had become obvious that Sandy was tired. She looked toward one of the dolphins and motioned for it to come to her.

The dolphin knew what was needed and scooped itself right under Sandy, causing her to flop awkwardly onto its back.

Breeze's hands were right there to make sure she didn't fall off. She remembered the words Sandy used when she wanted her to sit in that car-box. "SIT DOWN!" she commanded. Breeze pointed to the dolphin Sandy was lying on, smiled widely, and again commanded, "SIT DOWN!"

Sandy was speechless and shaking with fright. Her mouth was wide open. Her mask was hanging around her neck with the snorkel attached to it. The little bag of shells she'd found was still tied around her waist, and she was lying awkwardly on the dolphin's back, taking in big, fast gulps of air.

"YOU...DOING...OK?" Breeze was trying to remember just what Sandy said when she was afraid in the car-box. "SIT DOWN!" she again commanded. To show her just what was needed, Breeze flipped herself up on the back of one of the other dolphins and tried to lift herself into a sitting position. The tail was awkward on the back of the dolphin, so she conjured up her land legs.

Sandy let out a loud, long gasp. Her mouth dropped wide open, and her eyes grew as big as saucers. She couldn't believe what she was seeing...but there it was...right before her eyes.

Breeze pointed to the dolphin Sandy was lying on, gave a great big smile, and again commanded, "SIT DOWN!"

Sandy was still shaking with unbelief, but she put her hands on the dolphin and tried to sit up. The dolphin's back was slick and she was afraid she'd fall off, so she decided she'd rather keep her arms around the dolphin and remain in a lying position. Actually, she wasn't even sure she should BE on this dolphin... couldn't believe she was actually riding on a dolphin.

"YOU...DOING...OK?" Breeze asked again, copying words Sandy had used when she was frightened in the car-box. "OK?"

The dolphins started swimming toward shore with the girls on their backs. It didn't take but a few minutes before Sandy's fear slowly began to leave. She actually found she was enjoying herself. She did try to sit up...a little and, looking out of the corner of her eye, managed to give Breeze a slight smile. As they drew near to shore she realized…this was the sort of thing she'd been dreaming of doing all her life…and she really didn't want to stop. Looking over at Breeze, she smiled, quickly put her hand in the air, making a small circle out of her first two fingers…then shouted, "OK!"

"Home?" Breeze asked.

"NO! THIS IS GREAT! BREEZE, THIS IS GREAT!" Sandy was all excited with a big smile on her face as she started petting the dolphin and bent down to hug it. "I can't believe I'm here! SITTING ON A DOLPHIN…and YOU…YOU'RE…YOU'RE A…A…MERMAID!" She managed the courage to take one hand off the dolphin and pointed to Breeze's legs. "HOW DID YOU…YOU'RE…A…BREEZE?"

"MORE?" Breeze asked.

Sandy still couldn't believe what she was doing. All she knew was…she loved what she was doing. "Yes! Oh, YES! I LOVE THIS! JUST…LOVE THIS!"

Breeze conjured up her tail, flipped off her dolphin and headed back out to sea…with all the dolphins following…and with Sandy still on the back of one of them.

For some reason, it didn't seem to bother Sandy at all that Breeze was a mermaid. In fact, inside, she was wishing she could have a beautiful tail…like Breeze's whenever she wanted it. They played with the dolphins the rest of the afternoon. Sometimes Sandy was on the dolphin and sometimes she was off.

The sun was beginning to go down, and there was a rosy glow in the sky. Breeze did a flip in the air and dove to the bottom of the ocean. She came up holding a great big, beautiful shell that she handed to Sandy. "HOME?" She asked.

Sandy's bag was still strapped to her waist. The shell was so big it filled it completely. She looked at Breeze and said, almost under her breath, "Yes! Home! Are you coming home with me?"

Breeze didn't answer.

Sandy held out her hand toward Breeze. "Are you coming home with me?"

This time Breeze understood and answered, "Yes!"

Chapter 10

For over a week, Breeze stayed with Sandy. She was quick to learn the language, and they enjoyed sharing different experiences. She did not tell Sandy about Alex, but she did keep asking when the big cruise ship would be coming back. She told her she didn't want to miss seeing it. Once they could understand each other a little, Sandy started asking what she could do to be able to have a mermaid tail. She figured...if Breeze could change her mermaid tail into legs, she ought to be able to change her legs into a mermaid tail.

Breeze tried and tried to conjure up a mermaid tail for Sandy...even though, in the back of her mind, she knew Neptune would be angry if she succeeded. They went into the ocean and tried. They tried on the shore. Breeze showed her everything Neptune had taught her about conjuring up legs when she wanted them and then having her tail back again. Trying to teach this to

Sandy was just not working. Day after day went by, and Breeze was getting tired of trying to teach something that didn't seem to be working. Then, she had an idea. She was showing Sandy the same way Neptune showed her. It took her a little while to understand what to do. Maybe it didn't work because, on Sandy, it had to work BACKWARDS...like when she changed her own legs for her tail. Sandy already had legs so Sandy would need to be changing legs to a tail.

This time it worked! Sandy was so happy she could hardly contain herself. It didn't take very many tries before she knew how to do it all by herself. When she finally did learn, she wanted to take off on an adventure out to sea to see everything she had read and heard about.

Breeze was constantly asking when the cruise ship would arrive...not wanting to miss her chance for one more kiss from Alex. Finally, she got Sandy to walk to the ship's docking area and ask the ticket agent...said she had a friend named Alex who was on board. When she found out there were still several days left, they both made the necessary changes, left their bathing suits on the beach, and swam out to sea.

Sandy was in awe at the things Breeze was showing her. They swam past her father's fish cannery. She had already told Breeze that her father owned that cannery... that because she didn't agree with his methods they were not on very friendly terms.

Breeze was quick to tell about all the trouble she'd gotten into there....Then she told Sandy about the crab pods and how the men in black with spear guns had chased her. As they swam under the pier Breeze not only told Sandy, but showed her, how to break the lines of the fishermen…break off the ends that had the hooks with pieces of fish on them and how to allow the fish to get away.

Sandy delighted in helping to do that…wanted to do it again and again.

Feeling assured that Sandy knew how to use her tail…Breeze led her farther out into the ocean. She took her to one of the sunken pirate ships and was just starting to guide her through it when some of her mermaid friends showed up; among them were Shell and Barney, two mermen who had tried to show their affection for Breeze. After kissing Alex, Breeze wasn't the least bit interested in either one of them.

When they saw Sandy, both of them wanted to become acquainted with her and immediately swam to her side. Sandy couldn't believe what was happening and immediately became infatuated with Shell. Mermen are not like human men….When Shell saw she was interested in him, he immediately put his arms around her and gave her a big, long kiss. Sandy was immediately in love and didn't want to go any farther. She just wanted to be with Shell. On land she had found no one she was interested in. Here…by the pirate ship… it was love at first site.

Breeze started to explain to Shell that Sandy wasn't really a mermaid but Shell wouldn't listen.

He just kept kissing her…said he'd never met anyone like her…never ever wanted to be without her and to please just leave them alone.

Now, Breeze knew she was really in trouble. If Neptune found out about THIS, he would surely be angry...maybe even banish her from the kingdom like he did with Olympia....He'd banned Olympia to that sunken ship where no one could visit or else they'd also get into trouble. Breeze definitely didn't want that! "SANDY!" she shouted. "WE'VE REALLY GOT TO BE GETTING BACK. IT'S LATE! SANDY!"

Sandy was paying no attention whatsoever. She was completely involved with Shell, and they were too busy holding each other...kissing and hugging.

"SHELL!" Breeze thought she'd take a different approach. "SHELL, WANT TO KNOW A SECRET?"

Shell paid no attention.

Barney was watching all this and had become very jealous. "I'll break it up!" he said. "Just watch me!" He swam way back away from them....Then with all the speed he could gather he put his arms in front of him with his hands together and swam right into them, causing Shell to be knocked one way and Sandy the other. "THERE!" Barney yelled....Then he turned around and swam off a short distance in a fit of jealousy.

Taking full advantage of the situation, Breeze announced time out, grabbed Shell and pulled him aside. She tried to explain that Sandy was NOT a mermaid but was a human. Shell, of course, would not listen. To protect her freedom, Breeze swung around and flipped Shell right in the face with her tail. At the same time, she acted like she didn't see Sandy coming and did the same thing to her. This knocked poor Sandy for a loop. Breeze grabbed her around her waist and started swimming towards shore as fast as she could.

It took a few minutes for Shell to come to his senses. When he did, he began swimming after them.

Breeze was fast, and she was strong. She reached the shore before Shell…laid Sandy down on the beach, and managed to get her legs back.

Shell was close enough to see all this…saw that Sandy really was a human…saw everything. Shell had fallen madly in love with Sandy, and to him, it didn't matter. He thought if she was in the sea once as a mermaid, she could do it again….So he swam right up to them and voiced his opinion.

By this time, Sandy was wide awake…saw that she had her legs back…saw Shell swimming in the water looking at her, and started yelling at Breeze…. "WHAT DID YOU DO THAT FOR? BREEZE, THIS IS THE FIRST TIME I'VE EVER CARED FOR ANYONE! I WAS—"

Shell interrupted, yelling, "BREEZE, YOU HAD NO RIGHT TO DO THAT! I DON'T CARE IF SANDY IS A MERMAID OR A HUMAN! IT DOESN'T MATTER TO ME!

Sandy got up, walked to where Shell was and sat down beside him in the water.

"Listen!" Breeze said. "Listen to me real close! Shell! YOU know about Olympia, don't you?"

Shell hesitated for a few minutes. "Yes! Yes, I do. Everyone does… but what does that have to do with us? With you…Or with Sandy and me?"

Breeze went on…"You remember the reason she got banned from being among us, don't you?"

Shell put his arm around Sandy and said, "Of course I do. We ALL know that. She lived with a human and...and..." He then stopped right in the middle of his sentence. "Breeze...I love Sandy." He pulled her close and kissed her on the cheek. "I don't CARE if she's human or mermaid. I LOVE HER!"

Sandy put both arms around Shell, gave him a great big kiss, and asked, "Who is Olympia? All I know is... I've never felt this way before. I LOVE being a mermaid and don't care if I EVER go back home." With that, she conjured up her tail. Looking at Breeze, she added, "If Shell wants me...I'll just go anywhere with him. Wish we could stay friends but...this is what I've been dreaming of all my life, and I'm NOT GOING TO LET IT PASS ME BY!"

Shell looked at Breeze, gave Sandy a big kiss, and said. "Breeze, you've been my friend all my life. I don't want to get you into trouble! You get into enough of that all by yourself. I just want everyone to be happy. If Sandy wants to be with me...then that's what I want too. Trust me, Breeze. We'll just go someplace else and no one will know." They swam off into the sea together, and that was the last time Breeze saw either of them.

Chapter 11

Breeze couldn't believe Sandy just took off like that. She'd gotten to know her pretty well staying with her...knew how she loved the water and all that was in it but had no idea she'd actually prefer it to the life she had. Because of all this, she thought it best if she'd make Olympia's acquaintance. She didn't want to make the same mistakes Olympia made and thought if she got the information firsthand, she'd know just what to avoid. Breeze hung around with Barney for a day or so making up her mind...and to see if Sandy would change her mind and come back, but she didn't. Breeze never saw or heard from Sandy again.

Barney, of course wanted Breeze to stay, told her she was the best company he'd ever had...said he'd always wished she was his. He gave her a big kiss hoping she'd change her mind about seeing Olympia...but she didn't.

To Breeze, Barney's kiss was nothing like the one she had with Alex, and she wasn't about to settle down with Barney, no matter how nice he was. Breeze had made up her mind. She was going to see Olympia, and she was going to find Alex again. Now that she could understand human language, she knew it would be much easier. Breeze put her arm around Barney…told him he was a special friend but she wasn't ready to settle down with a mate…that there were lots of things she wanted to do first.

Barney promised Breeze he wouldn't tell where she went, left her to do whatever she needed to do, and then he reluctantly swam away.

Breeze swam off in the direction of the old ship Olympia lived in, but after traveling for about an hour, she turned back. The cruise ship was due in at any time, and she really didn't want to miss it…didn't want to miss having a chance to meet and kiss Alex again.

It was nearing dark when she arrived back at the dock. Sure enough, there was the cruise ship. Passengers were still unloading, so she knew it hadn't been there very long. She was about to conjure up her land legs when she realized…she didn't have any clothes on. Humans HAD to have clothes on…Why? She still couldn't understand.

She swam back to where the smaller boats were and was about to board one of them when she remembered… Sandy had clothes! She had lots of them, and they all fit her. She'd just swim over by Sandy's place and get some of her clothes. She'd let those poor little fish loose while she was there too. It was dark by the time she reached the shore. Yes! The swimming suits were still lying there on the beach where they'd left them.

Breeze conjured up her legs, slipped into a suit and walked up to Sandy's place. Sandy hadn't locked the

Breeze...the Mermaid

door, so she just walked right in. The first thing she did was to put all the little fish into small containers, take them to the seaside, and let them loose. No one would be there to feed them anymore anyway.

This accomplished, Breeze went back into Sandy's place, put some of the clothes on that were in her closet, put some others in a little suitcase that was there, and left. She was lucky. No one saw her.

Now to walk to that ship and see Alex. She couldn't wait to get another kiss.

As Breeze was walking along the highway, she saw a family of black and white cats trying to cross it. They were gorgeous! She watched them intently, observing that the white stripe going down their back and down to the tip of their fluffy tail gave them a special beauty. The little animals ran as fast as they could across the road but a speeding car hit three of them. The fourth, a young female, not quite grown, barely managed to escape with its life.

"Oh, my!" Breeze exclaimed as she picked up the pretty, fluffy black and white kitty that had managed to get away. She felt its little body shaking as it looked into her eyes. "Are you OK?" she asked as she cuddled it in her arms. Looking back across the road, she noticed more cars racing down it. They all seemed to take no thought about the tragedy one of them had just caused. Most of those cars did seem to be trying to miss the little dead animals, but they were lying right where they kept getting run over again and again. She noticed a strange odor that she'd never smelled before coming from them but didn't think much of it.

Right now she was concerned about the little one that had managed to escape. "You're REALLY a very pretty little cat." she said as she cradled the scared little animal in her arms. "I saw what happened to your family, and I'm really very sorry." The little, fluffy black and white cat looked up at her and seemed to be content that it was safe and being cuddled. Breeze noticed that this cat looked a lot different than the ones she'd met in that barn. She just loved its big, fluffy tail. "Are you OK, little friend. I saw what happened, and I'm sorry. Are you going to be OK? You're such a pretty little cat. I think the white stripe going down your back to the tip of your tail makes you look really special."

"My name is Sweetie." The little female skunk smiled. "Most people are afraid of me but I detect you're not a human. I also detect that you're not afraid of me. You look like a human but something about you is not like a human."

"My name is Breeze. Actually, Sweetie," Breeze said with a smile, "I'm not a human. I'm a mermaid, and I'm just here to see what it's like to be a human. I'm on my way to meet a human called Alex. He's on that cruise ship that's coming in." Breeze stroked Sweetie's fur and fluffy tail. "You seem awfully nice to me, and you're really beautiful. I can't understand why anyone would be afraid of you."

"Trust me! They all are! Even animals are afraid of me. I can't understand why you're not. Mind if I stay with you for a little while? I'm still frightened from what just happened, and I'm very young and haven't been very many places."

"Do you like the water?"

"Not really! Guess I can handle it if I get wet but I really don't like it."

"Then I'll not take you swimming with me. I know you probably feel bad right now since you no longer have your family. If it's OK with you...on the way to the ship I'll try help you find another family you can be with until you are all grown."

"Oh!" Sweetie said, as she snuggled in Breeze's arms. "I would like that. I'd just love to have some friends. Do you think you could find me some that are the same as me?"

"I don't know," Breeze answered. "I'll carry you for a while until you get over the shock of losing your family. Remember, I am on a mission! I'm going to see Alex and get another kiss. If you'd rather not come along—"

"Oh! Yes!" Sweetie interrupted. "I'd love to come along. No one has ever wanted to be my friend except, of course, my family."

They'd only walked for a little while when Breeze realized…this walking was a very slow way of traveling. She'd never get to that ship before it docked. She decided to turn back to Sandy's. Sandy had a car. "Sweetie!" She asked, "Have you ever ridden in a car?"

"NO! I've never ridden in anything. What's a car?"

Breeze thought for a moment then answered, "Sweetie, a car is one of those things that ran over your family."

"I DON'T WANT ANYTHING TO DO WITH THOSE AWFUL THINGS! DON'T YOU EVEN THINK I WOULD GET IN ONE…BECAUSE I WON'T! AND YOU CAN'T MAKE ME!"

"OK! OK! You don't have to get so angry about it. I'm trying to help you."

About that time, they passed a building where there were lots of half grown humans running and doing things. "Would you like to go in there, Sweetie? Maybe one of those humans would like to keep you for a pet. I learned that humans kept pets when I visited land once before. They feed them and everything."

"THAT SOUNDS GREAT! TAKE ME THERE!" Sweetie snuggled very close to Breeze, swished her tail in Breeze's face, and added, "I think it would just be wonderful if someone would be my close friend. I would shower them with love every day.

Breeze opened a metal gate and walked into the yard. Several of the smaller humans saw her enter, and as soon as the children saw what she was carrying they all ran over to see. One of the very small little girl humans walked right up to her and started petting Sweetie.

Sweetie became uneasy with this as she was still upset from what happened to her family and not used to attention in this way. Since she was safe in Breeze's arms, she allowed the petting. Breeze allowed the little girl to walk close as they went into the big building. The girl was very persistent and kept asking to hold the pretty kitty...said she wanted to keep her for her own.

Since Breeze wanted desperately to be on her way back to the cruise ship, she said that would be fine just as long as Sweetie got a good home and would be well taken care of. Carefully she put Sweetie in the little girl's arms. To make sure Sweetie would be OK, she followed the girl into a room filled with lots of small humans sitting in tiny chairs. When they saw Sweetie in the arms of one of their classmates, they all got up out of their chairs and came running over yelling, oh! Let me see. Can I hold it. It's so cute. What is it?"

Breeze said goodbye to Sweetie and started walking out of the room.

The big human who was sitting behind a big box stood up, took one look at what was in the girl's arms and started yelling, "WHAT IS THAT? AAAAH!... A SKUNK! A SKUNK! GET THAT SKUNK OUT OF HERE!" She pointed her finger toward the door and continued yelling, "GET IT OUT OF HERE! NO! NO! GET OUT! GET OUT! OH! EEEEEH! MY CLASSROOM!" All this yelling scared Sweetie. She sprayed the little girl who was holding her with love for wanting to keep her then leaped out of the her hands and ran back and forth from one side of the room to the other. Blinded by fright, the little skunk turned her pretty, black and white bushy tail this way and that, spraying perfume on everything within reach. Sweetie then leaped onto the little chairs, jumped from one to the other spraying perfume, and then jumped onto the big box that the large human was standing behind. Yes! The woman was still yelling!

Because of that human's actions and loud, screaming voice, Sweetie managed to shower her with more perfume than anyone else. The more she screamed…the more perfume she got. Looking around, Sweetie noticed Breeze walking out of the door and out of her sight. Frightened little Sweetie ran towards that door, between the legs of the little humans, under Breeze's legs, and out the door. She turned away from the direction Breeze was walking and ran down the long, wide hall.

Lots of humans were in that hallway opening little boxes that hung on it. When they saw Sweetie, they started running in all directions…screaming, "SKUNK! SKUNK!" The frightened little skunk zigzagged from wall to wall, managing to attach its scent to everyone and everything in its path. Realizing there was nowhere to run to, Sweetie turned around and ran back to where she had last seen Breeze.

Breeze couldn't stand all the confusion and loud screaming. She was really anxious to get away from the smell Sweetie was giving out and ran towards the outside door, fresh air, and freedom from that awful yelling. As soon as she opened that door, Sweetie ran between her legs and towards the gate they had come through earlier to get into the yard.

"Why did you do that?" Breeze asked.

The little skunk stopped for a moment to listen. Breeze had befriended her.

"You left a horrible strong smell everywhere!" Breeze continued. "That was not nice! No one is going to want to take you home if you do that. I'm glad you didn't spray me with that stuff. I don't want to smell like that either. Please don't shower me with any of your...STUFF! You were real sweet when I was holding you in my arms, and I thought you would be able to find a home here. That larger human called you a skunk. Is that what you are?"

"YES! THAT IS WHAT I AM...and...I don't think my spray has a terrible smell. I LIKE THE WAY I SMELL, AND I LIKE THE SMELL OF WHAT I SPRAY. YOU CAN'T SPRAY LIKE THAT, CAN YOU? NO WAY DO I WANT TO SEE ANY OF THOSE HUMANS AGAIN. I'M BIG ENOUGH! I CAN TAKE CARE OF MYSELF!" shouted the little skunk. "You were nice to care about me when I was sad. I'm OK now! See you later! MAYBE!" Sweetie ran out the gate and down the road.

Breeze noticed the humans had run out the door also and were swiftly running towards her...still yelling...asking her why she had brought a skunk into the classroom. Breeze was out of their sight before they even reached the gate.

Chapter 12

Only problem was...Sweetie had taken a lot of her time. Now that Breeze was alone, she was in a hurry. She was all dressed up and had land legs...and did not want to miss the cruise ship. Walking was a lot slower than swimming in the ocean. She realized it would take her a long time to walk all the way to the boat. Then she remembered....Sandy had a car. Yes! Breeze had ridden with Sandy several times. She saw how Sandy operated it. She could do this! If Sandy could do it...SHE could do it! She walked back to Sandy's apartment and plucked the keys off the hook by the inside of the door. Breeze again whispered to herself, "Yes! If Sandy can do it...I can do it!" With that bit of self-assurance, she walked out the door and down the sidewalk to the car.

Breeze opened the driver's side door, sat in the seat, and took a deep breath...then another. She put the key into the little slot on the steering wheel and turned it. "YES!" The engine started...just like it had for Sandy. A big smile came across her face. *That was easy*, she thought. Next, she remembered Sandy pushing buttons to make pretty music...so, she started pushing buttons. The windshield wipers started going back and forth and washer fluid sprayed all over the windows. NO! THAT wasn't what she wanted. She turned those off, leaving her windows wet with washer fluid all over them, then started pushing and pulling one button after the other. Her mirrors were soon tilted upward, the gas tank cover was opened, and the cigarette lighter popped out glowing red. After fiddling with the buttons for a while, Breeze was finally able to stop everything...except for the open gas tank cover. She put her hand on the stick that stuck up out of the floor. Breeze pushed it forward ever so slightly. Yes! The car started backing into the street. Breeze wasn't real sure how to stop it so she just pushed that stick toward her a little bit.

She heard a funny growling noise but the car did start to move forward...Moved right back where it started from. It didn't stop there though...just continued going till it ran OVER the curb and into the grass. This would never do! Breeze remembered watching Sandy's feet on the little black things on the floor of the car so she stomped on the center black thing...really hard. That stopped the car just before it hit someone's plate glass window.

Breeze took another big breath and pushed the stick forward again. The little car backed into the street... making an eerie scraping noise as it brushed against a big black car that had been parked next to Sandy's. Now she knew what the little center black thing was. Pulling the stick towards her again, she slowly began to move forward...straight towards a cute little red car with no top. Breeze turned the steering wheel first one way then the other till she found out just how it worked. She didn't touch the little red car at all. Pointing the car down the street, Breeze realized it wasn't moving any faster then she could walk. Something was still not right.

She looked down on the floor again. Sandy had to have done something else. She saw the bigger black thing sticking up on the right side of the floor. That had to be it. Breeze picked up her foot and jammed it down on top of that big black thing as hard as she could. The speed with which the little car took off almost knocked her out of her seat. She was traveling down the street all right. She ran right through a red light and barely missed several cars that screeched their brakes across her path. One car's front bumper did graze her back bumper and fender. The impact swung her around into a half circle.

"WOW!" Breeze thought, *this is really neat!* This was the perfect direction she wanted to go because it pointed right at the little harbor where all the smaller boats were docked. Her foot was still pressed hard on the floor, and the little car was accelerating…fast. It scraped the bumpers of several parked cars as it went speeding by. By now, Breeze was panicky-scared. She picked her foot up off the floor and jammed it down on the center black thing as hard as she could. This sent the little car screeching sideways…right over the curb…over the sidewalk…through the wooden railing and onto the deck of one of the cute little boats that was docked there. The boat, of course, began to sink with the weight of Sandy's car on it. Breeze panicked! Opening the door, she stepped out on what little boat

Breeze...the Mermaid

deck was left, grabbed onto the end of the remaining part of the fence that she'd just demolished, and swung herself onto the sidewalk. She stood there shaking...not saying a word as she watched the car—and the small boat it was sitting on—slowly sink out of sight.

All the noise and excitement had caused people to come running from every direction. By the time Breeze managed to swing herself onto the shore quite a large crowd had gathered. Among them was Alex.

He reached over and took her hand. "Think I need to get you out of here," he said, "before the police come. That was you driving the car that just sank with the boat...right?"

Breeze was so happy to see him, she didn't answer. She pulled her hand out of his, put her arms around his neck and gave him a big kiss.

Alex didn't kiss back this time. Instead, he forcefully took her arms from off his neck, then took her hand and led her away...walking as fast as he could. "You can't stay here! You're in trouble...if you were driving that car!" He paused for a second. "YOU WERE THE PERSON THAT WAS DRIVING THAT CAR...WEREN'T YOU? IS THERE SOMEONE ELSE DOWN THERE? DID SOMEONE ELSE DRIVE THAT CAR?" Then he remembered...everything...remembered seeing this mermaid when she went running across the deck of the ship and pulled him into the ocean with her. She never spoke at that time...probably hadn't understood a word he'd just said. Even though he knew she was a mermaid...something inside of him just didn't want to see her in trouble. He couldn't understand why he wanted to be with her and protect her...but he did.

They ran practically all way to the cruise ship's wooden walkway. Breeze followed right along. When they stopped, however, she again put her arms around Alex and gave him a big, long, passionate kiss.

Alex's first thoughts were to pull away...but he didn't. He kissed her back...then pulled away momentarily and looked at her pretty face. Taking a deep breath he smiled slightly, shook his head, put his arms around her, and gave her the most passionate kiss he could.

Breeze remembered what Neptune had said about kissing a human more than once, but she'd already kissed him more than once...more than twice....And she wasn't about to stop kissing him now. "Mmmmm..." She whispered..."I like the way you kiss, Alex."

Alex was stunned. He couldn't believe what he was hearing. Before...when they went overboard, she didn't say anything, only repeated his name. Now! NOW...

"...and...YES!" Breeze continued. "I was driving the car, or trying to. My friend Sandy went away, and I wanted to come to the ship...to see you, Alex...So I drove her car."

"OH! YOU DID?" Alex couldn't believe what he was hearing. He moved back a little and put his hands on her shoulders. "Don't tell anyone! Who's Sandy? Where is she? Does she know you drove her car?"

Breeze just stood there looking into Alex's eyes. She knew by the sound of his voice and the look in his eye that she'd done something wrong again.

Alex took a deep breath. "I don't think they know who drove the car...and you don't need to tell anyone!"

Breeze shook her head up and down. "Oh! I won't! I won't! You still remember my name?"

Alex put his arms around her again…took another deep breath and looked into her eyes. With a smile on his face he answered. "I still remember your name, Breeze. I remember your kiss. I remember everything… remember you pulling me overboard too. When I first met you…I thought you were dead when you ran into those propellers. Breeze…"

Before Breeze could answer people started coming up the wooden walkway…pushing them forward towards the cruise ship. Alex took her hand and led her up onto the deck. "We're leaving again real soon. You can't stay on board. I remember the last time you were on here. Actually, we're leaving in about half an hour." Alex looked her up and down. "Breeze…I…"

"WHAT?" Breeze was upset. As far as she was concerned, she wasn't finished with the kissing. She paused for a minute then asked, "Why? Why can't I stay here?"

"Breeze!" Alex cupped her face with his hands and continued. "People pay lots of money to take this cruise. They have rooms they've rented for this trip. I work on this ship…Ah…Breeze…um…are you…are you REALLY a mermaid?"

"Of course, I am!" Breeze smiled proudly. "Want to see?"

"No! No, I don't! Especially not here! Not in front of all these people. We'd have the same problem we had last time you were on this ship…REMEMBER? Please! Don't—"

"Don't worry, Alex," Breeze cut in. "I won't! I've learned a few things about you humans. I just wanted to—"

Just then the whistle blew.

Breeze was startled by its shrill loudness and asked, "WHAT'S THAT?"

Alex put his arms around her tightly, gave her a long hug, and said, "You'll have to leave, Breeze, before they shut the gate and take away the walkway."

"I don't want to!" She put her arms around Alex, stood on her tippy toes, and pressed her lips hard against his. Engulfed in the passion of that kiss, they were—for the moment—oblivious to their surroundings.

The whistle blew again, twice this time. The gate closed to the walkway, and the ship started moving.

Alex broke away. Gazing at the fast-disappearing shoreline, he exclaimed, "OH, NO! BREEZE! Breeze! As much as I don't want you to go…YOU CAN'T STAY HERE! THERE IS NO ROOM FOR YOU…And…and I have no money to get you one…and…" He looked towards the shore…"NO!…I'm not sure there's a way for you to get back."

Breeze looked up at Alex…gave him a great big smile, and pointed to one of the cots on deck. "I'll just sleep here."

"Can't let you do that, Breeze. The ship won't let you do that. You'll get in trouble. I'LL get in trouble because they've seen me with you. I'll have to tell them, and they'll let down one of those small boats to take you back to shore."

"OK! OK! If you don't want me here…" She gave Alex one last, passionate kiss, and put her hand on the side of his face. "You're what I'm here for. I like your kisses, and I intend to get lots more!" With that said she turned her back and quickly walked towards the railing. "See ya, Alex!" she said as she climbed onto the railing and dove into the ocean. Her clothes flew off as she conjured up her tail.

Alex just stood there with his mouth wide open. He was glad she didn't take him with her this time, but he didn't want to see her go either...especially THAT way. He could see passengers walking swiftly towards him...passengers that obviously saw the whole thing.

All sorts of questions and statements started coming his way. "Did she just jump overboard? Did you two have a fight that made her jump over that railing? Why did you let her do that? We need to alert the captain so someone can go get her. Aren't you worried about her drowning? What kind of man are you to just stand there and let her do that?"

With that last remark, Alex had had enough. "HEY!" he yelled. "NOT ONE PERSON HAS JUMPED OFF THIS SHIP! I'm sorry about what you all THINK you saw! Maybe the sun was in your eyes! Maybe you've all had too much to drink! I would not be standing here if I saw one of you jump off this ship. Whatever you all THINK you saw...you didn't see! All of you were way down at the other end of the deck. Check the passenger list if you don't believe me. Now!...Go and have fun! That's what this cruise is all about." With that, Alex turned and walked out of sight.

Breeze heard everything that was said on the ship and mentally commended Alex for the way he handled all those people. She decided that...rather than cause any MORE trouble; she would try to visit Olympia. Olympia had a human husband at one time, and she would probably know a lot. Breeze didn't, however, want to wind up like Olympia—an outcast! In fact, she, herself, would have to be very careful so not be noticed getting to Olympia's place or visiting her. Olympia was banned from Neptune's kingdom, and other mermaids were banned from ever seeing her. Breeze had to be very careful. She vaguely remembered where the ship that Olympia used as her home was located. She took one last look at the cruise ship as it sailed out of sight and, with Alex in her thoughts, dove deeper into the ocean and started swimming towards Olympia's home.

Chapter 13

It wasn't long before she was joined by her dolphin friends. They swam together for several hours, with Breeze hitching rides on first one then another. Nearing the old ship Olympia stayed in; they were met by sharks that seemed to be patrolling the area.

The dolphins loved Breeze. They always had a lot of fun together….So they let the sharks know…in no uncertain terms…that Breeze WAS going to visit Olympia.

Their loud sounds were heard by Olympia, who rushed right out of the door and into the middle of it all. Taking one look at Breeze, she pointed her finger at her and yelled, "YOU SHOULDN'T BE HERE, YOUNG ONE! DON'T YOU KNOW WHAT WILL HAPPEN TO YOU IF THEY CATCH YOU HERE? DON'T YOU KNOW WHAT WILL HAPPEN TO ME IF THEY CATCH YOU HERE? NOW…GET OUT OF HERE…BEFORE I SIC THE SHARKS ON YOU!"

Breeze stood her ground. She wasn't about to come all this way to be yelled at...by a fellow mermaid. "I'LL BE HERE IF I WANT TO BE HERE!" she yelled back. "BESIDES...YOU THINK YOU'RE THE ONLY ONE THAT EVER FELL IN LOVE WITH A HUMAN? WHY DO YOU THINK I'M HERE, ANYWAY?"

"YOU'D BETTER STAY AWAY FROM HERE... IF YOU KNOW WHAT'S GOOD FOR YOU! NEPTUNE FINDS YOU HERE AND YOU'RE IN REAL TROUBLE. WHAT'S YOUR NAME?"

"Breeze! My name is Breeze!...And I'll have you know...I AM NEPTUNE'S DAUGHTER!"

"Does he know you're here?"

"OF COURSE NOT! I came here to find out about you! YOU fell in love with a human, didn't you?...Had children by him...didn't you? I came here to get some information...so I won't have the same kind of problems you had...or...ARE STILL HAVING!"

"Nothing to tell about me! Really none of your business! THERE'S NOTHING TO TELL!"

"OH? Yes...there is! I would love to be alone with you for a while and just listen to your story." Breeze looked around.

The sharks were all there looking at them. The dolphins were there looking at the sharks. Some electric eels had gathered and were looking at all of them. The whole ocean full of living things that seemed to be looking at them. EVERYTHING was staring at them.

"Think you're getting a little PERSONAL... Breeze...but...YES! YES, I did fall in love with a human. Want to hear about some of my life and the reason I've been banned from the clan?"

"Yes! OF COURSE...THAT'S WHY I'M HERE! YES! I want very much to hear."

"Well, then I'll tell you some of it." Olympia straightened up and looked Breeze right in the eye. "I'll tell you so you don't make the same mistakes I did and wind up banned from the clan like me. Breeze, if you're not careful...you may wind up here...living here with me...banned from the clan! Now, come with me!" Olympia led her away from the crowd of on-lookers. "I'll tell you only what I think will help you."

Breeze didn't want that at all. She wanted to hear about everything, but this would do for a start, so she was all ears. She agreed and followed. Breeze was terribly excited. She was actually talking to the famous Olympia.

Olympia only went a little ways...just far enough to be alone with Breeze. "GO HOME, BREEZE! You shouldn't be here! You KNOW Neptune has banned anyone from coming here." She flipped herself around to where she was facing Breeze. "You KNOW you're forbidden to fall in love with someone outside Neptune's kingdom...let alone with a human." Olympia swam up next to Breeze to where they were looking each other in the eye at close range. She pointed her finger at Breeze and continued. "YOU ARE AWARE YOU ARE NOT SUPPOSED TO KISS A HUMAN MORE THAN ONE TIME...AND YOU ARE NOT SUPPOSED TO FALL IN LOVE WITH ONE! YOU ARE AWARE OF THAT...AREN'T YOU?"

Breeze was stunned by her change of attitude and was beginning to get upset. Olympia was yelling at her. "HEY! OLYMPIA! YOU DID! You fell in love with a human. You married a human, and YOU had children by one. What right do YOU have to tell ME not to do that? If YOU had it all to do over again...would YOU fall in love with a human? Would YOU marry him...and would YOU have his children?"

Olympia turned her back on Breeze and swam a little ways away. She didn't speak.

Breeze slowly followed her, leaned over her shoulder, and said. "Don't think you have the right to tell ME what to do! Just look..."

Olympia was quick to interrupt. "LOOK HERE, BREEZE! YOU REALLY DON'T NEED TO BE HERE! YOU NEED TO JUST...GO AWAY! YOU DON'T WANT NEPTUNE TO CATCH YOU BEING HERE!"

Breeze thought about that statement for a few minutes. She remembered Olympia making that statement a couple of times during their short conversation. "Olympia! Now...just HOW would Neptune catch me being here...IF HE DIDN'T COME HERE OCCASIONALLY?"

Olympia said nothing...just kept her back turned.

"Olympia! I don't think you're telling me everything."

Olympia still said nothing.

Breeze put her hands on Olympia's shoulders and flipped her around...looked her in the eye and asked. "OK, MISS...Ah...OLYMPIA! Just HOW would MY FATHER catch me HERE?"

Olympia put her lips together real tight. "OK! OK! I guess you should know. First of all....I knew your father before he ever met Oceana. We sort of grew up together."

Breeze was shocked. "You? You knew my father? You knew Neptune?"

"Oh, YES! I knew him. If it hadn't been for my adventurous nature…I'd probably be your mother right now rather then Oceana. I guess I was too much like your father. He couldn't tame me." She gave a great big smile. "I had to see EVERYTHING…had to know what it was like out of the water. Had to see what the HUMAN world was all about."

Breeze stayed really quiet. She couldn't believe what she was hearing. Couldn't be….The very words out of Olympia's mouth were…were like Olympia was reading her mind. These were the things she wanted. How could this be?

Olympia moved really close to Breeze, reached out, and touched her shoulder. "Breeze, you know those big, beautiful black pearls you and Galley found…."

Breeze let out a meek little "Yes!"…thought for a minute then exclaimed, "BLACK PEARLS! YOU KNOW ABOUT THE BLACK PEARLS?". She was glaring at Olympia, eyes open wide with a questioning look. "HOW'D YOU KNOW GALLEY AND I FOUND THOSE? HOW'D YOU KNOW THAT? NO ONE KNOWS THAT!" She backed away slightly. "No one but Oceana and…and…" Breeze couldn't believe what she was hearing. She continued to glare at Olympia "NEPTUNE! NEPTUNE? That means…NEPTUNE COMES HERE? He comes…HERE…um…to…to SEE YOU?"

"That's right, my dear little friend...No one knows but Oceana and your father." Olympia moved close again. "I know EVERYTHING, Breeze! EVERYTHING! You should never have kissed Alex more than one time. It was OK to save his life. That was a good thing. But you should have STOPPED!... SHOULD'VE STOPPED RIGHT THERE! You—"

"WAIT A MINUTE! YOU JUST WAIT A MINUTE! HOW'D YOU KNOW THAT?" Breeze was beginning to get upset. "YOU'VE NO RIGHT TO KNOW THAT! THAT...." She shook her finger at Olympia. "THAT'S MY VERY OWN PERSONAL BUSINESS, OLYMPIA! THAT'S MY BUSINESS... AND...AND...IT'S NONE OF YOUR BUSINESS!" Breeze felt like smacking Olympia...felt like smacking that self-assured grin right off her face. "WHAT ELSE DO YOU KNOW...OLYMPIA? WAY...WAY...OUT HERE...away from everything...and everybody, HUH? NO ONE IS ALLOWED TO VISIT...HUH? HEY, JUST HOW OFTEN DOES MY FATHER COME UP HERE ANYWAY? You...who all visitors are forbidden to see." Breeze reached over and took hold of Oceana's shoulders again. "HOW OFTEN, OLYMPIA?" Her face was right in front of Olympia's, and she was glaring into her eyes. "I ASKED YOU A QUESTION, OLYMPIA! HOW OFTEN?"

Olympia took a deep breath and calmly answered. "If you really want to know Breeze...I'll tell you tomorrow. You'll have to leave right now...and come back tomorrow. Come back real early. Don't want you to get caught here...with me. Would mean more trouble for you...BIG trouble!"

Breeze...the Mermaid

Now Breeze was really angry. "TROUBLE? WHAT KIND OF TROUBLE? YOU GOING TO SICK YOUR SHARKS ON ME OR SOMETHING?"

Olympia sat down on a nearby rock and just kept smiling. "See you tomorrow, Breeze!"

"YOU'LL TELL ME NOW, OLYMPIA! DO YOU THINK I CAME ALL THE WAY HERE FOR A FIVE-MINUTE CHAT? I NEED TO KNOW THINGS... NOW!"

"What for? Alex's ship doesn't come back for about a week and a half. You have plenty of time, Breeze."

"WHAT? YOU KNOW ABOUT THAT, TOO? IS THERE ANYTHING YOU DON'T KNOW ABOUT?"

"Not much...Breeze! Not much. Go play with your dolphin pals or something. See you tomorrow. Maybe I'll answer some more of your questions then."

"MAYBE! MAYBE? WHO DO YOU THINK YOU ARE? MAYBE... I WANT THE ANSWERS NOW, OLYMPIA! NOW! By the way...how did you know about Alex and when he'd be back from that cruise?"

"Tell you tomorrow, Breeze. LEAVE...NOW! Before it's too late! PLEASE!"

Breeze hesitated...looked Olympia up and down and said. "Olympia, I don't understand...but I will leave because you asked me to, and I will be back tomorrow. I'll be back first thing in the morning...TOMORROW!" She flipped her tail as she turned to go, making sure Olympia knew how disgusted she was that she was asked to leave.

Once out of sight, Breeze stopped, turned around, and found a good hiding place where she could watch things outside Olympia's place. She wanted to see what was so important that she couldn't stay. She waited for a long time. Nothing was happening. Breeze was beginning to think Olympia just wanted to get rid of her. She was about ready to leave the area…decided she'd just go find the dolphins and have some fun with them for a while….Humph! The more she thought about it, the more she thought she just might not come back at all.

She was just about to give up her hiding place when…up swam Neptune…swam right past her…right through the sharks and right into the old sunken ship Olympia was staying in. Breeze couldn't believe her eyes. It's a good thing she was still hidden or he would have seen her. Breeze swam close to the ship but couldn't hear anything. She knew she couldn't stay there, and she certainly didn't want to get caught….So she went back into hiding. With her father in there…alone with Olympia…she wasn't about to leave. In fact, she was getting angrier by the second. What could HER father possibly be doing in there? ALONE…with Olympia?

Breeze could feel the anger boiling up inside her. There he was! HER FATHER! Alone with a mermaid that had been banned from their society…that HE HIMSELF banned from their society. "I can't STAND this!" She muttered angrily, "Who does he think he is?"…Telling everyone what is right and what is wrong! Who they should marry and who they shouldn't…and who they should see!" She sat there a minute on a big clump of coral trying to keep from crying.

"I'm going in there!" She muttered to herself, "Yes! I'm going right in there…right now…and let him have a piece of my mind! Just who do they think they are? They're no better than me!" Breeze thought about her decision for a moment. "They're WORSE then anything I ever thought of doing or have done." She took a big breath and voiced her decision loudly. "I AM GOING RIGHT IN THERE…RIGHT NOW!…AND I'M GOING TO TELL THEM JUST EXACTLY WHAT I THINK!"

Her decision made, Breeze slowly started to leave her hiding place when she saw Oceana approaching. She knew this meant nothing but trouble so she quickly backed into her hiding place again. Oceana seemed happy enough. What was SHE doing here? Breeze watched as Oceana swam right past her. The sharks paid no attention to her either as she swam through them, through the door, and into the ship Olympia and Neptune were in. Oh boy! She knew there would be a fight…and she wanted to at least be able to hear it….So she quickly swam up to the ship…got as close as she could get…and listened. Nothing! Instead of the fight she expected to hear, she heard laughter…lots of it. All three of them were laughing. It was obvious now…. The three of them knew each other pretty well. At least Neptune was not cheating on Oceana. That was a big relief.

Sneaking up to the entryway, Breeze could see the door wasn't completely closed. *GREAT!* she thought. She'd try to listen in to their conversation.

Olympia was the one speaking…through bursts of laughter. "She did what? Neptune! You actually helped her pull those fish lines away from the humans?" More laughter! All their conversation was telling and re-telling things that she, Breeze, had done. They were even laughing about when she got drunk on the milk. Neptune thought it funny how he pulled her away from the farm, drunk on milk...with egg all over her face and hair. They all laughed and laughed.

Breeze listened for a long time through that open door...realizing they were laughing at her and the things she had done. The next thing they started talking about was Galley...how she'd finally taught Galley how to conjure up human legs.

This made Breeze really mad! No one was supposed to know about that. Galley had to be the one to tell this one because she kept their little secret. She didn't tell anyone. There was no one there when Galley got her legs...just the two of them. How could he know this?

Neptune continued. "Don't think I've told you two this story...."

Breeze could see through the crack that Oceana and Olympia were all ears...waiting for the story. She wanted to burst inside and spoil their little party...but she didn't. She wanted to see just how long Neptune had watched her that day.

"You'll never believe this one..." Neptune went on. "I like to watch Breeze because she's always in some kind of trouble, so I followed her. I follow her a lot! She doesn't know this, but I do. There they were, Breeze and Galley...as close to the shore as they could get. I'd just finishing chastising Breeze for stealing those giant pearls....Really something how she stole that big black pearl. Wish I could have been there and watched that."

"There they were, underneath the pier right at the shore line. Breeze set a big shell full of something beside the water and started explaining to Galley how she could conjure up her legs. She did this over and over. Galley tried over and over. All afternoon they worked on Galley getting legs. I almost went to sleep watching," Neptune added. "Finally, Galley understood and there they both were...with legs. This wasn't good enough for Breeze. I'll tell you everything as near as I can remember..."

"GALLEY, that's PERFECT!" Breeze yelled. "Now, I've got a surprise for you!"

"YOU HAVE?" Galley said, grinning from ear to ear. "What is it?"

"I've watched those humans for a long time. Some of them wear things on their feet that make them taller and make a clicking sound when they walk. I brought these!" She showed Galley what was in the big shell. "Are you ready to try them?"

"OH! YES!" Galley answered sitting down on one of the rocks. "What is all that in there?"

"Itty-bitty pieces of clothes...for you and me. I took them off that little boat some time back and saved them in case I needed them. Here! Put these on!" Breeze showed her how to put the itty-bitty bikini on. They picked up the shell and took it onto the pier.

Neptune paused for a few seconds laughing. "I had to conjure up legs for myself so I could watch them. I didn't want to miss any of this so I just reached up and took a bathing suit from one of those little booths on the pier. Those two mermaids were so busy getting into trouble that they didn't even notice me. Listen, there's more…"

"Now!" Breeze said as she picked up a couple of long, narrow shells and gave them to Galley. "Put these on your feet, and we'll be just like those humans over there. We'll be taller and make that neat clicking noise when we walk…just like they do." She pointed her finger toward a couple humans. "Look! They're wearing them!"

"Theirs don't look like ours!" Galley frowned. "But I'll put them on anyway."

The girls sat there for a few minutes getting used to the feel of their new feet. Breeze took Galley's hand and said. "Let's walk down to the end of the pier. OK?"

"OK!" Galley answered.

Breeze had her hand on the edge of a table at the booth that was next to them. When she pulled on Galley to stand up, they both fell against the booth, sending all its contents into the ocean.

The human at the booth started waving her arms and yelling. "GET OFF THE PIER! GET OUT OF HERE…AND TAKE THOSE SILLY THINGS OFF YOUR FEET! WHAT ARE THOSE, ANYWAY?" Then the human started picking up things and throwing them at Breeze and Galley.

The mermaids were now upset from being yelled at. They tried hard to run in those silly shell shoes… but they couldn't. Rather than take them off…to stay standing upright, they grabbed at everything within reach as they staggered down the pier. Now, it seemed everyone on the pier was yelling at them and doing anything they could to stop them. The mermaids were doing everything they could to keep themselves from falling. They grabbed onto umbrellas, edges of tables, and things that were on the tables. They even grabbed onto some of the humans themselves to try to keep from falling. One after the other...first the umbrellas, then the tables were pulled down. Most of what was on those tables went splashing into the ocean...along with the tables, umbrellas, and a couple of humans.

Neptune laughed again, and then continued...

"You should have seen the ocean! Stuff was floating all over! Humans have what they call police...people of authority that take charge when things go wrong. Two of these police came running down the pier blowing their whistles....Little things they put in their mouth that cause a shrill, high-pitched sound...hurts the ears. They each carried a big stick in one hand, blowing their whistles in the other, and were reaching out to grab our mischievous little darlings when Galley turned and shouted, 'I CAN'T STAND THIS! I'M NEVER GETTING LEGS AGAIN! BREEZE! HERE! YOU TAKE THESE! ENJOY YOUR...YOUR LEGS!'"

Galley threw her shells at Breeze. They missed Breeze but went right into the faces of those two policemen. This took the police by surprise. One of them grabbed Galley's hair just as she dove off the pier. The policeman didn't expect her to dive off the pier, was caught off balance, and went tumbling over the railing and into the sea. Breeze dove in close behind. They dove right through all the clothes, jewelry, and fancy things that had fallen from the booths. The policeman was weighted down so heavily with all the stuff he wore that he was having trouble keeping his head up above the water.

Neptune was still grinning when he finished the story…

"Breeze knew how to get her tail back…but Galley wasn't so good at it. With all the confusion, she just may have forgotten. Breeze had to pull her to shore to save her and get her tail back. Then Breeze noticed the policeman out there near the end of the pier thrashing around in the water. She swam out there and brought him to the shore too."

Neptune roared with laughter, pounded his hand on the table, and added, "You should have been there!"

Breeze was getting angrier and angrier by the minute. Neptune had no right telling about all the problems she had gotten into. They had no right to bring Galley into their conversation either. She felt like bursting into the room and spoiling their little party. She could see through that little crack in the door pretty well. Neptune was about to give one of his eloquent speeches. She could tell because he straightened up and puffed himself up as big as he could. "Well…Olympia!" Neptune boasted. "Hope you know why Breeze does what she does! You ARE her mother! And…SHE'S JUST LIKE YOU!"

Breeze sucked in a deep breath. "WHAT?" she exclaimed loudly…almost choking. Breeze hoped she wouldn't be noticed but she made a loud, scuffling noise as she scrambled away from the door. She could hear the three of them rushing towards the door to see what had made the noise. By the time they all got to the opening there was no one there. A very shocked, surprised, and out-of-breath Breeze was back in her hiding place. She felt awful! She loved Oceana. All her life she'd thought Oceana was her mother...loved her as her mother, and she knew Oceana loved her in the same way. Now! Now to find out she wasn't her real mother...that OLYMPIA was her real mother! This was just too much!

As Breeze watched the three of them swim back and forth checking out the front of the old ship she thought...*If Olympia is my mother...that means...Oh! My!* She hesitated even entertaining the thought. That means Olympia and her father....Oh! NO! Couldn't be! She'd have to confront the three of them. Later! MUCH later! Now that she heard THAT...she couldn't go through the rest of her life not knowing about her mother AND father. She was terribly upset as she watched the three of them swimming back and forth together...looking for whatever caused the commotion by the door. She felt like making a REAL commotion right then and there...but she didn't.

Then she heard Neptune's loud voice. "Hey, X! Did you look over there by the big chunks of coral?"

X! X? Hey, X! Hmmm, Breeze thought. Neptune called Olympia X. What would that mean...X? *No one's called X!* Right at this point, she wished she had never come to visit Olympia....OLYMPIA? Her MOTHER? Couldn't be...Just COULDN'T BE! With those thoughts weighing heavily on her mind, she managed not to be seen while she scooted away from the coral and swiftly swam to a safer distance. She couldn't see as well but she could still hear what was going on.

"Olympia!" Neptune continued. "That noise was not from any fish. Was Breeze here?"

"Breeze? Here? Thought you told me she was over by that cruise ship that's docked in town. She's been banned from this place, hasn't she? Don't think she'd go against your rules for that...would she?"

Neptune thought about her answer for a few minutes. "Guess not."

Oceana's voice was heard in the distance. "She's just like the both of you! Serves you both right for what you did way back then. Just so you know...I'll stand behind Breeze...no matter what, because I love her. She can't help her mischievous ways. It's in her heritage. BOTH OF YOU ARE THAT WAY! How do you expect her to be anything else? Personally...I THINK SHE WAS HERE! I think she's STILL here! Think she's somewhere near, listening to us. I just feel that. You'll see! Next time we see Breeze, she will be different...BECAUSE SHE'LL KNOW ABOUT YOU AND OLYMPIA...way back when."

Neptune and Olympia swam up to Oceana. Neptune put his arms around Oceana. "Oceana! You KNOW I love you. YOU KNOW—"

Oceana cut into his sentence..."I'm not worried about what happened between you and Olympia before you even met me. Not worried about that at all. I think you made the right decision." She smiled widely and looked at him sideways, then added, "...when you chose me." She gave him a big grin and winked at him as she flipped around and looked at Olympia. "Sorry, Olympia! But I still believe Neptune did right not allowing Breeze to live with you and that human. How your other children were raised...that was YOUR business. I know you're Breeze's mother...but I was the one that was always there for her, and I'll always love her as my own. No offense...but...HOW COULD YOU LIVE WITH A HUMAN FOR SO LONG?"

Olympia spoke up. "Oceana, we've gone over this before...LOTS of times and—"

Neptune cut in. "STOP IT! You two are friends! Remember? The past doesn't matter. If Breeze wasn't here...well...must have been something else at that door."

Breeze had heard all she wanted to hear for now. Her world seemed to be tumbling down on her. So! HER FATHER...NEPTUNE...ah...WOW! She wasn't sure she wanted to go back and visit Olympia in the morning. Maybe that's what Olympia wanted to tell her, but decided to wait until the next day. She'd sleep on it and think about it. If she did go back...she was sure she wouldn't let Olympia know what she'd just heard. Hmmm....It might be interesting to go back tomorrow morning at that.

First thing in the morning, Breeze decided she would go back to see Olympia...see just how long they all intended to keep this secret from her. Inside, she was angry at what had happened last night, and she was going to have to be really careful not to let them know what she'd overheard.

Breeze woke up before the sun was up. She wanted to get there really early and find out just what Olympia was waiting to tell her. She put two sea horses and a few small shells in her hair so she'd look her best.

Paying no attention to the sharks that policed Olympia's old wrecked ship...she swam right through them and up to the door. Breeze was determined to pretend everything was still OK. She shouted at Olympia from outside the door, "Are you in there, Olympia?"

Olympia came, opened the door, and asked her to come in and join her. She led Breeze over to the ship's old sea-bar as Olympia called it. She had some pretty neat food stashed under there, and as they ate they drank something Breeze had never tasted before. Olympia also mixed up something else to drink. She said it was laced with clam juice and only allowed her to drink a little of it...said it would make her feel funny. Breeze immediately asked. "Does it have the same effect as that milk humans drink?"

"Yes! Yes, it does, Breeze. How'd you know about that?"

Well! Breeze thought to herself. Her being drunk on the milk was one of the things they were all laughing about last night. "Well!" Breeze said, looking Olympia in the eye. "Neptune taught me how to change my tail for legs...and I went on land. There was a cat there and I drank its milk." She didn't want to relay the whole story that she knew Olympia had already heard...just told her enough to let her know she'd tasted the milk.

"So! Neptune taught you how to get human legs... did he?" Olympia took in a couple of deep breaths. "I'm kind of surprised that he taught you that. I learned how to get legs when I was young also. It's a long story. That's one of the reasons I'm here, Breeze...instead of with the rest of you."

Breeze was hoping she'd go on and tell everything... but she didn't. "Is it true you went on land...and lived on land with a human and...and had his children?"

"Yes! Yes! It's true! I even lived in a house and went for long periods of time without my tail."

Now! Breeze thought. Now, she'd try to trip her up. "You ever have any children, Olympia?" She looked her right in the eye. "Have any children by that human?"

"Yes, Breeze. Yes, I did."

"Where are they, Olympia? Are they humans...Or are they mermaids?"

"BREEZE! Do you really think THAT is any of your business?"

Right then, Breeze saw the opening she needed... thought it would be a good time to bring things out in the open. She looked Olympia right in the eye and said. "Oh!...but it IS my business, Olympia. If YOU had family members you'd never met...wouldn't YOU want to know who they are?"

"FAMILY MEMBERS?" Olympia looked inquisitively into Breeze's eyes. "What do you mean?... family members. My children had nothing to do with you...and they are none of your business! I think it's about time you leave, Breeze. I was going to tell you more about life without legs and what type of problems there are...but...I think you are stepping a bit out of line here, little girl."

Breeze gathered up all the courage she could...tried to puff herself up like she'd seen Neptune do so many hundreds of times before. "Olympia, just how many children have you had?"

Olympia thought about that question for a moment before answering. "I had two children from my human companion, Jim...and they both turned out to be just fine! Now, I think you need to leave!"

"NOT JUST YET OLYMPIA! Not just yet!" Breeze looked Olympia right in the eye and asked, "What about the child you had with Neptune? WHAT ABOUT ME?"

Chapter 14

Olympia couldn't believe what she was hearing. For a few minutes she was speechless. Then she remembered the noise at the door, composed herself, and asked, "IT WAS YOU LAST NIGHT...AT MY DOOR. WASN'T IT? YOU WERE LISTENING AT MY DOOR, WEREN'T YOU?" She looked at Breeze... looked her right back in the eye. "And...just what DID you hear last night, Breeze?"

"Heard it all Olympia! Heard it ALL! SO, YOU actually are my real mother...huh! You know what? I used to put you...WAY up there! Thought you were really something SPECIAL! All my life I've wanted to meet the GREAT...AND FAMOUS Olympia. HUH! CHANGED MY MIND, OLYMPIA. I could NEVER...EVER...not keep MY child. AND...if MY child came to visit ME after never seeing her...I'm real sure I would never be so RUDE as to tell her to leave as soon as she got here. SIT DOWN, OLYMPIA! I THINK WE NEED TO TALK! NOW!...And I WANT SOME REAL GOOD ANSWERS TO MY QUESTIONS...

MOTHER!" Breeze made herself comfortable, put her hands behind her head and said, "WELL, LET'S HAVE IT! NOW, I WANT TO HEAR EVERYTHING...And I think that's the least you can do for me...Olympia!... MOTHER!"

Olympia went to the old ship's sea bar, poured two drinks and added a little clam juice to each one. She handed one to Breeze and said, "Come with me, Breeze. I have something I think you'll like to see."

Breeze took the drink, said "OK," and followed Olympia down to the bottom part of the old ship. There were a bunch of square holes in a very large wood cabinet. Some had bottles in them and others had other things in them. "What is all this stuff, Olympia?"

Olympia pulled a long piece of thick cloth out of one of the square holes. "I've kept track of everything; Breeze...from the time Neptune made me leave and took you away until now. While I was with my human companion and lived in a house on land, I learned to read and write like humans do...even learned to draw things. I'll show you if you want."

She put her arm around Breeze. "Breeze, it was never my choice to not have you with me. This was Neptune's choice. He said you were HIS child and you were going to stay with him...said he'd always keep me informed about everything you were doing and how you were...but never wanted us to meet. He said it was because of my dealings with humans. I really don't think that was the only reason. All this hasn't been easy for me, Breeze."

Opening the scroll she'd just pulled out, Olympia pointed to all the writing. "I'll teach you to read and write if you want me to. It's a good thing...not bad. ALL things humans do and have are not bad....Some are good. The drawing is a sketch I did of your brother and sister when they were real small. They ARE half human, you know."

"Oh! YES! OH YES! I would LOVE that! I would love to have you teach me to read and write and make pictures like these." She quickly kissed Olympia on the cheek. "Can we start now?" Breeze took the piece of canvas out of Olympia's hands to get a better look at her brother and sister. "They both have a tail. Can they get legs too?"

"Of course! Actually, it's easier for them because they are half human. This is not a very good drawing, Breeze. It's hard to write and draw on pieces of canvas in the ocean. On land, the humans have paper and it's much easier to use. Things look more real with paper too, but...paper would not last long here in the ocean so I did all this on old ship's sails I've found."

"Tell me about them...About my brother and my sister! Where are they? Can I ever meet them?"

"Oh!" Olympia chuckled. "I think you already have, Breeze! You just didn't know it."

Breeze looked at her inquisitively. "I HAVE? Where are they? Do they know I'm their sister?"

"Well of course not! If they knew, they would have told you. I'm their mother, and they love me and come to visit me occasionally. Neptune doesn't know that... and he MUST NEVER KNOW THAT! You hear me! Never tell what I'm about to tell you to anyone...not to ANYONE! Promise?"

"I promise! I'll never tell. I'm good with secrets. WHO ARE THEY, OLYMPIA?"

Olympia just smiled...but said nothing

"You're not going to keep this a secret from me...are you?" Now Breeze was really upset. She had a brother and a sister. She knew them already...and she didn't know who they were. "OLYMPIA!" Breeze yelled. "THAT'S NOT FAIR! THAT'S...JUST NOT FAIR!"

"Oh! But it IS fair!" Olympia was still smiling as she explained. "You see...once the word got out that they were MY children...they would be banned from the group...and..." Olympia moved really close. "Breeze, you listen to me! Listen REAL CLOSE!"

Breeze was slowly becoming aware of how important it was to Olympia to keep this secret...so she DID listen...very closely.

"Now, Breeze, your father, Neptune, knows I have two children by a human. He just doesn't know where they are and who they are with. He need NEVER know who they are. Breeze! Even if you ever do find out... Neptune does not need to know who they are." Olympia drew closer. "LISTEN TO ME, BREEZE! They do come to see me. If you knew who they were...and he found out...he would not only ban them from ever being with you...HE MAY BAN YOU AND THEM FROM THE WHOLE CLAN ALSO."

Breeze's eyes were suddenly wide open. "BAN? ME? OLYMPIA! I'm his DAUGHTER!"

"Yes, I know that, dear! I know that! Actually you're not even supposed to be here now. Didn't he tell you not to come here? Someday I'll tell you why he banned me...But not just yet...and...Breeze...there's one more thing that's VERY IMPORTANT."

"What? What could be more important than what you've already told me?"

Olympia bent down really low, almost whispering into Breeze's ear. "Breeze, Neptune must NEVER know you've come here!...He must NEVER SEE YOU HERE! This must be kept our secret...just as it is my secret and your brother and sister's secret that they visit me occasionally." She backed up a little bit. "BREEZE, YOU DO UNDERSTAND WHAT I'M TELLING YOU...DON'T YOU?"

Breeze shook her head up and down. "YES! Yes, Olympia. I DO understand...and I will always be careful when I come up here, but I would really like to know who my brother and sister are." Breeze thought for a moment. "Olympia, Alex isn't my brother...is he?"

"No, my child! Alex isn't your brother. You've played with your brother and sister off and on all your life. Alex is not your brother."

Breeze let out a sign of relief. "That's good!"

"One more word of caution!" Olympia looked Breeze right in the eye and continued..."DON'T EVER LET NEPTUNE KNOW HOW MUCH YOU LIKE ALEX! It would not be good for you for him to know that. Promise me you'll not speak of him again to either Neptune or Oceana. Don't speak about him to ANY of your friends, either. I'm trying to save you from problems, Breeze. Remember what I've just told you."

"I will." Breeze smiled. "Can I look at some more of these?" She reached into one of the square holes and pulled out a small piece of canvas.

"Of course! You can look at all of them, except this one." Olympia reached into one of the large holes on the bottom and pulled out a great big piece of canvas wrapped around something. "This one is very special to me and not for anyone else's eyes. I'll just take it and put it someplace else. You're welcome to look at anything else in there you want."

Breeze put her arms around Olympia. "Olympia, I don't see anything about you that would cause Neptune to ban you from our society. To me…you seem to be just…just really OK. You're interesting to talk to and be around. I'm afraid I don't understand. Can you please tell me why?"

Olympia flipped around and was on her way out of the room. "I'm going to put this away. This is just not the time for me to tell you all that, Breeze….Hope you can understand!"

Breeze busied herself opening first one canvas then another and laying them aside to ask questions about.

As Olympia was floating down the stairway, she started asking Breeze questions again. "Breeze, looking at your life's history….It seems like you have always been on the edge of getting into trouble. You know we're not allowed to have serious relationships with humans… especially male humans. Yet…you kissed Alex twice. Is there more to that story that I don't know?"

"No!" Breeze said with a big smile. "But I am going to see him again when that cruise ship comes back. He knows I like him, and I think he likes me."

"Breeze!" Olympia said as she put her hand on her shoulder. "You certainly are…Neptune's wayward daughter. You should know….You are not allowed to marry out of your clan, and you are CERTAINLY not allowed to have serious relationships with humans…especially male humans. Looking at your life's history, Breeze…It seems like you have always been on the edge of getting into trouble."

"Olympia!" Breeze smiled. "You're right! I'm not really like the others. I like adventure. I like to see other things. I have always wanted to find out how humans live and what they do. Neptune was hoping I would choose one of the males I used to play with for a mate, but I'm…well…I'm just not interested in any of them…only as friends."

She hesitated for a couple minute "Olympia, I probably shouldn't tell you this but…somehow, I feel I can trust you not to tell. Last time I was on land…with my human legs…I met a girl named Sandy…."

Breeze told her the whole story, and Olympia was eager to listen. When it came to the part where Sandy fell in love with a merman, she quickly interrupted and asked what his name was.

"Shell! His name is Shell! And I've played with him most of my life. They were so much in love that…they just took off and I haven't seen either of them since. Shell said they didn't want any trouble. They just wanted to be with each other and…and they just took off." Breeze thought for a moment. "OLYMPIA, SHELL ISN'T…ISN'T YOUR…"

"No, Breeze! Shell isn't your brother. Do me and yourself a big favor."

"What?"

"Don't EVER show any of those humans how to get a tail…EVER!" Olympia glared at Breeze. "You have no idea how much trouble it can cause."

"OK! I can see that with what happened to Sandy. I really liked Sandy, Olympia…thought she was my friend." Breeze hesitated for a moment then added, "Ah…Olympia! Did you show Jim how to have a tail?"

"Yes, Breeze! Yes, I did…but Jim was different! He was already a person of the sea. Most people would not be able to handle having a tail. They would abuse the use of it by doing things they shouldn't.

"Humans are not like us, Breeze. Sandy will continue to think about you, but you'll probably never see her again. She already has what she wants." Changing the subject, Olympia asked, "Do you have any more questions about what you see there? I see you've taken out several sketches."

"Yes! Yes, I do! I do have more questions." Breeze wasn't sure if she should ask this next question or not… but she asked it anyway. "Olympia, what happened to your human husband? What did he look like? I know it's none of my business…but…I'd really like to know."

"Don't see any reason why I can't tell you that, Breeze. First of all…that little darker piece of canvas you have there…that's a sketch of my human husband, Jim."

Breeze unrolled the canvas and looked at it intently. "Olympia! Did he like the water? Was he good to you? What happened to him?"

"One question at a time…One question at a time! Yes, he liked the water. He was a diver."

"So...what happened to him?"

After a long pause, Olympia answered. "He's dead, Breeze."

"Is it hard for you to talk about it? What happened?"

"Yes! Yes, it is hard...but I will tell you. If he were still alive I wouldn't be here all by myself. We always liked to have picnics by the sea. Breeze, a picnic is where lots of food is packed up and taken with you so you can eat it someplace else. By this time, Neptune had already taken you away to live with them...said he didn't want any daughter of his living with some half-witted human, so he just came and took you away. You were VERY small when he took you away. I cried a lot over that. It happened soon after that your brother and sister were born."

"Back to the picnic! We had just gotten out of the car...and...yes! That's how we traveled on land...in a car. We pulled up to a beautiful spot by the sea. Other groups of humans were parked in the area too but they never parked or sat very close to one another. One little human girl had wandered away from her people. She was very small. No one seemed to be paying any attention to her. All of a sudden she started running towards the road...toward the fast cars. She was right at the edge of the road when Jim, my husband, saw what was about to happen. He threw down the things he was carrying and ran as fast as he could to try to stop her, yelling at her to STOP as he ran. She was right at the edge of the road when she saw Jim coming. He was almost close enough to touch her when she looked at him with a frightened expression on her face, turned around, and ran in the opposite direction."

"This put Jim on the edge of the road. One car went way out of its lane, for no apparent reason, and ran into another car. This caused it to crash into several other cars. Then, the car that originally came out of its lane purposefully skidded across the road and hit my husband. I couldn't see real clear, but I did see the driver's arms turn that steering wheel right towards my Jim. That driver didn't even bother to stop and see if he was OK…just drove off as fast as it could. Jim never woke up after that. I never go back to that area, Breeze! Whoever was driving that car did not need to do what he did. There was no reason for that driver to turn his wheels towards my husband!"

"Breeze, if Jim hadn't seen what was happening… that little girl would have kept running, and she would be the one not here now.

"Will you ever want to go back and live with humans?"

"No! No! I won't! Don't think so! Life is hard enough without being around memories you wish were still there. No, Breeze! I'll not go back! Nothing for me to go back to. It's not too late for you. Find yourself a handsome merman. Enjoy this beautiful ocean. You are free to go and do whatever you want in your life. Don't alienate yourself as an outsider by falling in love with a human."

Breeze looked at Olympia with raised eyebrows, thought about Alex, and said. "Olympia, if you had it all to do over again…would you still have gone with Jim?"

There was no hesitation in Olympia's answer. "YES! Oh, yes! The only thing I would do different is…I would NOT have gone to that place to picnic that day."

"Why didn't you keep your other two children with you? Seems like they should have stayed with their mother…and…WHY ARE YOU BANNED FROM OUR SOCIETY? I don't see anything you did that would cause that to happen."

"You have the habit of getting personal…don't you, Breeze?"

Breeze gave her a sheepish look and muttered a very soft little "…I guess so."

"Well! I'm not going to tell you everything….Not just yet. It would be sufficient for you to know that my children are being raised by some special friends…with their family. They all come to visit occasionally. I may tell you why later…and I may not. Think I want to get to know you a little better before I go telling you any more personal information. You ARE my daughter, and I have kept up with everything you've accomplished and been through. I do care about you, Breeze. You're more like me than I ever imagined. Now…about this Alex!"

Breeze made no comment. She knew how she felt about Alex, and she didn't want to hear Olympia telling her what to do. Olympia! Who was stuck way away from everything…all by herself. No! Whatever Olympia had to say about Alex…she didn't want to hear.

She picked up first one piece of canvas then another…looking each over with great intent. "Olympia, instead of worrying about me…and Alex, I'd like you to show me around this ship. I see lots of interesting things in here that you've collected. Maybe you could tell me—"

Olympia cut into her sentence sharply. "Listen, little daughter! I've been there! You haven't! I think you need to listen to what I have to say. You ALSO need to show a little respect for someone that's already been where're you're about to go."

Breeze straightened up and looked Olympia right in the eye. "I don't need a lecture about this. I get enough of those from Neptune."

"I'm not going to lecture you, Breeze. I just don't want you to fall into the same problems I did. Look at my situation. Take a real good look! I know all of you put me up on some kind of pedestal…because I'm different. I dared to be different! I went against the 'don't get too close to humans' clause in the 'How to be a Mermaid' manual…Did something none of them would even think of doing. I saved a human's life… Kissed him many more times than once…and dwelt in HIS territory for years until that fateful day. Breeze, most of those fancy little mermaids don't have any idea why I'm here. YOU don't even really know why I'm up here. Do you?" Olympia paused for a moment, looked Breeze over from head to the tip of her tail. "They just know I'm here and can't be there…and…TRUST ME! You don't want to wind up like me…alone in an old ship with just memories to keep me company. Now, come over here and listen.

"Part of the reason I'm here is because of your father. Neptune and I were pretty close…close enough for you to be born. We were always together. For a long time I kept thinking he would ask me to belong only to him…but I never heard that. He never asked me that. You were born during a time when I was very upset with him. He just…always expected me to be there when he wanted me there but that was it."

"One day I was swimming by an old wrecked ship and saw an air hose going into it. I knew a diver was in there because I'd seen them go in there many times before. The water was too deep for them where the ship was, and they always wore those silly looking suits. Usually, I just watched from far off. But this time… THIS time was different. I had a feeling something was wrong, so I went inside the ship. I was right! The diver was in trouble. He seemed to be struggling trying to get air through that hose. I just took his headpiece off and gave him a big kiss. He didn't seem to have any energy…probably from the lack of air. I knew he was in trouble so I took the rest of his suit off too. I kept kissing him. Kissed him all the way back up to the ocean's surface. He opened his eyes about then and seemed to be in shock seeing me there holding him without his suit on. The boat he had come on had drifted quite a long ways away. He asked me what I was doing swimming alone way out in the water. Then he realized I was a mermaid. I didn't wait for him to say anything. I just gave him another big kiss. This time, he kissed me back.

"Breeze, I knew with that kiss that I wanted to be with Jim for the rest of my life. He felt the same way. We swam to the boat, and I conjured up my land legs. Yes! Neptune taught me how to do that too. Surprised the heck out of Jim. He gave the other humans on the boat some story about finding me after being shipwrecked, and I went back to land with them."

"I went back for you, Breeze, but Neptune was there. He seemed to know everything….Said I would never be able to see you again, that he had someone else to raise you…Oceana! I found out then that he'd been seeing her all along. Breeze, since you were his child too, he would have taken you away from me even if I'd never met Jim. Neptune told me I could never again come around his area…his kingdom! Said I was banned forever and he would make sure no one ever came to see me."

"I was hurt! I didn't mean to do anyone any harm…I just fell in love. If your father…that…NEPTUNE…had cared for me the way he cares for Oceana…I would never have given Jim that second kiss."

"I see!" said Breeze as she picked up the canvas that had the sketch of her brother and sister on it. "Wish they were older in this sketch so I'd know who they are. Olympia, this doesn't explain why your other two children aren't with you. What happened there?"

"Breeze, Neptune was like their grandfather. He was always there for me.…Always has been…was there with each of the children when they were born. He knew Jim and they…well…let's say they tolerated each other because of me and the children. Ever since they were first born…" Olympia paused and gave Breeze a sly grin. "Thought I'd say their names…didn't you? Well, I'm not going to do that."

"Every since they were born, they could change from tail to legs at will…without hesitation! This can be devastating in a human society. When Jim was alive it was no problem helping them to remember not to change into their tails. After he died I took the children to some special friends I had so they would be raised with other mermaids. I knew I couldn't handle living in a human society all by myself. Jim was gone, and Neptune started to take over...thought he could just come in and tell me what to with myself and with my children. I didn't want this for them. I wanted them to be raised like any normal mermaid would be."

"Neptune was furious!...He said he would steal my children if he found them...said he didn't want any half humans among his group and I didn't need to be bringing them up that way...that he would take them far away if he ever saw them. I tried for a short time to keep them...but eventually I knew I couldn't. They are with some special friends of mine, and Neptune thinks they are theirs. After a couple years of me not telling him where they were, he decided I no longer belonged with the rest and banned me completely from ever coming back. That's not the only reason I can't go back, but the fact that I refused to tell him where they were caused him to have 'HAD ENOUGH' as he put it. So, here I am...And there they are! Oh, they come to visit all the time. They know I'm their mother, and I'm sure they love me. Most of their life has been away from me, and they seem to be happy. They'll be full-grown soon and be able to do what they want. Being raised the way they are, I doubt very much if either of them would want to live as humans. They were both very small when Jim died and really don't remember him or living the human way."

"Hmm...." Breeze looked at Olympia out of the corner of her eye, and a sly smile came across her face.

"BREEZE, DON'T EVEN THINK ABOUT IT! I know what you're thinking. Just DON'T!"

Breeze looked up at her in surprise. "Don't what?"

Olympia cut her sentence short. "DON'T THINK ABOUT ZAPPING UP YOUR LAND LEGS IN FRONT OF THEM ALL...Be one of the biggest mistakes you've made so far. If everyone saw you could do that...your brother and sister would do that too. They would instantly be labeled as outcasts, and all three of you might be banned from the society. Please! Just let things be as they are! Promise me you'll not do that!"

"OK! I see your point! I promise!" Breeze realized what would happen if she changed in front of everyone. Then she REALLY thought about it. "Olympia, do you suppose...Neptune taught me how to get land legs so I would...maybe conjure my legs up in front of my brother and sister?" Somehow she wanted to figure out just how to tell which of her friends were her brother and sister...without causing any trouble. There just had to be a way. "Olympia, do my brother and sister know they have another sister?"

Olympia, wise to Breeze's sneaky ways, said, "You're probably right about the reason Neptune taught you how to get legs. I'll not tell you any more about your brother and sister just now. Think it's about time you leave and go enjoy yourself for the evening. It's getting late, and I'm getting tired. You can come back again. Morning time is best. You don't want to get caught around here in the evening or at night. We may chat more about that next time. I'll put these things away. You're welcome to look at them any time you come to see me." She swished her tail, moved towards the front door, and held it open. "I really enjoyed your visit, Breeze. Come back soon."

Breeze was upset about being ushered to the door so fast and let Olympia know it in no uncertain terms. "Olympia, I THINK YOU'RE BEING RUDE HERE. I CAME WAY OUT OF MY WAY TO VISIT YOU! CAME HERE AGAINST NEPTUNE'S WISHES BECAUSE I THOUGHT YOU WERE SPECIAL... and...AND...I DON'T LIKE YOU JUST TELLING ME IT'S TIME FOR ME TO GO...all of a sudden...in the middle of our conversation. I THINK I PUT YOU ON THE SPOT! THAT'S WHAT I THINK! NOW! Do my brother and sister know you had a child by Neptune?"

"Breeze, it's time for you to go! PLEASE! You pry too deep into my private affairs, and I've told you enough for one night! MORE than enough!"

"MY AFFAIRS TOO! They ARE my brother and sister, you know."

"That's enough, Breeze! Please don't wear out your welcome by pushing too hard."

Breeze looked down at the deck of the ship for a minute. "OK! But...how would YOU like it if YOU had a brother and sister and just found out about it? Wouldn't YOU want to know who they are?" With that remark Breeze flipped her tail in disgust and swished out the door.

Olympia quickly went to the backside of the ship and slipped out. She knew if Breeze had waited in hiding once, and watched and listened, she would do it again. She swam a long distance around and met Neptune…told him she was changing things around and wanted to make sure that anyone who visited her came in from the back side of the ship.

Neptune knew in an instant why Olympia was doing this and questioned her. "Has Breeze been here?"

Chapter 15

"Humph!" Breeze muttered to herself as she swam away. "I hid once! I'll hide again. Won't tell ME who my brother and sister are, eh? I'll find out for myself! I'll just wait where I was before." And she did!…And she waited…and waited…and waited! Breeze waited till the ocean got black with nightfall. She fell asleep waiting and was awakened in the morning by her friends the dolphins wanting to play.

Breeze didn't feel much like playing. All she really wanted to do was find out who her brother and sister were, but she decided to go back home to her group of friends. For the time being she'd had enough of visiting with Olympia. She never was much for staying in one place and just talking anyway. And she surely couldn't just stay where she was…hiding and waiting…in hopes her brother and sister might just decide to drop by for a visit. Her world wasn't the same anymore. Her mother wasn't really her mother, and now she had a brother and sister she didn't even know she had.

It was time for some fun! "YEAH! I'LL PLAY WITH YOU! LET'S GO!" Breeze was disgusted! She had spent the night in an uncomfortable area…waiting…for nothing. "THINK I'D LIKE A RIDE!" She slipped onto the back of one of her dolphin friends and came up with a brilliant idea. She told the dolphins to keep an eye out for boats and ships…thought it would be funny for humans to see her riding on a dolphin way out there at sea.

It wasn't long before they came to a fishing boat. The nets had been let down, so they had to be very careful not to get caught in them. They dared not come too close to this type of boat. Even at the distance they were at, it was dangerous. Breeze could not resist conjuring up her land legs. She had the dolphins swim as close to the surfaceas they could. No one seemed to notice Breeze sitting on the dolphin. Breeze stood up on the dolphin…Still no one noticed. They were all too busy with the nets. Things were just not going right for her. She HAD to do something for some excitement…and fishermen definitely were not it.

Breeze was disgusted that no one had noticed her. She headed out to the deep sea with her dolphin friends looking for another boat. There was nothing! No matter which way she looked, all that wat there was the horizon. She would have been better off if she'd stayed near the shore. They spent several hours doing flips out of the water to see who could go the highest. To Breeze, this was boring. She'd done this so many times before. Even riding on their backs was boring.

After what Breeze called an uneventful afternoon, she announced that she was going back toward the shore…that there was nothing out there in the open sea that was interesting or different and she was going back towards the land. She looked at each of the dolphins, saw how disappointed they were, and said if they wanted to follow her they could.

Within a few minutes the sun glistened on something just coming over the horizon. Being the curious mermaid she was, Breeze changed directions and headed straight for it. Oh, boy! A cruise ship. It wasn't the one Alex was on…but there were lots of people on the deck. This was just what she needed. She did a big flip in the air, conjured up her land legs, and landed on the back of the biggest dolphin in the pack. Shouting with glee she rode all around the ship hoping for some attention.

Even the cruise ship seemed to pay no attention to her. Maybe it was the way the sun was hanging low in the sky. It didn't take long for her to get tired of exhibiting herself with no one looking. She slipped into a sitting position on the dolphin and motioned for it to head towards shore. There was sure to be some excitement there.

Sylvia Fraley

They left the area and on their way to the shore they found a sailboat. "Yes!" Breeze was thrilled. She again conjured up her land legs, straddled them over the biggest dolphin in the group and swam to within a couple hundred feet of the boat. Several people were lying on deck chairs, but no one seemed to be looking out to sea. She stood up on the dolphin's back and waved. Still, no one was looking. "I can't believe this!" She said, "I notice EVERYTHING! NONE OF THE HUMANS ON ANY OF THESE BOATS NOTICED

ME!" She sat back down and watched the boat for a few minutes. It was a beautiful, big sailboat with big, colorful sails.

Something was being lowered into the sea. Breeze coaxed the dolphins to swim closer. It was a platform with two humans along with two of those things humans sat on when they wanted to scoot over the ocean at high speeds by themselves. Both humans put their hands up to shade their eyes and looked straight at Breeze. "They DID notice me!" she exclaimed, delighted that at last she could have some fun. Again, she stood up on the back of the dolphin and waved her arms at the strangers.

She could hear the man-people yelling at her, but she couldn't understand what they were saying. The platform had disappeared under the surface of the ocean. The humans were seated on their little floaty sea things, and she could hear their engines start. The next thing she knew those two humans were headed straight for her and her dolphin friends at top speed. Breeze immediately dove off into the water, gaining her tail as she went, and motioned for the dolphins to dive deep to get away. The dolphins lost no time following her example. The two humans with their black skin and tanks left their floaty things in the exact area where they saw Breeze dive and were doing their best to catch up with her. At this point, they didn't know Breeze was a mermaid. Things just happened too fast for them to notice that.

The dolphins had scattered and were nowhere in sight. Breeze had been in this type of situation before. There were only two of them, and she knew they would try to catch her…especially if they saw she was a mermaid. A sly smile came on her face as she thought what she was going to do next. Swimming as fast as she could…in a big circle…she swam up behind them. The two humans were still swimming close together looking from side to side as if searching for where she might have gone. Breeze snuck up close behind them, reached for the back of their masks, grabbed them both at the same time, and ripped them off their heads. Immediately she flipped her tail around and swam off in the opposite direction taking the masks with her. She laughed at their awkwardness in the water. To make her joke complete…she swam up to the floaty things and hung one mask on each.

Breeze was about to dive back down and watch the two humans as they fumbled their way back through the ocean with nothing on their eyes. A quick glance toward the sailboat told her all the people on deck were watching, so she thought she'd just give them something to watch. She hoped her tail wasn't showing when she hung up the masks. It didn't take a second for her to conjure up her land legs again. She sat on one of the floaty things and looked for a way to turn it on. It couldn't be much different than that car of Sandy's. She looked for the keys. THERE WERE NO KEYS! There was NOTHING! All she saw was a small black thing sitting on the side. Maybe it was a radio or something.

Sandy always played pretty music when she was in her car, and Breeze liked that. She started messing around with that black button…expecting to hear music. All of a sudden the engine started. This was GREAT! For quite some time she just sat there with a big smile on her face listening to the engine running...until she saw the divers' heads pop up above the water. They saw her sitting on one of their machines with the engine running and started yelling at her.

That did it! Breeze hated yelling! In a fit of anger, she reached for the hand grips and squeezed them both as tight as she could. "OOOEEEE!" she screamed. If she hadn't been holding on to those handlebar grips she would have been thrown right off the back. She'd never felt anything like this before. "YEEES!" she shouted. Her hands were still tightly gripping those bars. Breeze was heading for the open ocean at speeds she didn't even know existed...with nothing in her way. "YAAA HOOOOO!" The sounds of the engine drowned out her screams. It also drowned out the loud yelling of the divers that were coming too fast behind her...on the other machine.

In her excitement, Breeze started leaning to the side...first one way then the other. Now she was having more fun then ever. She had discovered how to turn...by leaning from one side to the other. Water shot high into the air as she spun around. Her eyes then caught sight of the two divers closing in behind. Seeing them put an end to her excitement, and she let go of the handlebars. Immediately her machine came to an abrupt halt... almost throwing her over the front.

The divers sped right past her and turned around just in time to see Breeze standing on the machine... waving at them.

She looked right at them, winked, and gave them a huge smile...Then she dove into the water. Breeze had had enough fun with the sailboat crew. Well...Almost enough! Out of the corner of her eye she saw those silly divers put on their masks and go back into the water looking for her...again. She couldn't pass that up. So she stayed just out of their sight and watched. Doing things one time was never enough for Breeze.

She was just about to sneak up and take their masks off again when her dolphin friends showed up, bringing several of their brothers and sisters. This would be GREAT! A distraction! The dolphins thought so too. They began to swim around the divers, flipping up pieces of seaweed and bits of the sandy ocean bottom. This was great fun for them. Breeze lost no time reaching for and trying to snatch their masks. This time, she only managed to grab one mask. The other diver moved just out of her reach. Not wanting to be seen as a mermaid, she hooked the mask on one of the dolphin's noses and quickly flipped herself around and out of sight.

With all the sand and seaweed that the dolphins were churning up, the diver without the mask was lost and had to remain pretty much in one spot. The diver that still had his mask on knew there was no way he could catch a dolphin and retrieve the mask. He grabbed his friend's hands to guide him to the surface. This was not so easy...trying to swim through twenty or more good-size fun-loving dolphins.

Breeze was not the type to sit on the sidelines and watch the fun. She HAD to join in. Conjuring up her legs, she swam right through all the commotion...right past the diver with his friend and up to the surface. Just as the divers popped their heads above the water, Breeze again mounted one of the dolphins. With her sitting on its back, she coaxed the dolphin to swim right

Breeze...the Mermaid

in front of the divers, around them, then right past the floaty sea things. Before heading out into the open sea, Breeze had the dolphins flip around. They were headed directly toward the divers once again. Breeze just had to make one last statement! So...just when they were about to collide with the divers, the dolphins veered to the side. She stood up on her dolphin's back, turned around, gave them a great big smile, and waved as they headed out to sea.

Out to sea wasn't really what Breeze wanted to do—no excitement there. She just wanted to find something different. The dolphins were happy because they had their favorite playmate back. "Let's turn around!" Breeze suggested. "I don't want to go back to that sailboat but...there MUST be something else we can do."

One of the dolphins spotted a fishing boat. "That would be perfect!" Breeze said as she started swimming toward it. Soon, she realized...this boat was one of the boats that brought fish to that cannery she visited a while back. She remembered what Sandy had said...that part of her family owned it, that she was unhappy about the mistreatment of the fish and the way things were done in there. This would be a good chance to teach them a lesson. Their nets were out, and she wanted very much to set some fish loose. The dolphins stayed behind as she made her way toward the boat.

Breeze was disgusted to see the nets almost full of fish. She dove to the ocean floor, found just the right shell and broke it to where it had a sharp edge. She turned around and was on her way back to cut the nets when she was met by Galley and Barney, her old friends.

They told her Neptune sent them. He hadn't seen her in a while and wanted to know where she was and what she was doing. Breeze didn't tell them about Olympia, but she did tell them about the fishing boat and all the fish that were being held captive in the nets.

After showing them what she wanted done, and how she broke the sea shell… she told them that she was going to use it to cut the nets and let all the fish go. Galley and Barney thought it would be a great idea, and they dove down to the ocean floor to pick up shells too. They broke them just like Breeze did and swam up underneath the nets; together they began cutting. Pretty soon they had a hole in each net that was large enough for the fish to start swimming out….And they did…hundreds of them! Breeze, Galley, and Barney swam up towards the top of the water where they could see and hear what was happening on board the fishing boat.

The nets had been out all day, and the humans, thinking it was about time to pull up their catch, began reeling them in…one at a time. At first, they just couldn't believe nothing had been caught. After taking a closer look at the first net they discovered it had a big hole in the bottom where something had cut it. All sorts of foul language and yelling were heard. The second net was pulled up….Not one fish…And it also had a big hole that had been cut in the middle. The language got worse, and it got louder. When the third net was pulled up with no fish and a big hole was found cut in the middle, anger was not the word for it. The humans began scurrying around the ship, looking over the railing, shaking their fists and yelling. They seemed to think some other fishermen had sabotaged their nets.

Smaller boats began to be lowered towards the water with humans in them. They all had guns and knives in their hands. When the little boats reached the water they landed amidst the fish that were once in the net. The sea was thick with various kinds of fish churning the water trying to get away. This made the fishermen even angrier, but there was nothing they could do about it. The deed had been done. Now all they wanted to do was to find the person or persons that had the nerve to cut those nets.

Breeze, Galley, and Barney were laughing so hard they had to keep their distance from the ship and little boats so they wouldn't be heard. They did not want to get caught. All this noise and churning of the water brought the sharks. Oh! What a feast they had! The sharks were huge! Now the humans were frightened. They scurried to get their little boats back and pulled up onto the bigger fishing boat.

"Time to leave the scene!" Galley spoke up. "Breeze, I've really missed you! Life is so dull without you around. I'll even take back what I said when we were playing with those seashells at the pier. Um...Well...you know, your father is worried about you."

"About me? I don't think so. I think he just wants to keep close watch on everyone in his group...and I am one of his group."

"He loves you, Breeze!" Barney spoke up. "He talks about you all the time and tells us all about your adventures. Wish I had the nerve to do HALF of what you do....And you seem to get away with it all too."

Breeze squinted her eyes as she looked Barney up and down. "Barney! Do you remember when you were real little?"

"What are you asking me that for, Breeze?" With a questioning look, Barney continued, "Of course I remember when I was little. What does THAT have to do with what we're doing now?"

"Oh, nothing!" Breeze answered. "Just wondering."

"You coming back with us?" Galley asked.

"Don't think so, Galley….Too dull there! Wasn't it fun? What we just did? Didn't you two enjoy yourselves? Didn't we help a lot of fish?"

Galley looked at her with sad eyes. "Some of them got eaten by the sharks."

Barney flashed a big smile. "YEAH! BUT LOOK AT HOW MANY GOT AWAY! THIS IS GREAT, BREEZE! Let's go do some more neat stuff!"

Breeze thought a minute…then looked at Barney with different eyes. Could HE be her brother? He seemed to have an adventuresome spirit. "Got any ideas, Barney?"

"Me?" Barney looked at her with big eyes. "Ah… NO! Breeze.. You're always the one with the ideas. We all know that."

Galley spoke up. "You know, Neptune sent us here to look for you…see what you were doing…and bring you back."

"Galley!" Breeze corrected. "When you two swam up to meet me, you said Neptune hadn't seen me for a while and wanted to know where I was and what I was doing. I don't remember you saying I had to go back with you."

"Well!" Galley muttered. "You do! Neptune said he wanted to see you back home. I didn't tell you that right away because I didn't think you wanted to go back home yet."

"You're right!" Breeze looked her in the eye." AND…I'M NOT GOING HOME RIGHT NOW! There are some things I still want to do yet."

Now Galley was curious. "Like what?

Breeze remembered what Olympia had said about not telling how much she liked Alex….So she just said. "Oh! I've learned a lot of things….Like what we just did, saving those fish. It's just so wonderful to be able to do stuff like that and…well…I'm just not ready to go back yet. If you're going back, just tell him I'm okay…that I'm having fun….And I'm saving lots of our friends that are caught in nets."

"OK, Breeze! I AM going back, and I will tell him. When ARE you coming back? I really do miss your company?"

"Soon! Tell him I'll be back soon."

Barney looked at them both. "I'm going to stay here with Breeze, Galley. I think I like what Breeze is doing, and I want to do the same."

"OK!" Galley was upset, and she showed it. "You'll both be sorry. Neptune isn't going to like BOTH of you being gone." With that statement she flipped her tail and left.

Breeze wasn't too happy about Barney staying. If he were along she couldn't conjure up her land legs. "Barney! What are you going to do when Neptune gets angry with you for not bringing me back…and not coming back yourself?"

Barney looked down at the ocean floor. "I…I never thought of that, Breeze! I just want to—"

"I know you do, Barney." Breeze cut in…"I know you do…And I would love to have your company. I just don't want you to get into trouble because of me."

"Since you put it that way….It's probably best that I go back with Galley." He flipped around and started to leave…then flipped back. "Breeze! Are you sure you don't want me with you? I…"

"Barney! I'D LOVE to have you with me, but I'd feel bad if I caused you to get into trouble."

"OK! I'll see you later. I'll try to catch up with Galley."

Breeze wasn't sure just WHAT she would be doing next, but she was glad both of her friends were gone. Her dolphin friends didn't seem to be around any longer either.…So she decided to head for the area where the cruise ship had been.

Chapter 16

"YOU DID THE RIGHT THING, BREEZE... SENDING THEM AWAY LIKE THAT!"

Breeze flipped around and was surprised to see Olympia there...with a big smile on her face. "OLYMPIA, WHAT ARE YOU DOING HERE?"

"Came to see you, my dear daughter! Came to see you! I decided since you've gone out of your way and faced danger to come see me...I'd return the favor. Breeze, I know that no matter what is said...you are going to meet that human, Alex again." She looked Breeze right in the eye with a big smile on her face. "If it were me...I WOULD MEET ALEX AGAIN! I know! When you were visiting me, I tried to tell you not to meet him and not to get involved with a human. But...I've thought it over. When you asked me the question...Would I do it all over again? Yes, Breeze...I WOULD do it all over again...wouldn't think twice about it. Follow your heart, girl! You'll never be happy if your mind is always on someone else.

"Now, this is what I want to teach you! Let's swim to the shore. I have some things there, and we will need to change into our land legs."

Breeze was excited. "OLYMPIA, I can't believe you're here! Aren't you going against Neptune? Didn't he put restrictions on you...about leaving and...and coming to town...and..."

"Yes, Breeze....He did! I don't plan on telling him what we're doing! ARE YOU GOING TO TELL HIM?"

"OH! NO!... Of course not!"

"Then...let's go! My timing is perfect. The sun is on its way down, and things should be opening up for the night."

Olympia had picked a place away from everything. When they reached the shore Olympia made sure no one was there. She transferred into her land legs, reached under the dock and pulled up a small suitcase she'd hung there.

Breeze conjured up her land legs too.

Olympia pulled out two great big towels, handed one of them to Breeze, and said. "Here! Wrap this around you until we get to a place where we can change. The humans will think we have bathing suits on underneath. They don't like to see people with nothing on." This done, she attached the suitcase back under the dock.

Breeze couldn't get over the fact that Olympia was walking with her...ON LAND! They walked along the beach for quite a ways....Walked right into a real fancy building with big pictures of humans on the front. Olympia opened the door and walked inside. The first things Breeze saw were huge windows overlooking the ocean. The sun had just gone down. Looking through them framed a beautiful picture of the sunset. Several humans were seated on a place that was higher than the floor they were walking on, each one holding a different kind of instrument. "This is just GREAT!" Breeze commented. "I met Sandy in a place where they were playing music too. It wasn't as nice as this."

"They know me here, Breeze. My husband and I used to come here often. He taught me how to dance here. Now...I'm going to teach you." Olympia took her by the hand and guided her to the back of the building where their dressing rooms were. Several different people started up conversations with Olympia...asking how she was...commenting that they hadn't seen her for a long time...that they were glad she was back...and was she going to start coming here again. Olympia seemed to have no trouble at all carrying on a conversation with each of them. Finally she asked one of the man humans if there was a dressing room available. Then she asked him if he would do her the honors of teaching her daughter, Breeze how to dance.

Breeze couldn't believe her ears. Then she was introduced. "Breeze, this is Dan. He was a good friend of my husband's. I think he will do a fine job teaching you to dance."

Breeze wasn't sure about this...wasn't sure at all!

Olympia led Breeze into the dressing room, opened up a big suitcase that was sitting there, and pulled out two very pretty dresses, shoes, and something she called jewelry. She handed Breeze one of the dresses and said, "Here, Breeze! Put this on! I'll put mine on too. Put the shoes on. I think they will fit you. Leave the towels there and come over here to the mirror with me."

Breeze did as she was told. She didn't much like the shoes, but she put them on anyway and walked over to the mirror.

"Now, if you want to learn how to be a human…you need to know how to be a beautiful one. Humans put stuff on their faces. They think they are more beautiful that way. We're going to do that right now. Sit down! Here…In front of this mirror."

The mirror was huge…had lights all the way around it. The table in front of the mirror had lots of jars and tubes of stuff lying on it. Olympia chose several items… told Breeze to… "Hold still. I'm going to fix your face and hair up a bit."

When Breeze finally turned around and looked at herself in the mirror she couldn't believe what Olympia had done to her. "Olympia!" she exclaimed. "I'm really beautiful…Aren't I?"

"Yes, Breeze! You are…But don't let it go to your head. You've always been beautiful. You just didn't know it."

Just then, there came a knock at the door. It was Dan. He held out his hand for Breeze to take….Then he looked at Olympia and said. "My! My! Olympia! You do have a good looking daughter. If I were younger…"

"Don't even think it, Dan! I just think Breeze should know how to dance. She may surprise you with how fast she can learn."

"Already has surprised me," Dan said as he took Breeze's hand. "She's the prettiest girl here…outside of you, of course." He gave Olympia a great big grin and asked, "You ARE coming on the floor to dance aren't you?"

"Yes! I guess so. I haven't danced since…"

Dan looked at her. "This must be hard on you, Olympia. Haven't seen you in years and now….Now you show up with a beautiful daughter." He yelled across the room for someone called Spence. "Olympia, if it's OK with you, I'd like Spence to teach Breeze here. He's more her age, and I think they may just hit it off well together. He's a fine dancer. Actually, I'd very much like to spend the evening dancing with you…if that's OK."

Olympia was stunned by his offer…but said, "That would…be just fine, Dan. I think I'd like that."

Spence waltzed across the floor with another girl on his arm….He said his goodbyes to the other girl and stood there…in front of the three of them with his mouth open and his eyes open even wider…looking at Breeze.

Dan noticed that Spence was immediately taken by Breeze's beauty and tried to put him at ease. "Spence! Breeze here is the daughter of my dear friend Olympia. She brought her here so I could teach her to dance…but I think you would do just fine as her teacher…closer to the same age." He smiled and added, "Is that OK with you?"

"Oh! Oh! Yes…ah…yeah!" Spence held out his hand to Breeze. "You danced before…ah…Breeze?"

Breeze just stood where she was and watched as Olympia and Dan waltzed across the floor. She'd never seen anything like this before.

"Ah…BREEZE! Breeze!" Spence held out his hand to her again. "Would you care to dance?"

"Oh! Oh! Yes! I'm sorry. I've just never seen my mother dance before."

Spence watched Olympia for a moment, and then reached out again to take Breeze's hand. "She is a great dancer….And you can be just as great…if you'll allow me to take you onto the dance floor."

Breeze was a bit startled. She was busy watching Olympia. "Oh! Ah, OK!" She looked at Spence…gave a great big smile, and added…"Hey! If she can do it, I can do it!"…And she did! Breeze found out that dancing was one thing she could do with legs that was actually fun. She watched Olympia's every move and tried to copy them.

After a couple hours on the floor, Spence realized she was learning things as fast as he was teaching them. "You sure you haven't danced before?" he asked. "The way you're moving, it's like you've done this lots of times."

Breeze smiled to herself and winked at Spence. "Guess it's just in my blood. I can't let Mom have all the fun…can I?"

Spence stopped dancing…loosened his dance hold, and put his arms around Breeze. He looked directly into her eyes. "You're the prettiest girl I've ever danced with, Breeze." His hands slowly moved to where they were gently caressing her face…Then he pulled her close and gave her a great big kiss.

Breeze backed off, her eyes open wide with surprise. She pulled off her live crab earrings and quickly put them down the front of his shirt.

"HEY!" he yelled. "WHAT'D YOU DO THAT FOR? W…WHAT'D YOU PUT DOWN MY SHIRT?"

Spence looked at her questioningly. "YOU WERE SO PRETTY...I JUST HAD TO KISS YOU." About that time, he began to feel little tickles on his chest...like something was moving or running on it.

It took him a few moments before he realized exactly WHAT Breeze had done. He looked her in the eye, smiled, and asked, "Did you like it? Did you like my kiss?" Then the crabs must have started pinching because his eyes got very big. He sucked in his breath and did kind of a dance of his own...Then he started yelling and pulling at this shirt. "WHAT THE! OH! OW! UH! WHAT IS THIS? BREEZE...YOU..."

Quickly, he pulled off his shirt and found two little crabs clamping onto his skin with both claws. One was on his stomach and the other on his chest. He glared at Breeze.

"BREEZE! BREEZE? YOU...YOU PUT THESE? DID YOU DO THIS?"

"Well...YES! YES! I DID!" Breeze cut in. "Spence, YOU SHOULDN'T JUST TAKE ADVANTAGE LIKE THAT! We were dancing...and that was fun! Then! Then you had to go and complicate things." Breeze thought for a minute. "Spence, I already have someone I'm interested in. My mother just thought I needed to learn how to dance....That's all. I didn't come here to... to be kissed!"

Spence pulled the crabs off, put his shirt back on and gathered himself together. Then he calmly said, "You didn't answer me, Breeze. Did you like me kissing you?"

"Well! Yes! But...but...we were having so much fun dancing. I..."

"That's why I kissed you. I really enjoy being with you, Breeze. You didn't have to put those crabs on me. You know...I really like you and want to be with you more than just tonight...more than just on this dance floor. I want to see you often." He looked into her eyes and smiled. "I want to be with you even more since you stuck those crabs in my shirt." Spence put one arm around her waist and the other behind her head and pulled her close, their lips almost touching. "I liked kissing you, Breeze. I liked it very much. I like your name. I—"

Breeze cut his last statement short. "Spence, we dance really well together! I'm glad you taught me what you taught me." She caught Olympia's arm as she and Dan waltzed by. "Mother! Do you think I could dance with Dan for a while? I'd like to see if I can do as well with him as I do with Spence."

Spence stood aside with his mouth open. He knew he'd stepped out of line by sneaking that kiss.

Olympia had seen what happened....She took Spence's hand and said, "Let's dance, Spence. This is Breeze's first time dancing and she wants to make sure she can dance just as well with whoever she is with."

Dan looked at Olympia. He was a bit reluctant. He'd seen what happened to Spence also. Olympia nodded her approval. Breeze took his hand, and they danced until way after closing time. "You are a fast learner, Breeze. I'm sorry, but I thought what you did to Spence was funny. It was all I could do to keep from laughing. I know Spence pretty well...and he really likes you, Breeze. I own this place, and it's time to close for the night. Come with me while I announce it. By the way...you don't have any more crabs on you...do you?"

"No...No! I don't! I just thought it was the thing to do at the time. I like to wear those crabs for my earrings. Spence just took me by surprise. That's all."

"Good! I like a woman with some spunk." Dan's arm went around her waist and they walked to where he made his announcement...Then he turned off the lights....Then HE took Breeze in his arms and gave her a big kiss.

"DAN!" Breeze said as she pulled away. "I liked dancing with you very much...BUT...Spence did the same thing you're trying to do. I wish I did have more crabs! Wish I had big ones. I don't give my kisses away to just everyone. I think—"

"YOU ABOUT READY TO GO?" It was Olympia. She'd seen Spence kiss her earlier....And now...she saw her friend Dan do the same thing. She reached out and took Breeze's hand. "It's getting late and I think we need to be going." As they walked through the door, Olympia yelled back across the room, "THANKS, GUYS! Thanks for the lessons and the fun evening.... We'll have to do it again sometime!"

Once out the door, Olympia started explaining to Breeze how she shouldn't just let everyone kiss her. "Breeze, humans are not like mermaids. You kiss a human more than once and it's almost certain you'll fall in love with them...and they'll fall in love back with you. You go around allowing different humans to kiss you more than once...and you're in for a lot of problems. Don't even test this one out, Breeze. Please listen to what I have to say."

She had barely finished her sentence when Breeze said. "Olympia, Spence was nice…But he's NOT Alex! Dan? Well, Dan….He's nice enough, too….But I just didn't feel like kissing him at all…I don't feel like kissing anyone but Alex. Wish I'd worn BIG crabs! Would have been more fun watching him. Olympia! Is that all men want to do? Kiss?"

Before that question got answered, Spence came running up and grabbed Breeze's hand. "Breeze!" he said, as he stopped to catch his breath. "Breeze, if I offended you in there, I'm sorry. I just have to tell you! Dancing with you is unlike anything I've ever imagined. I could dance with you forever. You catch on so fast! You're a great dancer and…well…ah…" He turned to Olympia. "Olympia, I really like your daughter…in spite of the crabs!" He winked at Breeze. "I want to see her again and again. I want to dance with her all night. I just REALLY like your daughter…Hope you don't mind."

"Not at all!" Olympia smiled. "She's a big girl and can make her own decisions." She turned to Breeze, looked her in the eye, and said, "Can't you, Breeze?"

Breeze couldn't believe what she was hearing. Olympia stood right there and allowed that…allowed that Spence to…"Spence!" she said as she turned toward him. "You don't even know who I am. All you did was teach me to dance…kissed me without asking and…and…"

"When I kissed you, Breeze…it was like no other kiss I've ever had. I'm sorry if I offended you but—"

Breeze cut in before he could finish. "Spence, I told you earlier! I've already found someone I like. I...I'm sorry!"

Spence was persistent! He quickly reached out with both arms, grabbed Breeze and pulled her close. "Well! I guess this is good bye then!" He quickly put one arm behind her head and the other around her waist, leaned her over backwards and kissed her once again. "Had to do that, Breeze! One last kiss from the most beautiful girl I've ever met."

Breeze was stunned. Now she had kissed TWO different guys...TWICE! She just stood there for a moment...with her mouth wide open. "You...You! You really shouldn't have done that Spence. You just don't know! You—"

Olympia cut in this time. "Time to go, Breeze. Spence, that was a naughty trick! You ought to be ashamed of yourself. I ought to tell Dan on you."

"WELL! YOU DON'T HAVE TO TELL DAN! DAN SAW...SAW EVERYTHING!" He had quickly walked up behind the group to say one last good bye to Olympia. "Been a long time, Olympia. You and Jim used to come here all the time and I haven't seen you since...since....Where are you living now? I'd kind of like to...come and see you once in a while...maybe go out to dinner...stuff like that. Maybe we could—"

"That's sweet Dan...but I don't think so. I've moved pretty far away....Didn't want to look back at memories all the time. The only reason I'm here now is to visit my daughter. I'll be going back home later tonight. It was nice seeing you again and dancing with you....And it HAS been a long time." She took Breeze by the hand

and smiled. "Maybe some other time, Dan. Maybe! Maybe! I'll think about it."

They had walked along the beach for only a short distance...just far enough to be out of eyesight from the dance studio. Olympia stopped under a palm tree and sat down on the park bench next to it. "Breeze!" Olympia said, in a stern voice. "Now you've done it! You've kissed TWO different humans more than once. Haven't you listened to anything I've said? Don't you remember what happens when you kiss a human more than once?"

"Olympia!" Breeze smiled. "I didn't kiss that human twice. As a matter of fact...I didn't even kiss him ONCE. HE kissed ME! There IS a difference!"

"I suppose so! You SURE you didn't kiss him back? I'm just trying to save you from trouble."

Breeze was beginning to get a bit upset. She was not used to being so 'mothered.' "OLYMPIA! I may tease a little bit. I may cause some trouble with the fishing boats....They ask for it...killing so many of my friends. I may be adventurous and occasionally do things that are a little...well...ah...that I probably shouldn't...but... I'm NOT going to go around...just kissing humans."

"I hope not, Breeze!" Olympia said as she started taking off her clothes. "This is where I leave you." She stood up, dropped her dress onto the sand, walked across the moonlit beach and into the water. With a big smile, she added. "That cruise ship should be coming back any day. Say hello to Alex for me...will you?" With that remark, she dove into the sea and...with one flip of her tail...she was out of sight.

Breeze sat down on the bench. Olympia's pretty dress and shoes lay on the ground in a pile at her feet. She sat there for some time looking up at the eerie, luminous glow of the full moon surrounded by thousands of stars that twinkled in the sky. Sitting there, alone in the night in her human form, she found herself actually missing Olympia and was tempted to follow her….But she didn't. A smile crept across her face as she remembered Olympia's last words…."Say hello to Alex for me!" That was wonderful! That meant she understood….And it was OK.

Chapter 17

For the first time in her life…Breeze felt alone. She'd had so much fun dancing and being with Olympia…enjoying the music and excitement of dancing that now…in the dimly lit darkness of the still night…she felt alone. She looked down at the dress lying on the ground…picked up the hem of the dress she was wearing and looked out into the sea. She'd never felt lonely there. There was always something to do or someone to pal with. Here, in the human world…there was either lots of excitement and things to do or there was nothing…and the nothing was what she was experiencing now.

Breeze stood up and gazed out to sea. She took her dress off and let it slip onto the ground on top of the gown Olympia had worn. She stood there feeling soft wisps of the summer winds caress her body. Looking across the sea toward the horizon, she could see the lights from a huge ship. Her loneliness was instantly gone! She scooped up the dresses and the shoes and ran down to the pier where Olympia had originally left her small suitcase. It was still there, attached under the dock. She hurriedly stuffed the dresses into it...ran a short ways to the end of the dock, dove into the sea, and of course gained her tail as soon as she touched the water.

She wanted in the worst way to meet that ship before everyone got off...wanted to meet Alex and had no thought that she just might need to be wearing clothes. It wasn't until AFTER she reached the shore where the ship was to dock...and after she conjured up her legs that she remembered. Breeze also remembered all the trouble she'd had before...with no clothes on. Immediately, she changed back to her tail and swam back to the dresses that she'd just put into the small suitcase hanging under the dock.

THE SUITCASE WAS GONE! It couldn't be! She'd just put it there! Popping her head up a little further out of the water, she noticed a couple children playing...with the dresses that were in HER suitcase. This would never do! Those were the only things she had to wear! "HEY!" she shouted. The top half of her body was out of the water, and she was rapidly changing into her human legs. "THOSE ARE MINE...AND I NEED THEM... NOW! DROP THE SUITCASE AND LEAVE MY DRESSES ALONE! CAN'T A GIRL GO FOR A SWIM WITHOUT SOMEONE STEALING HER CLOTHES?"

The children just stood there with their mouth open...shocked that a grown person would be swimming with no swimming suit top on.

The dresses were still in their hands when Breeze pulled herself up onto the shore. "I SAID, DROP THOSE

DRESSES!" She stood there for a brief moment with her hands on her hips glaring at the children. "I SAID..."

"OK! OK!" the children yelled. They dropped the clothes and the little suitcase, turned around, and ran away.

Breeze picked up the dresses, shoes, and the suitcase. She slipped into her wrinkled dress, put the other dress and both pairs of shoes into the suitcase, and started off walking to the ship. Her feet were a little sore from dancing most of the night, and she just didn't feel like wearing those funny shoes right now. They looked like they had a nail on the back of them anyway. Walking was SO slow.

The cruise ship docked long before she got there, and a few people were still getting off the boat. Lots of people were getting on the ship with their luggage. A lump came into her throat as she joined the crowd that was getting on.

When she reached the entrance, she was met by a stern looking, uniformed lady. "Which room are you in, Miss...AND WHERE ARE YOUR SHOES?"

Breeze held up the little suitcase. "In here!" she answered.

"Where's the rest of your luggage?"

Breeze thought for a minute. "Oh! It's coming behind me. Someone's bringing it behind me. I have lots of luggage. Ah...it's coming! Can I go to my room now?"

"Which room are you in? I'll tell you how to get there."

"Oh! I know where it is. You don't have to do that. I really need to change out of this dress...this dancing dress...Danced all night, you know." Breeze scurried past the lady as fast as she could, trying not to be too obvious. She didn't look back for fear the lady would say something to stop her.

Luck was on her side because several large groups of people were following close behind asking directions.

Breeze sucked in a big breath and let it out again in relief. She felt better now that she was on the ship and headed right for the ladies' restroom to get as pretty as she could for Alex. This took a while because she had nothing to work with. She snuck the use of a hairbrush from a little girl when her back was turned and stole a pair of sandals from an older lady who was rummaging through her purse then quickly exited the room.

Now, to find Alex! For some reason the ship just didn't look the same this time. She remembered things in different places than they were, and the ship seemed much larger than it was the last time she was on it. Not thinking too much more about that, she put the sandals on and started walking down the long deck. Each person she saw with a ship's uniform on, she asked. "Where's Alex? You seen Alex?"

Of course, no had seen or even knew an Alex.

By now, the ship had sailed pretty far out to sea. Breeze walked the deck of the second floor. No Alex! No one knew of or had ever heard of Alex. She walked the deck of the third floor. Still, no one knew or heard of Alex. She went into a dining room and noticed all the food that was being brought out. "Oh boy! FOOD!" she said as she let herself in the door. Breeze did not bother picking up a plate. She just reached down and helped herself to whatever looked good. She was the only person in there eating. Humans with big funny white hats came running out and told her all the food wasn't ready yet…that she needs to come back in about half an hour. She just told them she didn't care and went on eating.

By now, she'd walked the deck and checked out everything she could on the fourth floor. Breeze sat down in one of the wooden chairs, propped her feet up, sat the little suitcase down beside her and looked out over the sea. Land was nowhere in sight, and the sun was high in the sky. She sat there for quite a while remembering when she dove off this ship and how she'd knocked Alex off with her….And that kiss! She REALLY remembered Alex and the kiss he gave back to her. A frown came across her face as she thought about it. She'd been all over that ship, and it didn't seem near as big as this one. Walking over to the railing, she noticed that was different too. The distance down to the water was about the same as when she dove off…but she didn't remember this type of railing. Maybe it was just this floor that had different railing. She picked up the little suitcase and went to the fifth floor and walked all over it, asking everyone if they'd seen Alex. Of course, no one had. The sixth floor was the same. No one knew of or had seen Alex.

Breeze was just about to go to the top deck when one of the humans in uniform came up to her and asked. "You looking for a man named Alex?"

"Oh! Yes! Yes, I am. Do you know where he is?"

"He's in the room where they navigate and steer the ship. He's in there handling the ship right now. I'll take you there if you like."

Breeze was excited. "YES! OH, YES! CAN WE GO NOW?"

"Sure! Follow me!" The man led Breeze into one of the halls and stopped in front of a green light blinking overhead. He pushed a button, took Breeze's hand and led her into an elevator.

"This the first time you've been on this ship, young lady?"

"NO! I was on here a few weeks ago...with Alex."

"Couldn't be...Ah...what did you say your name was?"

"Breeze! My name is Breeze."

"My name is Larry, Breeze. The last time this ship was at the docking point we just left was SIX months ago. You couldn't have been on this ship a few weeks ago because we weren't even here a few weeks ago. Now, are you sure you're on the right ship?"

This really took Breeze by surprise. "Of course I'm on the right ship!" She looked the man in the eye. "Don't you think I know where I'm going?"

"Not to be impolite, Miss." They stepped out of the elevator. "Follow me! I'll lead you to where Alex is working. He doesn't get many visitors, you know...pretty busy man." When they reached the door of the room, Larry said, "Wait here! I'll see if he can see you now. He does know you, doesn't he?"

Breeze smiled. "YES! OH YES! We know each other...real well."

"You stay right her. I'll be right back." He went into the room, shut the door behind him and immediately came back out...frowning. "I thought you said you knew Alex. He said he's never heard of you."

Breeze couldn't believe her ears. She just stood there and started crying....Then she got angry. "WHAT ARE YOU TELLING ME? I KNOW ALEX WOULDN'T TELL ME THAT! JUST...GET OUT OF MY WAY!" She pushed Larry aside and burst through the door only to stop dead in her tracks. Her eyes grew as big as saucers. She gasped and glared into the room. There were several humans, in front of lots of buttons, levers, and pictures that moved..."WHA...AH! OH! WELL...um...I'm sorry! Thought there was someone I...I knew in here."

The older, heavier human got up out of his chair and, in a gruff, commanding voice said, "GET HER OUT OF HERE! LARRY, DON'T YOU KNOW BETTER THAN TO BRING THE PASSENGERS UP HERE?" He turned to Breeze and said, "Young lady, I don't know what you think you're doing in here, but you'll have to leave! Go back to your room. Go somewhere, but you can't stay here. By the way, my name is Alex, and I've never seen or heard about you before. NOW, TAKE YOUR LITTLE SUITCASE AND GO BACK TO YOUR ROOM. GOODBYE!"

Breeze couldn't believe what she was hearing. No one but her father, Neptune, had ever spoken to her in that tone of voice. She stood there for moment thinking about what he said....Then she pointed her finger at him and blurted out her answer. "MISTER! MR. ALEX! YOU ARE A VERY RUDE MAN! EVER SINCE I'VE COME TO YOUR PART OF THE WORLD, I'VE FOUND MOST OF YOU HUMANS TO BE VERY RUDE AND CRUEL...AND I WOULDN'T EVEN THINK OF COMING BACK UP HERE

Breeze...the Mermaid

AGAIN!" After a moment's pause she continued, "AND I HOPE I NEVER SEE YOU AGAIN! YOU HAVE NO FEELINGS...JUST LIKE MOST OTHER HUMANS I'VE MET!" With that remark, she turned around, slammed the door, and left. Turning to Larry, she added. "I don't find that about you. You were nice. Thank you."

Larry looked at Breeze. "I'm sorry for the way he yelled at you. Did you say your Alex worked for this cruise ship?"

"Well, he did a couple weeks or so ago. I said goodbye to him on the bottom one of these floors."

"Couldn't have been this ship then. We haven't been in this port for at least six months."

Now Breeze understood why everything looked different. She felt empty inside and upset with herself for not recognizing it to be a different ship. "I guess I'll be leaving then. I'll just go back to the shore and wait for the other ship."

"What did you say your name was, Miss?"

"Breeze...My name's Breeze."

Larry thought a minute. "And...which room did you say you were in?"

"I didn't say I was in a room. Only asked to be taken to Alex."

"You're on the wrong ship, aren't you?"

"Yes!"

Larry pushed the elevator button to open the door and calmly said, "We can't turn back now...and we can't send you back. You'll just have to stay with us till we get to the next port. I'll make sure you have a cabin and are fed. Is your luggage here?"

"NO!" Breeze answered, stepping into the elevator and waving the little suitcase in his face. "I don't have any...LUGGAGE... only this...And...and I'm NOT staying on this ship until you reach the next port. I'm leaving...RIGHT NOW!" Breeze had been on the elevator at Sandy's and on this one for only a change of 1 floor but this time, but she was not ready for the sensation she received when the elevator picked up momentum dropping down several floors this time it jerked and, to Breeze, it felt like the bottom was dropping out from under her. Breeze sucked her breath in and almost screamed. She was in no mood to hear what Larry was going to say next.

"I'm sorry, Miss. You can't do that You can't just... leave right now!"

The elevator door opened into the hall of the lower deck. Breeze walked through the door...turned and looked right at Larry, and said, "OH! , YES!, I CAN! Just WATCH ME!" She flashed him a big smile, shoved the little suitcase into his hand and swiftly headed straight for the deck's railing.

Larry followed close behind...thinking she was upset enough to jump overboard. "There's no where to go, Breeze." He begged. "Come on! Please! Let me show you to a room."

Breeze was now standing at the railing. There were several people sitting in the lounge chairs and walking on the deck. There was also Larry...trying to be helpful. She looked at everyone, who by now were all looking her way. She turned to Larry and said, "Thank you Larry. Thank you for being kind to me."

With the swiftness of a cat, she leaped on the railing, unzipped her dress, and let it fall to her feet as she dove into the sea. Her dress caught on one foot and was soon flipped off as she regained her beautiful tail. The sheer fabric of it was like a parachute that not only hid her from the sight of the fast gathering crowd but followed her all the way down to the sea and lay like a huge mushroom on top of the water.

Larry dropped the suitcase and reached out to grab her, but she was too fast. He wasn't even able to catch hold of the gown that she had slipped out of. Between the sharp, shrill bleeps of his whistle he was yelling. "NO! OH NO! OVERBOARD!…BLEEP…BLEEP…BLEEP…SHE JUMPED OVERBOARD!…BLEEP…BLEEP…HELP!" The ship came to as sudden a stop as it could. So many people were gathering in that little area of the deck where she had jumped off that they were now not just leaning over the railing trying to see but were beginning to be pushed into the railing. More and more people began to pack into the area, and the little railing began to sway. At the beginning their yelling and screaming was to let everyone know that someone had jumped overboard. Before long though, people began to get uncomfortable…started fighting for elbow room. The crowd began growing larger and larger, and soon the shorter people were finding it hard to breathe. Some were even being injured because of the pushing and shoving. Ship personnel streamed out of the elevator to try to disperse the crowd, but it was of no use. No one was listening.

All this time, a small lifeboat was being lowered into the water with three divers in it to rescue Breeze.

They heard what was happening on deck, realized what was about to happen, and started yelling. "GO BACK! GO BACK! GO BACK TO YOUR CABINS! THERE'S NOTHING YOU CAN DO HERE! NOTHING YOU CAN SEE! PLEASE! GO BACK TO YOUR CABINS!" As soon as the little boat hit the water, a long portion of the ship's railing broke and all the people that were pressed against or near that railing went tumbling into the sea...screaming.

The little boat that was sent into the water to rescue Breeze was way too small to rescue that many people. Lots of life preservers where thrown into the ocean from the deck, and three other lifeboats were let down at the other end of the ship so they wouldn't land on the screaming people. Those screaming people had landed pretty much on top of one another and were awkwardly thrashing around in the water....Some couldn't swim and were in trouble.

Breeze was quick to see the problem she'd caused, felt bad, and noticed there were a lot of humans who didn't seem to know how to swim. She was shocked that this whole problem was caused by her one simple action...jumping off the ship. She swam back to help. One after the other, she grabbed the people she saw who couldn't swim and either handed them a life preserver or brought them to the boats. At first, with all the confusion, no one recognized her as the person that had jumped ship and caused all the trouble.

As things began to get under control and the majority of people had been rescued and put on a boat...Larry, who had manned one of the rescue boats, stopped to take a really good look at the girl in the water who was aiding in so many rescues. His eyes got big and his mouth dropped wide open. "YOU! IT'S...YOU!" he yelled and pointed his finger. "WHY DID YOU DO THAT?...AND...AND..." Then he realized...Breeze had nothing on...At least she didn't have a bra or a swimming suit top on...He stared wide eyed at her for a moment then asked. "WHERE'S YOUR CLOTHES?... WHY DID YOU DO THAT? WHY DID YOU JUMP OVERBOARD? ARE YOU OK? GET INTO THE BOAT, MISS! I'LL MAKE SURE EVERYTHING IS OK TO GET YOU HOME."

Breeze flashed a big smile in his direction. This guy was really worried about her. Interesting! She had made sure none of the people she rescued were put in Larry's boat. As she helped the last of the soaked passengers, one of the guys reached out his arm to help her onto the boat; Breeze just smiled and said she'd go to the next boat. She stopped at the boat Larry was in, stayed about two feet from the boat, and said, "I hope I didn't cause too much trouble for doing what I did."

Larry turned around, went to the side of the boat she was at and reached out his hand to pull her on board.

"Oh! I'm not going back to that ship!" Breeze said with a big smile. "I'm going back to shore to wait for Alex."

Larry, not realizing she was a mermaid, thought she'd lost it mentally and was even more eager to get her on board the ship. He threw Breeze a life ring tied to a rope. "Come on, Miss! You know I can't leave with you out here. You need to get into this boat."

"Why?" Breeze asked. "There's no one I know on that boat. It's going in the wrong direction. The only reason I boarded it in the first place was to meet Alex, and he is not on your ship. I'll just swim to the shore and wait for him there."

Now Larry knew she had lost her mind. The shore was miles away and out of sight. "Miss!" he begged again, reaching out his arm. "You really need to come closer so we can help you onto this boat."

By now, the other two boats had been lifted back onto the ship. The people had gotten out of them and were standing there...watching the rescue boat that was still in the water below trying to pick up the last remaining person...Breeze. A yellow rope had been pulled across the opening where the railing used to be. No one was anxious to get close to that rope.

Larry was beginning to lose his temper with Breeze. "Miss!" He said firmly. "I'll have to order you to get on this boat. You really don't want me to come in there after you....Do you?"

"You'd do that? You'd come in here after me? You don't need to do that. I'll just leave and you can put your boat up and put those humans that are helping you back on deck."

"NO!" Larry insisted. His voice got louder and louder and was filled with anxiety. "AFRAID I CAN'T LET YOU DO THAT! YOU'LL HAVE TO COME WITH ME!... HERE! PLEASE!... DON'T MAKE ME YELL. MISS! TAKE MY ARM!" He extended it out as far as he could reach.

Breeze was getting a little tired of him telling her what to do...and now he was yelling. She hated yelling, so she reached out and took his hand....But...instead of Larry pulling her on board, she gave a mighty yank, and

Larry went into the ocean. Breeze backed up a ways, gave a great big smile, and started laughing. "Teach you to order ME! Now who needs to be pulled back into the boat? Need some help, Larry?"

Larry was still sputtering water when he asked, "Why did you do that, Miss? Don't you know I'm trying to help you?"

Breeze swam up to where she was looking him in the eye. "If you're trying to help me...you'd leave me alone! You wouldn't have yelled at me! Here!" She put her arms around Larry's neck...flashed another big smile, and said, "This is for all your trouble and for caring about me." She put her hands on his shoulders and pulled him close, then put her arms around him, and gave him a big kiss. "THERE! That ought to make up for any trouble I've caused." She smiled again at the astonished Larry...backed away from him a few feet, tossed him the life ring, chuckled, and said, "Larry, you don't know it yet... but...you've just been kissed..." She flipped her whole body into the air, then back into the water again. "...by a mermaid...and...I WILL leave you now and swim to the shore."

It took a few minutes for Larry to gain his composure. He would never forget that kiss....And he couldn't believe what he saw. "Couldn't be...Just couldn't be!" he said to himself...But it did happen. Everyone in the boat saw it happen, and their mouths all hung wide open in disbelief. After being pulled back into the boat, Larry spent several minutes looking down into the water...but there was no one there.

Chapter 18

Breeze smiled to herself thinking about all the commotion she caused simply by diving into the ocean. She really chuckled about the kiss she gave to Larry. Oh! There would only be that one kiss to Larry... for being so nice to her.

Turning her attention to Alex, she started swimming toward shore...hoping to meet up with her dolphin friends along the way. The ship had traveled in a different direction and a bit farther than she thought. The sun was just beginning to go down when she popped her head out of the sea. Not only did a beautiful sunset greet her eyes, but beautiful music came into her ears. On the shore there were lots and lots of differently colored lights moving in different directions, and she was anxious to get to the shore. She just had to check this out...but again, there were no clothes. She knew she could never get by wearig...no clothes. The humans just wouldn't accept her.

There was the pier, and it was all lit up too. Breeze knew there were lots of small booths on it and some of them had clothes hanging in front of them. The beach was crowded and lots of people were still swimming. Beach towels were scattered all over with no one sitting on them. Then Breeze had an idea. With the sun practically gone, it would be hard to see WHAT she was wearing. She swam back out into the deeper part of the ocean and broke off a few long strands of seaweed…the kind that had big leaves. Nearing shore, she conjured up her land-legs and draped the seaweed around her shoulders and waist.

With a slight chuckle, she ran across the beach picking up several towels along the way. No one seemed to notice. This was GREAT! She discarded the seaweed and wrapped one of the towels around herself. As she strolled up the beach toward the peer, Breeze saw an unguarded paper bag. Looking around, she noticed no one was there and no one seemed to be looking her way, so she picked up the bag and stuffed it under the towels that were hanging over her arm. She was just sure that bag would be full of clothes.

Well! It wasn't! It was full of jewelry, candy, lotion, and a bunch of other stuff she couldn't wear…So she dropped the bag back on the sand where she found it. By this time, the stars were beginning to come out and the moon was up. Breeze loved to just sit and watch them. There didn't seem to be any clothes lying around so she thought she'd just sit down on the bench facing the ocean with the towel wrapped around her, enjoy what was there, and watch the sky for a while

"Is this seat taken, pretty lady?" It was Alex. He sat down beside her and put his arm around her. "What are you doing out her all alone?"

Breeze couldn't believe her eyes. "Well!" She smiled. "I guess I'm...waiting for you."

"Have you been on any of the rides yet?"

"No! I...ah...I sort of lost my clothes," Breeze blurted out. "I...ah..."

Alex cut into her sentence...looked her in the eye, and smiled. "You don't have to pretend with me, Breeze. I know you're a mermaid. That doesn't keep me from caring about you."

Breeze couldn't believe her ears. She flashed a big smile and said, "Really? You do? You care about me?"

"Yes I do, Breeze! I care about you a lot. I was really glad to see you last time but wasn't very happy that you found me just when we getting ready to start our voyage. I knew the ship was ready to leave and we wouldn't have any time together." Alex pulled her close and kissed her softly on her cheek. "Want to go on some of those rides with me?"

"Alex...I..."

"I know! You don't have a thing to wear!" He stood up and took Breeze's hand. "Don't let go of that towel or we'll both be in trouble. Let's just go get you something to wear. Can you stay with me this whole evening?"

"Oh! Yes! YES, I CAN!" Breeze said as she laid the other towels on the bench and flashed a big smile.

"I have to be on the ship first thing in the morning... about 5:30 actually...Have to be there before any of the customers come on board."

Alex led Breeze to the pier...stopped in font of a booth full of shorts, tops, and swim wear, and said,

Breeze...the Mermaid

"Your choice, pretty lady. Pick out something you like."

Breeze stood there for a long time looking at all the things.

"Would you rather I pick something out for you?"

"That would be great! Yes! You do it!" Breeze put both hands around his neck, pressed her body against his...almost losing the towel...and gave him a long, sexy kiss.

Alex was quick to reach behind her with one hand and grab the towel. That kiss lasted until the saleslady yelled at them, "HEY! YOU TWO! CAN I HELP YOU WITH SOMETHING? THE BEACH IS DOWN THERE!" She pointed down towards the water.

"Oh! Sure!" Alex replied, making sure the towel was still draped around Breeze. He picked out a pair of cut-offs and a shorty type top then turned to Breeze and asked, "You think you'll like these?"

"Oh! Oh, yes! I love them. Are you going to pay real money for these?"

"Yes! Of course I am!" he said, laying down his card with a chuckle. "Let's go someplace where you can try them on."

They chose a restroom...one of those green, portable, temporary restrooms. Breeze wasn't in there more than a minute. She flung the door open hard looking like someone that just stepped out of a magazine, then slammed it shut. A big smile was on her face. The towel was in one hand, and she was pinching her nose shut with the other hand. Breeze made a quick comment. "NOTHING smells like THIS where I come from!

NOW I KNOW why you didn't come in there with me!"

"I knew those would look good on you. You look GREAT, Breeze…..Just GREAT!" Alex reached out his hand. "Ready to get started?"

Breeze thought he meant ready to get started kissing. She threw the towel in the air, yelling, "OH YES!"…and practically flew into Alex's arms…kissing him all over his face, neck, and mouth. "I'M REALLY READY!" The towel landed behind her, hanging on the handle of the restroom door.

Alex, of course, returned all the kisses…was in ecstasy with what was happening and…since he was being kissed by a mermaid…lost all thoughts of doing anything else. The two of them stood there hugging and kissing for a long time.

"HEY! YOU THERE! YOU TWO! WHERE'D YOU GET THAT TOWEL FROM?"

The loud, gruff voice was coming from a tall…very muscular looking man wearing tight, skimpy, light blue swimming trunks. He was deeply tanned and dripping wet from just coming out of the ocean. There he stood, glaring at them with his hands on his hips…and he didn't look very happy.

Alex backed up a bit from Breeze, turned and stood in front of him. "What towel?"

"THAT'S A SMART ALECK ANSWER!" he bellowed. Shaking his finger, he pointed to the towel Breeze had just thrown onto the outhouse door handle. "THAT TOWEL! THAT'S WHAT TOWEL! HOW'D IT GET THERE? DID ONE OF YOU LIFT IT OFF THE BEACH?"

Breeze and Alex just stood there together, hand in hand, looking at him.

The man stepped up and snatched the towel off the door latch. "LOOK!" he said as he shook the towel at them. "THIS ISN'T JUST ANY ORDINARY TOWEL." He waved it again, right in their faces. "HAS MY NAME ON IT! SEE! SAME NAME THAT'S ON THIS SWIMMING SUIT I'M WEARING" He pointed to the name on his skimpy swimsuit bottom. "SPECIAL GIFT! NOW! HOW'D YOU GET MY TOWEL?"

Breeze should have kept her mouth shut...but she didn't. "Mister...if I were you and had something special...I would have kept it in a special place and taken special care of it...not just left it crumpled on the beach next to an empty beer bottle. Did you know that bottles should not be left on the beach? Someone may step on the broken glass. When bottles are left on the beach and the tide comes in...it could break as the waves hit it."

Alex was quick to let go of Breeze's hand and step in front of her again.

The guy was angrier than ever!...He balled up his fist, yelling some obscene words as he pulled his arm back ready to deliver a punch.

As fate would have it, that punch never landed. Mr. Muscles, for want of a better name, was still standing right in front of the outhouse door that he'd just picked his towel off of. The door was suddenly flung wide open with force by a large, heavyset woman that wanted no part of the smell inside. She did not look where she was going...just wanted out. She burst out of the door without looking and charged down the steps...and ran right into

Mr. Muscles. The both of them went tumbling down onto the sand yelling and screaming at each other.

"Think it's time to leave!" Alex said as he put his arm around Breeze. "Leave his silly towel here!" They walked across the sand then across to the parking lot to where the fair was. Standing in line for tickets, Alex kissed Breeze tenderly on the cheek and said, "I admire your spunk for standing up to that guy…but…I'm the one he was going to hit, and he was a lot bigger than me."

"Will this help?" Breeze pressed her body against Alex and gave him another long, sexy kiss. They were still kissing when it came time to purchase tickets. They definitely weren't paying any attention to the ticket agent. She had to repeat herself several times before they heard…"NEXT!"

The guy behind them heard, though. He waited for a couple minutes then nudged Alex in the back. "Hey! Listen, fella…I know you've got a great girl and all that…but…ARE YOU GOING TO GET TICKETS… OR ARE YOU TWO JUST GOING TO STAND THERE SMOOCHING?"

Alex pulled away, blushing. "Um….Sorry, I didn't realize we—"

"That's OK!" he said with a chuckle. "Just get your tickets so we can get ours. If I were in YOUR shoes…I wouldn't even bother with the tickets. I'd just go sit on that park bench over there."

Alex looked at him again. "Sorry!" He bought his tickets, turned to Breeze and asked, "What ride do you do you want to go on first?"

"Oh! I...I've never seen any of these." She put her arm around Alex. "I'll just do what you want to do."

Alex chose the Ferris wheel first and put his arm around Breeze as soon as they sat down.

Breeze looked at him with a big smile. The big, brightly lit wheel started turning. At first, everything was OK, but as they got higher and higher in the air and the seat started rocking back and forth, Breeze thought they might tip over. She started screaming.

Alex thought she was just happy for what they were doing.He pulled her head towards his and gave her a big kiss.

Breeze didn't kiss back. She grabbed the side of the seat with one hand and Alex's leg with the other, stiffened herself up, and let out a shrill, high-pitched scream unlike anything that had ever been heard in the human world. It drowned out the music and was so loud and hurt Alex ears.

"Breeze! Honey! It's OK! I ride these all the time! Relax and look out at the pretty lights and the ocean. We're all alone up here. Look at the beautiful moon." His arm was still around her, and he pulled her as close as he could. "Everything's OK, Breeze! Promise!"

This calmed her down a bit, but her heart was still racing. Breeze just knew those swinging seats would tip over...So she did the only thing she knew to do, turned sideways, put her arms around Alex and gave him a big kiss that lasted until they were stopped at ground level. She didn't get out of her seat when the man came by to let them out...just smiled and said, "Can we do that again?"

After that second ride, which they also spent kissing each other, Alex stopped at a refreshment stand. BIG MISTAKE! Breeze ate a hot dog, some French fries, and a candy apple. She felt brave now that the Ferris wheel was conquered and wanted to ride on the octopus...said the name reminded her of the sea.

She showed no fear this time and seemed to be really enjoying herself. Because of the fast, jerking, whirling motion, her crab earrings flew off and latched themselves onto passersby who were walking underneath.

One landed on an old man's bushy mustache and started pinching his lips. The other landed inside a lady's low-cut blouse and managed to get inside her bra. It started pinching with both claws. Both the man and the lady started screaming, clutching at the spots where the crab grabbed on and began stomping their feet up and down. The man managed to pull the crab off his mustache. It was happy to just pinch into his fingers with both claws. The other crab...the one that went down inside the lady's blouse was not so easy. The lady was in tears, screaming at the top of her lungs and stomping her feet. Finally, she lost control and didn't care who was watching...reached down inside her bra to see what was hurting so bad. The crab found her finger and bit into it with one pincher. The other remained attached where it was.

About that time, Breeze started feeling sick from what she had eaten. As their cart whirled by the lady who was still screaming, Breeze heaved out the food she'd eaten earlier. Most of this landed on the lady. Some of it also landed on the man who had just pulled the crab out of his mustache and was now trying to shake it off his finger. Some landed on other people as they were passing by.

The lady was not only screaming and stomping up and down because of the little crab that was still in her blouse, but was now half yelling and half crying as she shook her fist at the octopus. She finally ran off towards those smelly restrooms with one hand still inside her blouse.

"I'M SORRY!" Breeze yelled after her. She turned to Alex, smiled, and said, "HEY! I'M SORRY! I didn't know my crab friends would let go. I nearly always wear them…for earrings."

All this time, Alex was laughing. He laughed so hard he couldn't answer. When the ride stopped he was still laughing but managed to put his arm around Breeze to give her a close hug. "HONEY!" He laughed. "I've never had so much fun at a fair! Want another hot dog?"

"Yes! Yes, I do…But not till after I kiss you again." With that, she tippy toed up to meet his lips and gave him a big kiss. "Mmm…Alex…I do love the way you kiss."

Alex put one hand behind her back and the other behind her head. "I always want us to be like this, Breeze. I never want to lose you. When you dove off that ship the last time…my heart went with you. I don't know if it's possible.…" He kissed her with all the passion that had been building up inside him since their first kiss. "Breeze!…Is there any way…?"

"THERE YOU BOTH ARE! SONNY BOY, I'M GOING TO TEACH YOU NOT TO LAUGH AT ME!" It was Mr. Muscles himself, still wearing his itsy bitsy light blue swimming trunks with his big fist was doubled up ready to continue what he was going to do when he was so rudely interrupted earlier…by that lady coming out of the restroom door.

Breeze pulled Alex's head down and whispered something in his ear….Then they both started laughing and took off running toward the beach as fast as they could go…with Mr. Muscles close behind. They ran across the street, across the narrow beach, and up onto the pier…stopping in front of a fresh seafood stand. Breeze made a very low-pitched sound, reached into the glass tank with both hands, and filled them full of giant crabs. "PRESENT…JUST FOR YOU!" she yelled as she whirled around and flung the crabs at 'Mr. Muscles.'

Mr. Muscle's fist was no match for those large, pinching crabs. He blindly stumbled towards the pier's railing. One crab had landed on his face, one on his chest, one on his tummy, and the other…well the other landed someplace it shouldn't have. Caught off guard by the pain of the pinching crabs…Mr. Muscles was not ready for Alex, who rushed up and pushed him over the railing into the ocean. Because he was such a rude person, Breeze threw his suitcase in after him.

Breeze looked at Alex, smiled, and asked, "Want to go swimming?"

"I don't think so." Alex smiled. "I don't have a suit…and I only have a few hours left before I have to be at work. Besides, I'm not really interested in keeping company with 'Mr. Muscles."

"I just want to make sure that guy never bothers anyone again. He was not nice! He's just like so many other humans I've seen. I want to scare him real good. Just a minute, Alex. This won't take long. Come on in with me."

"Breeze, all these places are closed. I don't have a suit and—"

"Don't worry about a suit. The ocean's my home. Come on! Just take your shirt and pants off and it'll be just fine." She pointed her finger towards Mr. Muscles floundering in the water below and laughed.

Alex looked down and momentarily watched the struggle going on down below. "He may drown down there with those crabs on him the way they are," Alex said with concern in his voice.

"That's why we need to go swimming." Good thing it was late and no one was there. Breeze walked close to the railing, stepped out of her shorts, and slipped the blouse over her head....Then she pulled Alex's t-shirt up over his head...grabbed his hand, and said, "Let's go!" Over the railing they went. Breeze immediately conjured her tail back.

It was a ways down to the water. When Alex came up for air he mumbled. "These pants are weighing me down."

"Told you to take them off...You have anything in those pockets you want to keep?"

"Yes! Of course! My wallet! My keys! Some change. You pulled me in pretty fast, Breeze. I don't want to lose these things...but it's not easy to swim with these pants on."

"Take them off! Leave the stuff in the pockets. I'll take them and put them someplace safe. Want me to help?

"NO! NO! I think I can manage this all by myself."

Breeze smiled and put her arms around Alex… holding him high in the water. "Here!" she said as she gave him a big kiss. "Maybe this will help. You do realize…as long as you are with me in the water…you'll never drown."

"Oh really? I didn't know that."

Breeze took his pants, made sure they were wrapped tightly together so nothing would fall out of the pockets, and swam over to the pier, placing them in a notch where two boards met.

All this time, Mr. Muscles was struggling and yelling to get those things off him.

"Watch this!" Breeze smiled. She swam right over next to Mr. Muscles and said, "OK! You can let go now." Immediately, the crabs let go and were gone.

Mr. Muscle's eyes were open as wide open as his mouth.

"You don't look so big and mean in the water!" Breeze chuckled. "Are you as good at holding your breath as you are at doubling up your fist?" With that remark, she did a flip out of the water, grabbed his feet and pulled him down deep…towing him underwater to the edge of the shore. She swung him around as she let go, popping her head out of the water just long enough to add, "Next time…maybe you need to make sure just who you're messing with….Much easier to just be nice!" She smacked her tail hard in the water as she left…sending a huge spray of salty water into his face.

Alex had stayed his distance…watching. "WOW! Breeze, I had no idea you were going to do all that. I'll have to make sure I always treat you right."

Breeze cupped Alex's face in her hands, smiled, and kissed him tenderly. "You're safe in the water when you're with me," she whispered. "You'll see." She kissed him tenderly and they began to drift downward in the water.

At first, Alex hesitated…but…Breeze's kiss was like no other he'd ever had. He was drawn to her in a way he didn't understand with a passion he'd never known before. Mesmerized by her kisses and caresses, Alex let himself fall under the spell of love. With her lips pressed sensually against his and her body gently pressed against his chest, caressing him with a slight motion caused by the slow swaying of her tail…they sank into the sea. The two of them slowly submerged under the water and into the love they had found in each other.

Alex had gone to sleep in Breeze's arms. She knew he had to be at the ship early so, as they came back to the surface of the water, she woke him with a kiss. "Time to wake up, my sweet love. I think YOU have to be at work." She gave him a close hug and then reached over and carefully took his pants off the wooden crosspiece. As she started swimming toward the shore she said, "These aren't going to feel very good, being cold and wet. I'll take them to shore for you…then we can go on the pier and I'll put those pretty things back on that you bought me."

"Can't believe we spent the night the way we did." Feeling solid ground under his feel again, Alex put his arms around Breeze and kissed her tenderly. "I'll never forget this night. I'll dream about it forever. I want you forever, Breeze. I don't want to go on that cruise…and I don't want us—"

"I'll be here when you come back," Breeze interrupted with a big smile. "Put those silly wet pants on and let's walk onto the pier." She conjured up her legs, gave him a swift kiss on the cheek, and ran up the pier to where she'd left her clothes.

By the time Alex had dragged his drippy self to where Breeze was, she was dressed and holding his t-shirt out at arm's length. "This is dry!" She smiled. "You're not ALL wet!" She put her arms around him and gave him a big kiss. "Here, put this on….Think I'll hug your t-shirt. It's DRY. Teach YOU to come swimming with me with long pants on."

Alex put the t-shirt on and reached out for another hug. "You going to ride with me to the ship?"

"Of course!"

Alex put his arm around Breeze's waist and walked her to his truck. He opened the passenger side door, opened the suitcase that was setting on the seat, and pulled out a pair of kaki shorts. With a big smile on his face, he held the shorts, waving them high in the air, and said. "You thought I was going to have to go to work in those wet pants…Didn't you?" Before she could answer, Alex had looked around to make sure no one was there. The pants came off and the shorts went on. "There! I always pack a suitcase when I have to go to work. I'm usually gone a week or more." Motioning for her to get in, he added, "We still have time to get something to eat…if you want."

They stopped at a pancake house almost across the street from where the cruise ship was docked. Just inside the door...there sat Mr. Muscles. He took one look at the two of them and got up out of his chair...glared at Breeze with disbelief, held up his arms, and said, "YOU WIN! Then he pointed his finger directly at Breeze. "YOU! YOU'RE...YOU'RE A...A—"

Breeze walked right up to him, stood about two feet from him, and cut into his sentence. Very softly she said, "Yes! You'd better believe I am what I am...and don't you forget it. I have LOTS of friends also...that are the same as what I am. So...sit down and finish your breakfast! Oh, sorry about that eye...Must have caught it with the tip...OF MY TAIL!"

They took a seat in the booth just across from his table. Alex was a bit upset that Mr. Muscles was in there eating. He had been taken by surprise by Breeze and her daring remarks to the man just now, and it caused him to expect another encounter...but there was none. Instead, Mr. Muscles asked them to join him at his table.

"I've never met anyone who stood up to me like you two did," he said as he took a bite of his omelet. "Name's Sam...Sam Steelman....Go by the name Samson when I'm wrestling. You've probably heard of me." With a smile on his face, he reached out his big hand for each of them to shake. Then he reached into his pocket, pulled out a couple cards, and said, "Free tickets if you ever want to come and watch me wrestle. Sorry about the towel incident. I'm used to people just taking things behind my back because they know who I am." Turning to Breeze, he added, "Did I see what I thought I saw in that ocean last night...or was it just my imagination?"

Trying to protect Breeze, Alex stood up and said, "We were trying to have a quiet moment alone before I have to get on that ship...didn't expect you there."

"I like to swim in the ocean," Sam explained... "Makes me stronger." Again, he turned to Breeze. "Little lady, what did you use on me last night?" Putting his hand over his eye, he added, "I've never had a shiner like this before."

They finished their breakfast without much else said. When the waitress brought their bill, Sam gave her his card and said he'd take care of everything. "Are you two going on the cruise too?"

Alex answered, "Breeze isn't...but I am. I work there."

"Oh!" Sam said. "Be nice if you could both be there together."

Alex took Breeze by the hand. "Thanks for breakfast. If you need anything on your cruise, my name's Alex. I'm the only Alex on the ship, so just ask for me."

As they entered the ship's walk-up, Alex said, "Can't believe that! That guy was REALLY obnoxious... Turned out to be OK after all." He turned to Breeze and gave her a kiss on the cheek. "Maybe what you did knocked some sense into him. He seemed to be proud of the shiner you gave him." He chuckled as he added, "If he only knew he's just been smacked by a piece of tail." Alex started chuckling to himself as they stepped on board ship. "Loved watching that, Breeze. You don't know how much I loved watching that. I'm going to miss you. You know...last night was...was..." He set the suitcase down, put his arms around Breeze, and said, "Breeze. I don't know what to do here. I..." He took a deep breath, put his arms around her and gave her a long, passionate kiss. "I just want us always to be like this."...another passionate hug and kiss. "Last night... I've never spent a night like that...Never dreamed..."

"There's a lot more where that came from." Breeze said as she kissed his neck. "I really liked last night too." She threw her arms around Alex and put her head on his chest where she could hear his heart beat.

The whistle blew, signaling it was time to pull the ramp away. With their arms around each other, Alex kissed the top of her head and whispered, "I'm really going to miss you, Breeze...Wish I didn't have to go. You going to be here when I get back?"

"Mmmm Hmmm."

Their lips met for one last passionate kiss. "Honey, I think you'd better go. Don't want what happened last time to happen again."

"Mmmm hmmm...I know! I know!" Breeze looked into Alex's eyes. "Just one more kiss."

That one kiss was way too long. The walkway was gone, and there they were...locked in the embrace of each other's arms.

The ship's loud whistle sounded again, signaling its departure. Alex took a deep breath and said, "Wish you could stay....Wish we could be like this forever.... OH! Breeze! Last night..." He caressed her face with his hands, placed a gentle kiss on her forehead, and said, "I'd keep you with me if I could. I'd keep you forever...if I could."

Breeze put her arms around Alex's neck, whispered in his ear and said, "You can…if you want to." With a nibble on the ear she added, "I'd like to be with you too, like to kiss you forever. You're not going to get in trouble because I'm on here…are you?"

"Probably! It's OK if we say our goodbyes on board but not OK if we have someone stay on here. I don't want you jumping overboard again though. It's a long way down to that water and I don't want you hurt."

Breeze put her arms around Alex's neck again and gave him a goodbye kiss. "No one's watching. Let's go over by the railing." They walked to the railing, and she slipped off her shorts, then the top and handed them to Alex as she gave him one last kiss. She quickly stepped on the railing and dove off…leaving him holding the shorts and top as he watched her plunge into the sea. "LOVE YOU, ALEX!" she yelled as her head popped up out of the water.

"I LOVE YOU TOO!" Alex yelled back.

"Can't believe what I just saw!" Sam said as he walked up and stood next to Alex. He looked over the railing and saw Breeze in the water waving. His mouth hung wide open. "She IS a mermaid, isn't she? Last night wasn't a dream. Was it? I wasn't very nice yesterday…in front of that smelly outhouse. I had just—"

"Don't worry about it!" Alex interrupted as he continued to gaze into the sea.

Breeze had seen Sam walk up so she slipped down under the water.

"You didn't answer me, Alex. That girl you were just with…Don't believe she ever said her name. She IS a mermaid! ISN'T SHE?"

Still Alex didn't answer. He just took a deep breath, turned his back to the sea and asked, "Sam…can I help you with something?"

"I'm lost! It's the reason I hung around the deck. I didn't want to break into any of those kisses but…I don't know where my room is. SHE IS A MERMAID! ISN'T SHE? I SAW WHAT I SAW LAST NIGHT! DIDN'T I? DID THIS BLACK EYE COME FROM HER TAIL?"

"Sam, let's just find your room. What number are you in?"

Chapter 19

Breeze watched as the ship sailed out of sight…with the person on it that she wanted most to be with. Last night had been so wonderful. Now? Now she felt all alone…more alone then she'd ever felt before. She should be on that ship right now. All of a sudden she realized…humans aren't that smart after all. In her kingdom…excuse me…in Neptune's kingdom… there is none of that. When something or someone is wonderful…you just keep it or stay with it. Happiness was supposed to be a now thing, an all the time thing… not something that might happen down the road if you have time. Alex had no time. There he was…on that ship. He didn't want to be there but there he was. Nope! She didn't understand humans at all.

She watched until the ship got out of sight, thinking about how humans were different. Those silly clothes humans make themselves put on. She never had to think about such a thing…but on the land, with humans, they have to be worn and they have to be bought. She saw Alex PAY every time he did something…ate something…

even for the clothes he got for her...he paid what they called money...pieces of paper and little pieces of metal. Nothing was PAID for in the ocean. All was free for the using and taking. Silly humans!

Looking out to sea wasn't going to bring Alex back any sooner. Breeze didn't feel like going back home... didn't feel like visiting Olympia, and didn't feel like playing with the dolphins. She thought about money. That's what she'd do next....She'd just go back on land and find out all about money...how humans got it and why they had to have it in order to eat or do anything.

Again! She had no clothes, so it was back to sneaking on someone's little boat to get some. She chose to sneak onto a small yacht that was docked in the harbor. Boats like that always had clothes on them. She watched it for a long time to make sure no one was on it....Then she swam up to the back, pulled down the ladder, conjured up her legs and went on board. Breeze knew to be very careful just in case there was someone there. Before opening any doors, she listened to make sure no one was inside. The first door she opened was filled with folded up furniture for the deck. The second door she opened was a bathroom

The third door....The third door opened into a large area with funny looking furniture. There were different shaped benches with long sticks hanging over them with round pieces of metal on the ends of them...lots of small sticks with different size round pieces of metal on them sitting around on the floor...mirrors all around the walls...and pictures on the walls that didn't have mirrors. The people in those pictures didn't have many clothes on. She even saw some that didn't have any clothes on at all. Definitely, there was nothing to wear in this room. She'd try another door. Walking through the room, she opened another door. Oops! This room had two people in it sleeping, and THAT was the room the clothes would be in. She saw lots of clothes hanging in a small room near where she was.

Breeze didn't want to wake those sleeping humans but she DID want to get some clothes. Glancing around the room, she noticed the humans had dropped their clothes on the floor, scattering them pretty close to where she was standing. Well, she thought, it didn't matter what kind of clothes they were. Whatever they were would be just fine. Trying her best not to make a sound, Breeze gathered up all the clothes and everything else that was lying on the floor, and left.. There was no time to see what she had. She had to leave before getting caught.

She walked through the oddly furnished room and out onto the deck, wadded the clothes into a tight ball and walked towards the ladder where she'd come on board. Then she heard voices, loud, angry, yelling voices. At first it was a man's voice yelling, "WHAT HAPPENED TO MY CLOTHES? WHAT HAVE YOU DONE WITH MY CLOTHES? MY WALLET! MY WALLET'S GONE! WHERE'S MY WALLET? MY MONEY WAS IN THERE!"

Then she heard the woman yelling. "MISTER...I DIDN'T TAKE YOUR CLOTHES...AND I SURELY DIDN'T TAKE YOUR WALLET! WHAT DO YOU THINK I AM? HEY! WHERE'S MY PURSE? TALK ABOUT A THIEF!"

That was enough for Breeze. SHE had the clothes she'd picked up off the floor along with a big fancy bag that caught her eye…and wasn't about to give them back. Not even waiting to get to the ladder, she tucked what clothes that would fit into the bag, wadded the rest of them up and put them under her arm along with the bag…then stepped onto the back deck and dove off.

Immediately, her tail was back and she swam to the backside of a different boat and laid everything out on the little deck. The clothes were wet but she didn't care. She'd just say she got caught by a wave or something.

There were shorts and matching top that must have belonged to the lady. They were kind of big, but that was OK. The man's shirt was huge and so were his pants so she just took everything out of the pockets and let the rest fall down into the ocean. Inside the pants was a big wad of paper money, lots of little round metal pieces, a black thing filled with more money and several little cards. Inside the fancy bag was a little bag. She unzipped the little bag and found that it had that same kind of paper money in it. There were little tubes that came apart with red stuff in them, a brush, and a bunch of other things Breeze had never seen before and didn't know what they were. Those things were dropped down into the sea along with the clothes she couldn't use. She stuck the paper money, pieces of metal, and the black thing in the bag, zipped it back up, put the long strap that was attached to the bag over her head, and headed for shore.

Just before stepping out of the water, she conjured up her legs and slipped on the shorts and top. Breeze noticed a bunch of humans hitting a round object back and forth, some occasionally falling in the sand as they tried to catch it. She also noticed another group of humans throwing the same type of object through a round piece of metal. Now THAT looked like fun! She dropped the purse in the sand and started walking toward that group…had second thoughts about the bag lying there unattended and went back to cover it with sand so no one could tell it was there. After all…it had that paper money stuff in it.

Breeze sat on the sand for a few minutes watching. Only male humans seemed to be doing this, and they seemed to be having lots of fun. She decided she'd just join in that fun but she didn't want to just go up there with nothing to throw through the metal ring. Still dripping wet from her swim to shore, she decided to go back into the ocean and get some things to throw through that ring.

A few minutes later, with her hands full, she walked right through the humans, interrupted their game and stood in front of the metal ring. Everyone started yelling at her to get out of the way. Breeze turned around gave them all a big smile and said, "I can do this too!" As she threw a big starfish through the hoop, she added, "See! I can throw these through there just as good as any of you can." A big crab was next, followed by an octopus.

One man walked right up to her and yelled, "GET OUT OF THE WAY! WHAT DO YOU THINK YOU'RE DOING? WE'RE IN THE MIDDLE OF A GAME HERE!"

Breeze didn't answer. She just threw another starfish through the hoop, totally ignoring the man and his angry statement.

Being ignored made the man very upset. He reached out and took hold of her arm. BIG MISTAKE!

Breeze had a huge crab under that arm that the man didn't see, and it clamped onto his hand with a vengeance. The man instantly pulled back and began yelling and cursing. "WHO ARE YOU?" As he reached over to pull the crab off his hand, the crab immediately snatched his other hand. Now both hands were under the grasp of the crab. His hands were bleeding, and there was nothing he could do. His friends ran up to help. One had a knife and was about to cut the claw off the crab when Breeze intervened.

She put her hand right on the wrist of the man with the knife. "Why don't you just ask it to let go?" she asked with a smile.

The man couldn't believe what he'd just heard. He looked at Breeze and frowned. "WHAT?" he yelled. "LET GO OF MY WRIST! WILL YOU? CAN'T YOU SEE WHAT I'M DOING?"

"Yes!" Breeze answered calmly, "but it's much easier just to ask." She put her hand on the crab and calmly said, "You can let go now." The crab immediately let go of both hands. She looked each human right in the eye…threw the crab right through the ring, followed by three starfish, one after the other, then she tossed a couple of octopuses and three big clams…each going right through the ring. To the humans' astonishment she snatched the ball from the hands of one of them that were standing there with his mouth gaping wide open and said. "I can throw this just as easy. Want to see?" The ball went through the hoop also. "I can put everything I throw right into that little ring…." She smiled. "...but I really don't think I want to do this with you. You are all just rude!" The whole group of men watched with their mouths open as she picked up all the sea creatures one by one, cradled them in her arms, uncovered the fancy bag and walked into the ocean with them.

She conjured her tail back to swim down the beach a ways. First, her shorts, top and that fancy bag were put under a big rock for safekeeping. Then she started to leave the area. Breeze didn't give another thought to the men in the basketball court who by now had called the Coast Guard because they never saw her came up out of the water. Maybe she would look up her dolphin friends. At least THEY were sociable. Slowly she began to move towards the open sea paying no attention to what was happening behind her...or above her.

Several divers plunged into the sea looking for her, almost landing on top of her. They landed in front of her and in back of her. The one that landed right in front was face to face with Breeze. He opened his eyes wide with surprise when he realized what he was looking at: a mermaid, and an unusually beautiful one at that. His mouth dropped wide open. If his mouthpiece wasn't attached to his goggles he would have lost it.

Instantly, Breeze knew why they were there. They were there for her. They thought she was a human who just got swept away with the sea. By now, all the divers were coming her way. They'd all seen what she was. The diver who was right in front of her was quick to regain his composure and started to reach out for her. This would never do. Breeze knew she was out-numbered. She let out the loudest call for help she could in hopes her dolphin friends would hear. The diver in front of her heard the loud, shrill, high-pitched screech she made, and it caused him to immediately put his hands to his ears. This was all Breeze needed to make her getaway. She took a deep breath, gathered up all the energy she had, and propelled herself head first…right into him, knocking him through the water towards the other divers. With her tail on the sandy bottom, she stirred up the sand, making it hard for them to see. Then she began pulling masks off first one diver than another and scurried out to sea.

Chapter 20

She was met by some of her dolphin friends, but they were too late to be part of the excitement. They seemed unhappy and nervous. Some were bruised and had cuts on them. They all started talking at once… telling her what was happening to their friends and what almost happened to them.

Breeze had to slow down the conversation. That was not an easy thing to do because they were all nervously chattering at the same time and it was hard for her to understand what the trouble was. Come to find out, fishermen were herding great numbers of their dolphin friends and relatives, and some whales too, into little inlets, blocking them off so they couldn't get out. Some dolphins and whales were being taken away, but most of them were being killed.

She knew this was too big a problem for her to handle by herself, so she yelled out to them…"NEPTUNE! WE HAVE TO GET NEPTUNE TO HELP! MY FATHER WILL KNOW JUST WHAT TO DO." Motioning for them to follow, they headed for her home area.

Neptune, however, was nowhere in sight, and Oceana was just getting ready to leave. Breeze was out of breath from traveling so fast. "WHERE IS HE? WHERE'S NEPTUNE?"

"I...I...ah...I don't know...Ah...he was just here a minute ago."

"You're not a very good liar, Oceana. Now, WHERE IS HE? MOTHER, THIS IS TERRIBLY IMPORTANT! And just where are YOU going?"

"Um...Nowhere! I'm not going anywhere."

"Yes, you are! You were just leaving! Were you going to follow Neptune?"

"NO! I...I WASN'T! I..."

"I'VE HEARD ENOUGH!" Breeze put her face right in front of Oceana. "Listen to me, Mother! And listen real close! There are hundreds...maybe thousands of my friends...OUR FRIENDS, THAT ARE IN BAD TROUBLE...AND IF YOU DON'T TELL ME WHERE NEPTUNE IS..." Breeze put her hands on Oceana's shoulders. "I know where he's going! I KNOW WHERE YOU WERE GOING! You two were going to see Olympia! WEREN'T YOU?"

Oceana pulled back in shock. "OLYMPIA! OLYMPIA? You know we aren't supposed to go there. Whatever made you think..."

"Oceana! I was there! I saw you! I saw the both of you there. I was at the door...listening. That's the noise everyone heard. NOW, ARE YOU COMING WITH ME...OR NOT?"

Oceana took a deep breath. "Breeze...If you go there, you're going to be in big trouble."

"WELL, I'M GOING! ARE YOU COMING... OR NOT? DOESN'T MATTER TO ME! THERE'S TROUBLE OUT THERE, AND IF MY TRYING TO CORRECT IT GETS ME IN TROUBLE...THEN LET IT!" With that remark, Breeze turned on her tail and left...with Oceana following close behind.

They caught up with Neptune just before he entered the old pirate ship Olympia was in. Breeze placed herself right in front of the door and explained the situation.... Then she added..."If you don't help...I'll just try to do this all by myself!"

Olympia opened the door just then and said, "What a surprise! Can't believe you actually brought Breeze along."

Neptune was furious! The last thing he wanted was for Breeze to know they visited Olympia. For a few minutes he said nothing...just gave frowning looks...first to Breeze for discovering his visits...then to Oceana for allowing Breeze to come...then to Olympia for saying what she had just said.

First and foremost, Neptune was a warrior, and his duty was to protect the sea. This little family problem would just have to wait. "WHERE ARE THEY?" His loud voice boomed out orders. "OCEANA! GO BACK AND GET ALL THE YOUNGER MERMEN! DO IT!...NOW! HAVE THEM READY WHEN WE GET THERE! OLYMPIA, DO YOU STILL HAVE THOSE SWORDS AND WEAPONS AND DRY GUN POWDER I ASKED YOU TO SAVE FOR ME?"

Olympia went inside and immediately produced what he asked for.

"OLYMPIA, THIS TIME...YOU CAN COME WITH US. YOU'RE JUST SNEAKY ENOUGH TO BE OF SOME REAL HELP HERE."

The three of them gathered up the swords, weapons and gun powder and set off to meet with Oceana and the younger mermen. On the way, Neptune turned his attention to Breeze. With a loud, firm voice he said, "BREEZE! DAUGHTER! YOU WERE LISTENING AT OLYMPIA'S DOOR A WHILE BACK...WEREN'T YOU? I HAD A FEELING AT THE TIME THAT NOISE WAS CAUSED BY YOU. YOU KNOW YOU'RE IN TROUBLE! YOU KNOW THAT... DON'T YOU?"

Breeze didn't want to ruin any rescue efforts that might take place so she kept the comments she wanted to make to herself. She meekly answered. "I saw you leave and asked Oceana where you went. We wound up here...at the pirate ship."

The timing was just right to save the conversation from becoming unhappy. Oceana was there waiting with the mermen. Breeze knew all them....Carefully, she looked each one over. One had to be her brother... but which one?

"LET'S GO! LEAD THE WAY, BREEZE, SINCE YOU KNOW WHERE THIS IS HAPPENING ! YOU STAY HOME, OCEANA! NO PLACE FOR YOU DOING THIS!"

This upset Oceana, but she said nothing.

"HERE COME THE DOLPHINS!" Breeze yelled, pointing in their direction. "THEY'LL LEAD US THERE. Just look at them. They barely escaped."

When Neptune saw them...saw their wounds and bruises, he yelled, "MOVE IT! NOW! LET'S GET THIS PROBLEM TAKEN CARE OF."

Chapter 21

Neptune had them swimming in rows of five across. Breeze, Olympia, and himself were in front following the dolphins, who were leading the way. He said it would be easier that way...that they would need discipline and order to do battle. In spite of their wounds, the dolphin didn't waste any time leading them right to where the action was.

A short distance away, Neptune stopped abruptly and started shouting out his orders. "STOP! KEEP YOUR FORMATION! STAY HERE! I'M GOING TO SLIP AHEAD....GOING TO CHECK THINGS OUT! NO NOISE!...AND DON'T GIVE AWAY OUR POSITION!" He looked over his troops and glared at them for a couple minutes to make sure everyone was listening.

They were! Not one of them would dare go against Neptune's orders. They knew better. Breeze, of course, couldn't wait to start doing something...anything to stop this abuse to her friends....But she, too...waited.

Neptune wasn't gone long, and he didn't waste any time issuing his commands. "YOU WHO HAVE THE SWORDS...AND THE KNIVES....I WANT ALL OF YOU UP HERE WITH ME! NOW!" Once that move was accomplished, he added, "LISTEN CLOSE! I'M ONLY GOING TO SAY THIS ONE TIME! THERE ARE TWO LARGE FISHING BOATS OUT THERE, AND THEY HAVE A NET STRUNG BETWEEN THEM...DRIVING DOLPHINS, WHALES AND WHATEVER ELSE IS IN THERE PATH UP INTO A SMALL INLET. BE CAREFUL! TAKE YOUR SWORDS...AND KNIVES! GO WAY DOWN DEEP, UNDERNEATH, BY THE BOTTOM PART OF THE NET...WHERE YOU CAN'T BE SEEN. START FROM THE BOTTOM OF THE NET...AND CUT IT UPWARDS! DOTHIS AS FAST AS YOU CAN!" He glared at his audience, and then continued, "THIS HAS TO BE DONE VERY QUICKLY...MAKING NO MISTAKES! DON'T ALARM THE DOLPHINS AND WHALES THAT ARE BEING HERDED! WAIT UNTIL THE NETTING HAS ALL BEEN CUT AND IS IN LITTLE PIECES...AND...DON'T GO YET. WAIT TILL I GIVE THE SIGNAL."

He swam back and addressed the rest of the group. "OK!" He shouted. "NEXT GROUP! I'LL NEED EIGHT...NO...TEN OF THE STRONGEST OF YOU TO COME UP HERE TO ME." They obeyed instantly. Neptune continued to shout out his commands. "I WANT FIVE OF YOU TO BE AT EACH BOAT...CLOSE AS YOU CAN GET TO WHERE THE NETS ARE UNDER THE WATER. AS THESE NETS ARE CUT, I WANT YOU, ONE BY ONE, TO TAKE HOLD OF

THEM AND KEEP THEM TIGHT SO THE HUMANS IN THE BOATS WON'T BE ABLE TO TELL WHAT WE ARE DOING! ONE MISTAKE, AND WE MAY ALL WIND UP WITH THE DOLPHINS. DO YOU ALL HEAR WHAT I'M SAYING?"

They nodded their heads in unison.

"GOOD!" Neptune continued, "NOW...FOR THE REST OF YOU, YOUR JOB WILL BE TO SWIM UNDER ALL THIS...GET IN FRONT OF THE DOLPHINS AND WATCH FOR MY SIGNAL. WHEN THE NETS HAVE BEEN DESTROYED, YOU WILL USE EVERY EFFORT...BE AS SWIFT AS YOU CAN...POINT EVERY DOLPHIN...EVERY WHALE...AND EVERY CREATURE THAT'S BEEN DRAGGED TOWARD SHORE IN THAT NET...BACK OUT TO SEA. THIS MUST BE DONE SWIFTLY AND WITHOUT ANY HESITATION! ANY QUESTIONS?"

There were none.

Neptune saw that all was in order and ready. "ALL RIGHT! NOW!" He shouted. "GO GET INTO YOUR POSITIONS! THE FASTER WE MOVE, THE FASTER WE CAN GET OUT OF HERE AND THE LESS CHANCE OF ANY OF US GETTING CAUGHT! GO! NOW!" Neptune turned to his daughter. "Breeze!" He smiled. "I think this has been a long time coming. I WILL deal with you later, my child, make no mistake about that. And, you, my sweet Olympia. Brought you along because I know how much you love this sort of thing. You and Breeze can be a big help with the next part of this rescue. I have a feeling I'll have to deal with YOU later also."

Olympia just smiled and said nothing.

The siege didn't take long at all. Everyone did their part well. Neptune watched, and as soon as he saw the nets were cut and free, he motioned for the turn-about to take place. The nets were kept tight until every last living creature was well out of sight of the nets and into the sea. Then they let go of the nets and followed Breeze and Olympia toward the inlet where the remaining captives were.

The humans on the ships were so carried away with what they were doing; they failed to realize what was happening even after the nets were left to hang loose. When they finally did look to check them and found them cut off short by each boat, they started yelling. Both boats put their engines in high gear and headed for the little inlet that still held hundreds of dolphins and whales captive.

Neptune had planned for this also. He had sent a few good mermen ahead with the dry powder. When the boats came near to the inlet that powder was touched off...opening up an area large enough for all the remaining dolphins, whales and other large fish to gain their freedom. They swam right between the two boats and out to sea. There were a few stragglers that had been injured during their capture. Right under the eyes of the fishermen, Breeze, Olympia, and the mermen that had held the netting were there helping them to safety.

As they passed the fishing boats, they could hear the men yelling and cursing. With millions of dollars lost, the fishermen were livid with anger. There was nothing they could do but watch their money swim away. There they all were running back and forth on the deck of the fishing boat yelling…swearing they would get even. They would, no matter what, rid the sea of the demons that ruined their plans. Dolphins and whales sold for big money, dead or alive….And now that money was gone. They swore an oath to hunt down…and destroy every living creature that sabotaged and ruined their dreams.

With everyone safely out to sea…past the trouble and the sight of the ships, Neptune gathered his group together and praised them for their quick and relentless efforts and told them they could all leave and just go back to what they were doing. Then he looked at Olympia out of the corner of his eye and said. "Stick around, Olympia! Think we'll need to talk."

He turned towards Breeze next and said. "NOW! BREEZE! I told you I would deal with you later. This is later! And you'd better tell me the truth!" Again he looked at Olympia out of the corner of his eye…then continued, "Was this the first time you were ever at Olympia's….Or have you been there before?"

Neptune puffed himself up as big as he could, as he always did when he wanted to make a point or was angry. With him glaring down at her, Breeze felt like running away. She didn't want to tell she'd been at Olympia's before because she didn't want to get Olympia in trouble. So…she said nothing…just looked down at the ocean floor and said nothing.

Olympia broke the silence. "Neptune! I think I've about had enough of your ordering me to stay in that ship…Ordering your 'followers' not to ever see me. Seems like you didn't mind bringing me here though." She started yelling. "NEPTUNE, OLD FRIEND!

Today…YOU ASKED ME TO COME ALONG…ON THIS DANGEROUS MISSION…TO HELP. DIDN'T WANT OCEANA HERE, THOUGH. OH, NO! SHE MAY GET HURT…BUT ME!…YOU ASK ME!… HUMPH!"

Neptune started to speak, but Olympia cut him short. "LISTEN CLOSE, NEPTUNE! I REFUSE TO BE BANNED ANYMORE! BY NOW…EVERYONE knows you asked for my help today. EVERYONE! YOU will be the one that looks silly if you continue to BAN ANYONE FROM SEEING ME!" She got right in his face. "NEPTUNE, WE USED TO BE PRETTY CLOSE…YOU AND I. I STILL hold you with the utmost esteem, and I wouldn't want you ever to be embarrassed if someone should ask about this situation and why I was here and not Oceana. Oh, I know Oceana is not cut out for this kind of stuff. Actually, she is just a good homebody type wife…and there's nothing wrong with that. That's just what YOU need!

"To answer the question you just asked of Breeze… She'll not answer you because she doesn't want to get ME into trouble. YES! She stumbled upon my place a while back. I sent her away because I knew you would be angry, Neptune. This was about the same time you, followed by Oceana, came to my door and entered my place. She probably saw you two and ducked out of sight because she didn't want you to see her…AFRAID YOU WOULD GET ANGRY…JUST LIKE YOU ALWAYS DO!"

Olympia put her hand on Breeze's arm and pulled her close. "Isn't that about right, Breeze? You can answer now. I'm not going to get into any more trouble than I'm already in." She smiled and said, "Go ahead! If you WERE listening at the door...you can tell him so now."

Breeze felt a great relief that Olympia had stood up to Neptune....So she told all. Well, not quite all. She told Neptune that she did see them come...that she was shocked to see them there and just had to find out why. She took a deep breath as she continued. "Neptune! DADDY! I LOVE YOU VERY MUCH. WHY DIDN'T YOU EVER TELL ME OLYMPIA WAS MY MOTHER?"

Neptune was speechless for a minute...shocked at her statement. "What did you say?" He questioned.

"I SAID. I HEARD EVERYTHING! SO, I KNOW OLYMPIA IS MY MOTHER....I ALSO KNOW YOU ARE STILL MY FATHER! I GUESS YOU TWO WERE...PRETTY CLOSE." She took Olympia's hand and added, "I think...since you took it upon yourself to bring Olympia out in the open to help with all this...I would kind of like to GET ACQUAINTED...WITH MY MOTHER !" She pulled at Olympia's hand as if to leave. "OH! I AM SORRY I SPOILED YOUR LITTLE SECRET....BUT YOU WERE THE ONE THAT GAVE IT AWAY...IN YOUR OWN CONVERSATION!"

Neptune puffed himself up even more and commanded. "I WANT YOU BOTH TO LISTEN... REAL CLOSE!"

Olympia smiled and said. "BREEZE, I THINK IT'S ABOUT TIME WE DID GET ACQUAINTED. WE'LL SEE YOU LATER, NEPTUNE...BACK AT YOUR PLACE." With that she and Breeze turned and left.

Chapter 22

The first thing Breeze did when they were out of Neptune's sight was to ask…"Was my brother here helping free my friends?"

Olympia smiled. "Yes, Breeze, he was…but I'm STILL not going to tell you who he is. It just wouldn't be a good thing to do at this time. Trust me in this. Will you? Now, just what would you like to do to get acquainted? Did you like dancing the other night?"

"Oh, yes! Yes, I did…but, if we're going to go there…before we go there I want to see if the cruise ship is in. If it is…I have someone I want you to meet."

"I'll go dancing with you, Breeze.…Maybe show you how to do some other things humans do…explain things about them that you may not know.…But I really don't think I want to meet Alex. Not just yet anyway. I would really just like to spend time getting to know you. You have no idea how…all these years…I've missed you, Breeze! I've missed being your mother!"

"Well, Olympia!" Breeze smiled. "If that ship is in…I'm going on board to find Alex. I would very much

Breeze...the Mermaid

like you to come with me. We can find clothes in one of those boats." She pointed towards all the boats docked in the harbor. "That's what I always do."

"We don't have to do that, Breeze. Come with me. I'll show you something." They swam to the back of the dance studio and swam under the floor they had been dancing on the last time they were together. The water got shallower and shallower as they got farther underneath the building. When it became awkward to swim, Olympia said. "OK! Time to conjure up your land legs! Follow me!" This done, she took hold of a long, round piece of metal and pulled on it. It dropped down quite a ways. Next she pushed on the wood floor, and a big square of it opened upward. Olympia stepped up on the round piece of metal then into the building and disappeared. "Follow me, Breeze!"

Breeze did...but couldn't see a thing. "From now on...when you come on land...just come in here." Suddenly the light came on. "Pull this chain so you can see and pick yourself out some clothes. Only thing is...when you're finished wearing these things, they need to be put back exactly where you got them from. You don't need to take chances any longer going to humans' boats and stealing their clothes. Most of these are prop clothes...used for plays, musicals, parades, special dances...things like that. I have put some clothes that people use every day here in this box." She patted on the chest she was sitting on. "Let's get dressed and see what we can find to do." She pulled out a pair of shorts and a shorty type top, handed them to Breeze, and then pulled out the same for herself. Olympia gave her a great big smile. "Breeze! I've changed my mind. I think I would like to meet your Alex."

"GREAT!" Breeze smiled back excitedly. "What do you do, Olympia…when you want to leave here…just walk through the front door?"

"Yes! That's right. I just walk through the front door….Right through anything that's happening at the time. I've been doing this for a lot of years, and no one has said a word. This place is too busy for them to notice everyone."

"That was too easy! I'm not used to it being this easy to come on land."

Breeze was excited. As they walked down the beach together, she could see the cruise ship docked. The wooden walk was down, and no one was on it. "Can't believe you're doing this with me!" She smiled. "You'll see! He's really not like the other humans. He's—"

"HEY, BREEZE! BREEZE!" It was Alex. He was just pulling himself out of the water. "BREEZE!" He panted. "WAIT A MINUTE!" He ran up towards her with his arms outstretched and a big smile on his face. "Don't mind if I get you a bit wet…do you?" He was just about to give her a big hug when he realized she was not alone. Alex stopped dead in his tracks and said, "I'm sorry!" Turning to Olympia, he added, "I was so excited to see my favorite person that I—"

Olympia smiled back, cut into his sentence and said, "You must be Alex. Don't let me stop you from hugging your girl. Breeze told me about you and we were…just…on our…way…to…" Olympia's mouth opened wide, and she never finished her sentence. "WHO IS THAT BEHIND YOU? ALEX?"

Sam took one look at Olympia and stopped dead in HIS tracks. "SAM, Ma'am! Name's Sam!"

Alex put his arms around Breeze and gave her the hug he originally intended. Then he whispered in her ear. "Breeze! Who..."

Breeze was so excited to see Alex that, for the moment, she forgot all about the fact that Olympia was with her. "Oh! My!" she said. "I'm sorry, Olympia! Mother, this is Alex...and..." She gave a great big smile and pointed to Sam. "And THIS...IS SAM! We met him just before Alex left on that last cruise."

Sam was so taken with Olympia, he found it hard to catch his breath. "Olympia! Olympia!"

Olympia walked up to Sam with a big smile on her face, held out her hand and said, "Sam. You have no idea how glad I am to meet you. Do you like to swim? Want to go for a swim?"

Sam was stunned at the question. Usually when people meet that is not the question that is asked. "Why...YES! Yes! As a matter of fact, Olympia, I LOVE to swim." He looked at Olympia...then he looked at Breeze...remembering what took place on the ship.... That he saw Breeze actually take off her shorts and top, and hand them to Alex, then step on top of the railing and dive off the ship...into the ocean. No! He wasn't about to forget a thing like that. He took a deep breath and boldly asked, "Breeze, I was standing in the doorway when I saw you take off your things...saw you hand them to Alex, here. Then you stepped on the ship's railing and dove off...into the sea. I SAW YOU DOWN THERE...IN THE SEA...WAVING AT ALEX. No one just...does that!" Sam squinted his eyes and looked her right in the eye. "Breeze, are you a…a… MERMAID?"

Alex stepped right up to Sam, was just inches from his face and was about to tell him to get lost for being so rude.

Olympia reached out and took Sam's hand. "ARE YOU AFRAID TO SWIM WITH A MERMAID, SAM? I'M A MERMAID…AND SO IS MY DAUGHTER HERE. YOU MIGHT AS WELL JUST KNOW THAT RIGHT NOW. WHY DO YOU THINK I ASKED YOU IF YOU LIKED THE WATER?" She flashed a big smile at him and added, "I think, Sam…that you're that special kind of a guy that wouldn't mind being friends with a…a mermaid. Want to go for a swim?"

Breeze was shocked that, Olympia…HER mother, would be so bold. She remembered their conversation back in the pirate ship…when Olympia told her she wouldn't want to go back to living like a human. She said nothing. Neither did Alex. They just watched as Sam closed his big hand around Olympia's and answered, "Olympia, I would like nothing better then to go for a swim with you…and…NO! I'm not at all afraid to swim with a mermaid, especially one as beautiful as you." He pulled gently on her arm, pulling her close. Then he put his arm around her waist, and they vanished into the sea.

It was only a moment later that Breeze reached down and picked up the clothes Olympia had been wearing. She pressed her lips together, folded up the clothes and laid them on a small rock that jutted out of the sea. Then she looked at Alex and said, "All my life I didn't know she was my mother. Alex, I only found out a short time ago. Hope she and Sam don't do like another friend I had. Her name was Sandy. I showed her how to get a mermaid tail. She met one of my friends, and I never saw either Sandy or my friend any more." Breeze went on to tell him the whole story.

Alex listened intently, cupped her face with his hands and pressed his lips against hers ever so gently. Putting one arm behind Breeze's head and the other around her waist, he looked into her eyes and said, in an almost whispering tone, "First time I saw you, Breeze... something about you...I guess I fell in love with you right then. I didn't know you were a....Then when you pulled me into the sea...and I almost drowned...woke up with you kissing me. I've never forgotten that kiss, Breeze...never stopped wanting to kiss you. I love you, Breeze...I want us to be—"

At that moment, Alex found himself thrown into the sand with Neptune standing over him, fists clenched, and a loud, angry voice in his ear. "LEAVE MY PRESENCE, HUMAN! THIS IS MY DAUGHTER! AND YOU'LL NOT TOUCH HER AGAIN!"

"NEPTUNE! What a pleasant surprise!" Olympia said as she and Sam came walking back from their short swim. She smiled as she quickly stepped into her wet shorts and slipped the shorty top on over her head. She briskly walked right up and stood facing Neptune... stood between him and Alex.

Turning to Sam, she boldly added, "Sam...I want you to meet my good friend, Neptune...King of the sea, he is. Why earlier today, he saved thousands of dolphins and whales from a cruel death." She put her hand on Neptune's arm, smiled gently, and continued,

"Neptune! Tell us all about what you did saving them... REALLY GREAT... what you did. Please tell us!" Then she stepped aside and took Sam's hand, waiting for a response. To make things look even more relaxed, she pulled Sam towards the ground and they sat down on the sand near Alex. Breeze followed, worried about what might happen next.

As puffed up with pride as Neptune was...he couldn't resist telling the story...He boasted about his ideas and how everything worked so well. Then he turned to Olympia, looked down on her, and said, "I know what you just did...and what you've just done! You and...and..." He waved his arms around because he couldn't remember the name.

"SAM!" Sam stood up tall and held out his hand for Neptune to shake. "Name's Sam!"

"Well...SAM! Hope you had a good swim with my woman here! She IS mine, you know."

Olympia was shocked at the statement and so was Breeze. They both stood up...and in unison said, "What did you say?"

"You heard me! I said it to Sam here." Neptune made no attempt to shake Sam's hand..."HOPE YOU HAD A GOOD SWIM WITH MY WOMAN!" He turned to Alex...bent over...pointed his finger at him and said. "I NEVER want to see you again, son! You have no business with my Breeze either." Then he turned to Breeze. "As for that...HUMAN sitting down there on the ground...Breeze, you KNOW my feelings on that! DON'T BOTHER TO COME HOME IF YOU DECIDE TO CONTINUE TO SEE EACH OTHER. IF YOU DO...YOU'LL HAVE NO PLACE WITH ME!"

He glared at Olympia and added. "Remember what happened to Jim...at that picnic you were having? You're MY WOMAN, OLYMPIA! AND DON'T YOU EVER FORGET IT!" With that gruff remark, he turned and huffed off into the sea.

Alex, finally gaining his composure, stood up and took Breeze by the hand. "I don't want to get you into any trouble. Was THAT your father?"

"Yes! Yes, he is my father...but he is NOT going to run my whole life. I love you, Alex...and...if that's the way he feels...well..." She looked at Olympia. "I'll just not go back there for a while. I'll stay with my mother, Olympia...and, by the way, Sam...Olympia is NOT his woman."

Olympia had been giving some thought to Neptune's statement about what happened to her late husband. She was not dismissing the fact that, for all she knew, Neptune never really knew exactly what happened to Jim...just knew he had died. After a couple minutes of deliberation she spoke up. "You bet I'm not! I haven't been his woman since Breeze here was born! Neptune likes to think everything in his territory is HIS. I haven't been his for a lot of years!"

Turning to Alex, she added, "Alex! Why don't you just take Breeze for a little swim while Sam and I get better acquainted?"

Alex started to speak but Breeze cut him short...put her arms around him, and gave him an unexpected kiss. "Mmmmm...Good idea, Alex," she whispered as she kissed him again. "Let's do that! Come go for a little swim with me. Leave these two alone for a while?"

"Breeze!" Alex said as he pressed his body close to hers and returned her kisses.... "Breeze! You KNOW what'll happen if we get in that water together again. I remember last time we did that. You almost had me hypnotized with your affections. I want so much to be with you, but not at the cost of your family."

"I have an idea," Olympia said as she took Sam's hand. "We can ALL go for a swim, Alex!" She added, "Breeze is always welcome to stay with me. In fact, I'd like that very much....And, if you two really love each other...Neptune will get used to the idea sooner or later."

"OH... OLYMPIA! I DO LOVE HER!" Alex said, holding Breeze tight. He turned to Breeze. "I've always loved you, Breeze, loved you when I first saw you...in trouble on the ship. I loved you when you pulled me into the sea and almost drowned me. Really knew I loved you when you kissed me and saved my life...and that second kiss...OH! Yeah! Breeze, I do love you. Only trouble is...you're a mermaid and I'm a human. I'm just not so sure how that would work."

Olympia smiled inside as she spoke. "Alex, you know that I'm a mermaid, right?"

Alex answered. "I guess I know that...but I haven't seen you as a mermaid."

Sam put his hand on Alex's shoulder. "Trust me, son! Olympia IS a mermaid! Fell in love with HER at first sight too." He winked at Olympia, slung his arm around her waist and drew her close. Then he laced his fingers through the back of her hair to where he was holding the back of her head. His eyes slowly scanned the beauty of her face, and he kissed her lips ever so tenderly. "Olympia!" he said, in an almost whispering tone of voice. "I'm not a man of a lot of words. I know what I like when I see it...and YOU are what I like. OK by me that you're a mermaid. I want you for my woman, Olympia! I LOVE YOU...OLYMPIA!" Sam again gently pressed his lips against hers, delivering another slow and very passionate kiss.

"I'm a wrestler, Olympia...Go by the name Samson. That's what I do to make my money, that and some promotional stuff. Before that, I was a boxer, and before that I had combat training and lots of training in the marshal arts. Olympia, my love...I'm a warrior. I can hold my own with most any man in most any situation. The reason Neptune said what he said is...Well! We warriors recognize one another. Maybe it's written on our face or in our mannerism, I don't know....But...that's why he said what he said and why I said nothing. He knew I would be right there, ready...if need be. I didn't want you in the middle of a confrontation, Olympia. That's also why he left the way he did. Now, will you be my woman?"

Olympia put her arms on either side of Sam's face and gave him a big smile. "YES, Sam! OH YES! I will be your woman! I would be happy to be your woman! I would LOVE to be your woman!"

"OOOOH! YES! YES!" Sam yelled out with excitement, picked her up high in the air, and swung her around in circles. "Darlin'! You've just made me the happiest man alive! I'll move real close to the ocean... Build us a house, if you want...right here! So we can be just as close as we can. I know you're a fabulous creature of the sea...but that doesn't matter to me. I'll—"

Olympia interrupted his sentence with another kiss...then added, "SAM! My handsome warrior...I have a surprise for you! Come with me!" She turned to Breeze and added, "I know I told you never to do this...but I've changed my mind. Might just be a good idea, since you and Alex are so much in love...if he learned how to do this too."

It didn't take much showing. Sam and Alex soon learned how to conjure up their tails. Sam took to the tail right away, but Alex was a bit apprehensive...afraid he'd never get his legs back.

Breeze watched as he went from legs to tail to legs to tail. This went on for some time. Finally, Olympia said. "Let's go to my place! Lots of interesting things along the way."

"YAH...HOOO!" Sam yelled. "WHAT AN ADVENTURE! WHAT A SURPRISE! LEAD THE WAY, OLYMPIA, MY DEAR!"

Breeze had to give Alex a big kiss for reassurance. He wasn't too sure he wanted to travel very far just yet. She told him she'd be sure to bring him back when he was ready...pressed her body really close to his and gave him another sexy kiss, and they all swam off.

It didn't take long for both Sam and Alex to get used to their tails.

Chapter 23

Once out of sight of the shore, Sam began to feel adventurous. Instead of swimming PAST a sunken ship, he stopped and wanted to swim THROUGH it. "LOVE THIS, DARLIN'! BEST THING THAT EVER HAPPENED TO ME!" He reached over and put his arm around Olympia, pulled her to a stop, and planted a big, sexy kiss onto her lips. "LOVE YOU, OLYMPIA! DARLIN', I COULD STAY IN THIS OCEAN HERE WITH YOU FOREVER! JUST LOVE THIS TAIL!... WOW!"

Sam swam around in big circles, picked up speed and dove right at Olympia. He put his arm around her waist, swung her around in circles, and yelled, "OH! HOW I LOVE THIS MERMAID!" He planted a huge kiss upon Olympia's lips. "LOVE YOU, DARLIN'! LOVE ALL OF YOU...RIGHT DOWN TO THE TIP OF YOUR PRETTY LITTLE TAIL!"

Alex put his arm around Breeze as they watched. "Sam's quite a character, isn't he?"

Breeze just looked at him and smiled.

"I supposed you want the same treatment?" Alex asked as he gave Breeze the tenderest, sweetest kiss he could."

"Alex!" Breeze answered softly. "What I want from you is for you to stay just the way you are. Oh, I like Sam…but you're the guy I'm interested in…the guy I'm in love with…and I like you just the way you are."

"COME ON!" Sam yelled. "LET'S ALL GO INSIDE…OPEN UP ALL THE DRAWERS AND THE CLOSETS AND SEE WHAT'S THERE! NOW THAT IT'S IN THE SEA…THE SPOILS BELONG TO WHOEVER FINDS IT…RIGHT?"

"NOT EXACTLY!" Olympia spoke up. "…And just what will you DO with all the stuff you find in that ship? Can't bring it to my place. Can't take it to your place. Who knows how long this stuff's been down here. You bring it up on land, and it's liable to just fall apart. You take it to my place…and there's really no room. Besides…I have enough stuff already…more than any self-respecting mermaid should have. Sam! You don't NEED all those things! When you're in the ocean, all the ships that are sunk in the ocean are the same as yours. There's no set place to live down here. The whole ocean is our home."

"I choose to stay in the pirate ship…well… because…" She looked at Sam, then at Breeze and Alex. "OK, I'll tell you, Sam! I was once married to a human. We lived on the land because his things were there. His family was there. He got run over by a car trying to save a child. I still have some of his things in my pirate ship." Olympia again remembered Neptune's statement about what happened at that fateful time. She made a mental note to address him about it the next time she saw him.

Sam put his arm around Olympia. "So...my pretty little mermaid, loving one of us humans is not new to you...eh?" He kissed her tenderly on the cheek. "I want that same thing for us, Olympia. I love the sea. I love to swim in it. I LOVE YOU! And I want you to be my wife. I don't believe in waiting around wasting time. Want what I want...and I want you...NOW! Don't want to lose one precious minute with you. I want to MAKE something happen. I want us to have a home on the land, but I want us to have one here...in the sea too." He put his arms around Olympia and swung her around again—as much as he could under the water—and gave her a big, long kiss. "Well?" He said, kissing her again. "Will you? Will you marry me... HUMAN STYLE?"

"Sam!" Olympia joked, "All this time we've known each other....Thought you'd never ask! Of course I'll marry you...Just name the time and the place.

Breeze was shocked. "Olympia! Did I hear what I thought I heard? You two just met. Are you really getting married already?"

Olympia put her arm around Sam and answered. "If that's what Sam wants...then, YES! We're really getting married. Breeze, do you know why I've been single for so long...Lived in that pirate ship for so long?...Put up with Neptune's orders for so long?" She smiled. "I never thought there would be a SAM!" She gave Sam a big, long kiss. "Sam's perfect for me, Breeze. He's everything I always wanted...And, YES! I'll be his wife today...Tomorrow...Whenever he wants!"

Sam held Olympia up as high as his arms could reach. "RIGHT NOW, DARLIN'! Let's leave…RIGHT NOW! We'll catch a plane…And just do that! Right now!" He looked at Breeze and Alex holding their mouths open with surprise. "Son, if there's something that needs done…always best to do it right then. Something happens to one of you…at least you'll have the pleasure and happiness of knowing each other for that short time. You two coming along? I'M PAYING! THIS IS MY NIGHT!" He smiled and looked first at Alex then at Breeze…and said, "Bet that old Neptune would be fightin' mad if you two tied the knot same time as us!" Sam opened his mouth wide, threw his head back, and roared with laughter. "Looking at you two, it's going to be that way anyway sooner or later…May as well let him have the news all at once." He laughed some more. "Just get whatever you need and let's go. I'm itchin' for a hitchin'!" He gave Olympia another long, hard kiss. "WELL, ALEX?...BREEZE? Don't just stay there swishing your tails in one spot. Let's get movin'. Time's a wastin'." He looked at Breeze, then at Alex with his eyebrows raised. "WELL…YOU TWO COMING…OR STAYING? If there's not a flight out of here, I've got a friend that'll fly us wherever I want to go…for a price…and I've got the cash for the price."

Breeze smiled and answered, "I'm going!" Then she looked at Alex.

"Breeze!" Alex put his arms around her and held her close. "I love you, Breeze! Loved you since that day you pulled me overboard. My mind is whirling with thoughts of the possibility of being with you for the rest of my life. I had no idea you…being a mermaid…

could…" He stopped in the middle of his sentence, looked first at Sam then at Olympia, and then gave her a long, passionate kiss.

Turning to Sam, he asked, "How long do you think we'll be gone?"

"Son, are you worried about that piddlin' little job with the cruise ship? Forget it! With your build and good looks…I could get you in the circuit…be a wrestler like me. I'll teach you everything you need to know. Forget that silly cruise ship…No money there anyway! YOU TWO COMING OR NOT?"

Alex looked Sam right in the eye with a slight frown and asked, "You think?"

"I don't think, son," Sam answered, interrupting his sentence. "I KNOW! I've been in this business a long time. Coming?"

Alex put his hands on Breeze's shoulders, pressed his lips tenderly against hers, and then answered. "OK! OK! I'm coming with you!" Turning to Breeze, he added, "What do YOU want? Love me enough to spend your life with me? Love me enough…if I had no money? Probably lose my job doing this, you know."

Breeze kissed his cheek. "Don't need money where I come from, Alex. That's a human thing…and…YES! I love you enough to spend the rest of my life with you….And I don't CARE about the silly money. Don't understand it anyway."

"What about your father? What about Neptune?"

"Well!" Breeze answered. "I'll just have to deal with him later. It's my life! So…LET'S JUST GO!"

As they were nearing the shore, Olympia spoke up. "We need to stop by the dance studio. I've got some papers hidden underneath there, birth certificate, stuff like that...that Jim had made up for me. I also have one for you, Breeze, for when I thought I would be able to keep you with me. I had to have it when Jim and I got married. Breeze, Jim and I got married there, in the studio...and all the papers are still there, hidden. They had the place fixed up real pretty for us."

"Only need a driver's license where we're going, but bring them along anyway," Sam muttered as he gave Olympia another long kiss.

As they neared the dance studio, Olympia put her arm around Sam and said, "Hope you're not disappointed, Sam. I just got to thinking. There may not be any clothes your size in here. You are a pretty big guy."

Sam laughed and said. "My sweet, loveable mermaid, I have clothes...Have a whole suitcase full of clothes. Just don't you worry about me."

"Yes...But you'll have to have something to wear when we come out of the dance hall until you can get to your clothes."

"If there's a beach towel around, I'm good to go. Let's get in there and see what you've got."

Olympia led them underneath the dance studio, opened the little door, pulled down the step and went inside. She was right. Sam had to wear a big, pink, flowered beach towel. "I'll get you for this, mermaid!" He smiled. "Just wait and see!" He picked her up and gave her a long, passionate kiss. "Just you wait and see!"

Sam did change after he picked up his suitcase.

Chapter 24

They entered the big airline terminal only to find nothing available for where Sam wanted to fly to.

Breeze had never been to an airport or even seen an airplane take off and fly into the air. She stood in front of the window with her mouth wide open, watching the humans go into the airplane and then have it just leave the ground and turn into a bird in the air. "Are we going to do that?" she asked.

Sam answered, "Yup…But not in one of those. None of them are going where we want to go." He pulled his cell phone out of his pocket and called his friend, Burt, who offered to fly them for a small fee.

They grabbed a bite to eat and then took a taxi to the other end of the terminals. There awaiting them was a very small airplane. Sam introduced Burt and gave him a big wad of money. He smiled as he got in the little airplane, looked at Alex, and added, "Olympia and I are taking the back seat…More privacy for smooching. Watch your step now. Can't step just anywhere. You have to put your feet in the designated spots." He smiled and let Olympia enter first.

Breeze didn't know what designated meant. She started to step where she shouldn't and Burt yelled at her. "HEY…NOT THERE! DON'T STEP THERE!" He reached around her and pointed to the places where she could step. His voice went back to normal as he added, "These wings are very fragile, Breeze. If you step in the wrong place it could cause major trouble."

With that said, all seemed to be OK. Breeze stepped where Burt showed her and made her way inside. Already she didn't like it that Burt yelled at her. She'd had a lot of that from lots of different humans and…if Alex weren't there she wouldn't have even gotten on the airplane.

The door was shut, and there they were all inside. Breeze looked around at the tiny cabin, noticed the closeness of the seats and remembered the first time she rode with Sandy in her car. This couldn't be worse then that, she thought. No one else, including Olympia, seemed to be nervous about this ride…so she shouldn't be either. She looked around again, then looked at Alex and tried to sit there and be calm. Alex put his arm around her, which helped some. Next came the roaring sound of the engines starting up. They were much louder than Sandy's car. They sat there for what seemed like a long time to Breeze, with the noise getting louder and louder. As the little plane started to vibrate and slowly move forward, she made a mental note that if things got too much for her…she'd just leap out that door.

Breeze...the Mermaid

"MAKE SURE YOU'RE ALL BUCKLED UP! WE'LL BE IN THE AIR IN A FEW MINUTES." It was Burt yelling again.

Alex leaned over, put both arms around Breeze, and made sure her seat belts were fastened properly. Then he pressed his lips against hers and gave her a big kiss. "I can tell you're nervous. I'm right here, and everything's going to be OK!" He leaned over close to her ear, gave her a short kiss on the neck, and whispered, "I love you, Breeze, and I'll always be here for you."

Breeze took a deep breath as the plane sped up. Looking over at Sam and Olympia...they didn't seem to be concerned at all. They were too busy kissing each other. She thought that car of Sandy's went fast...but this! THIS...WAS JUST TOO FAST...AND GETTING FASTER. As much as she enjoyed Alex's arm around her, it just wasn't enough. As the airplane turned its nose up towards the sky and she felt the jolt of it being lifted off the earth. Breeze sucked in her breath, bit her lip, unfastened her seat belt, and leaped over the front seat towards the door.

Alex already had his arm around her, but he wasn't prepared for what she did. She slipped through his grasp and would have made it out the door if Sam hadn't dove over the seats to tackle her. With his strong arms around her waist, he managed to keep her from opening the door. This caused the plane to go bumpety bump back onto the runway...which caused Sam to break his hold on Breeze and land head first on the floor with his legs sticking up above the seat beside Alex. By Sam letting go all of a sudden, it caused Breeze to be thrown head first into the front seat beside Burt.

Burt had his hands full just setting the nose of the plane back down and keeping it from skidding off the runway. With Breeze's legs kicking back and forth on top of his shoulder and hands, it was no easy task. He did, however, manage to bring the little plane to a safe stop. Burt ground his teeth and shoved Breeze's legs out of the way. In a fit of anger he braced his arms against the instrument panel and glared out into the landing strip. For a short time, he turned his head around and sat there watching the two of them struggle to regain their seats.

Breeze was now in the front seat, lying on the seat with her legs over the back of the seat where Burt had flung them. Her hand was on the door handle. Alex was drooped over the seat and had his hands on Breeze's shoulders trying to calm her down. Sam...well, Sam was still upside down with his hands on the floor and his body pressed next to Alex. His legs were kicking in the air trying to find a spot of stability so he could right himself in the seat. Olympia was still sitting in the same position she was to start with, grinning from ear to ear...laughing.

"I can't remember when I've had so much fun!" Olympia said as she sat there laughing. "Burt! I think we need to put Breeze and Alex in the back seat." She put her hands on Sam's ankles and gave them a strong yank towards her.

"Sam, my love! You OK?"

Sam pulled himself together in the seat, put his arms around Olympia, and said, "Woman...With you by my side..." He pulled Olympia close and gave her a passionate kiss, then continued, "Of course I'm OK.

Saved her from jumping out didn't I? Nothing like a little excitement! Burt, think you can get this thing back up in the air so I can make this little gal mine?"

"Not so sure I want to fly with...with..." He pushed Breeze's feet to the floor. "With...THAT...THAT BREEZE girl in my airplane! Going to cost you extra Sam...old buddy, old friend....Going to cost you extra! Almost lost my plane!"

"WHAT GOT INTO YOU, BREEZE? WHY DID YOU DO THAT? YOU ALMOST WRECKED MY AIRPLANE!" Burt yelled.

Breeze...now sitting beside him, looked into his face and answered, "Burt, I've never been in one of these things before! I don't like your yelling! And... and...that's what started me being upset in the first place. You yelled at me! Just like you're doing now! When I first started to get into this thing...I didn't know anything about these noisy flying boxes...and I didn't know I had to step in a special place just to get in here. You didn't have to yell at me to tell me that, Burt." She put her face closer to his and looked him right in the eye. "DON'T YELL AT ME ANY MORE! I DON'T LIKE THAT! If...if you want to go again, I won't jump out. Burt! What is it about you humans? You always think you have to yell? I could have heard you just as well if you were talking nice to me."

With everyone in their seats, Burt again started the engines. This time Breeze was content to ride. After a short time she even began to enjoy herself, pointing out all the neat cloud formations. About an hour into the flight, Breeze kissed Alex on the cheek and said, "I want to do this, Alex. I want to fly one of these. It's really pretty up here looking down at the clouds and everything. Hey! I drove Sandy's car OK, didn't I?"

Alex tried to answer. "Well…"

"I did drive it OK…Not my fault it went into the ocean. Driving this would be a lot easier…No roads to follow and no ocean to fall into." She immediately hopped into the front seat with Burt and announced, "Burt! Can I drive this for a while?"

Burt looked at her out of the side of his eye, put the plane on autopilot, and answered, "Breeze, you see that steering column in front of you? Just take that in your hands. Keep it pointed to where the sun is always in the same spot in your window and…there you go. I'm just going to sit here…relax and watch you. Whatever you do…don't touch any of the buttons or any of the other controls!"

"I won't!" Breeze smiled back, delighted he'd given in so easily. After a very short time, she noticed Burt wasn't paying much attention to what she was doing. He was just carrying on conversations with every one else. No matter how she turned the funny looking wheel, it didn't seem to make a difference about what the plane did. She'd been noticing a little green light that seemed to be on all the time. Maybe it didn't need to be on. Burt wasn't paying any attention anyway so she thought she might just switch it off. First, she looked around to see if anyone was watching. No one was watching.

As she scooted over to reach for the switch, her knee hit a long red thing. This, she thought, was put in the wrong place…right in the way of her knees. Bracing herself against the panel of switches, she took hold of the handle and pushed with all her might to get it out of the way. MISTAKE! The switch she'd been leaning on was the auto pilot switch. It was now off. She also bumped the fuel on switch, turning it off and…while pulling on the handle, the long red thing suddenly let go, knocking her off balance and releasing white stuff that began spraying all over. With it still in her hand, she turned around. Breeze had her back to Burt as she swung the red thing across the seats and back around toward him, spraying everyone and everything with fire extinguishing spray. Burt started yelling! Alex and Sam were yelling, and so was Olympia…yelling so loud Breeze put both hands to her ears, causing the extinguisher to drop over into the middle seat. It landed on the handle…spraying Burt in the back of the head. All this happened within a few seconds, and the plane began to do a nosedive downward.

"YOU ALL DON'T NEED TO YELL AT ME!" Breeze frowned. I didn't know it would do all that! All I did was—"

While trying to brush the spray off his face, Alex cut her sentence short. "Get back here with me, Breeze! I need to buckle you up. I think we may be in for some trouble."

The engines started acting funny causing Burt to notice that Breeze had turned the fuel switch off. This he attended to first. It took a while before he managed to pull the little plane back into its flight pattern. All the while, both Olympia and Sam were staring at Breeze with their lips pressed firmly together, frowning. Spray from the fire extinguisher was everywhere…all over each of them! The whole inside of the plane was covered with white, fluffy fire extinguisher spray.

"Breeze!" Sam said calmly in a very low, slow, matter-of-fact voice. "Get back there with Alex! Sit down! Hold Alex's hands...And don't move again until we land!" He turned to Olympia, who was still staring at Breeze, and tenderly started wiping the spray off her face. "You OK, Sweetheart?"

To make matters worse, before Olympia could answer, Breeze started laughing. She climbed over the seat and into the seat next to Alex, laughing almost uncontrollably. "Do you all know how funny you look?" She laughed some more! "I don't seem to have any of that stuff on me."

That did it for Burt, but before he could yell out his obscenities, Alex put his arms around Breeze and said, "Burt! She has some on her now! Don't you go blaming my Breeze here for what just happened. You were the one that allowed her in that seat. You were the one that put the plane on autopilot and took your attention away from what she was doing. Don't you go blaming my Breeze!"

Everyone was silent. Burt finally broke the silence with laughter. "Hey... Alex! You're right! I never should have allowed her to handle the plane...pretend or otherwise. I apologize to all of you...Just thought she'd sit there and pretend." There was more laughter. "Guess we do all look pretty funny. Well! Put on your seat belts...if you don't already have them on. We're coming in for a landing." He reached for a drink of water, took one swallow and couldn't contain himself. He spewed the water out in front of him as he burst into another roar of laughter. "Sam...old pal! You know, I'll send YOU the cleaning bill!" More laughter!

They were all still laughing as they stepped down off the plane. Soon everyone that saw them in the airport was pointing and grinning. It didn't take long for a huge crowd to gather...most of which were laughing and pointing their fingers.

Alex was embarrassed! But not Sam! There just happened to be newspaper reporters there for some other reason. Sam saw them and announced, "WANT A NEWS SCOOP, FELLOWS? NAME'S SAMSON! YOU'VE PROBABLY HEARD OF ME! ONE OF THE TOP WRESTLERS ON THE CIRCUIT. Normally, I have my press agents handle things like this...but it all came up so sudden." As the croud gathered around, Sam put his hand around Olympia and gave a great big smile for the photographers who were snapping pictures like crazy. "Me and Olympia here..." He kissed her on the cheek. "Me and Olympia came here to get hitched. SHE'S GONNA BE MY WIFE." He picked Olympia up and swung her around in a circle. "OH! Suppose all of you want to know why we have all this white stuff on us....Fire extinguisher just broke loose while we were flying up there." With a big smile on his face, he shook his head, pointed to each of his companions and continued, "BIGGER MESS IN THAT AIRPLANE! Now we've all been christened for the wedding. That's all, folks."

Breeze looked first at Olympia then at Sam. "You always announce yourself like that, Sam?"

Alex put his arm around her waist. "Think we'd kind of like to remain anonymous, if you don't mind."

"OH!" Sam added. "JUST A BIT OF PUBLICITY, SON. GET YOUR NAME OUT THERE! LET 'UM

Sylvia Fraley

KNOW YOU'RE ALIVE! THAT'S WHAT SELLS TICKETS, SON. THAT'S WHAT PUTS THE MONEY IN THE POCKET. STICK WITH ME! YOU'LL SEE!"

Alex didn't say anything...just raised one eyebrow, looked at Breeze, and put his arm around her.

Sam hailed a taxi and away they went.

Chapter 25

Looking out the window, Breeze began to realize the difference in the terrain. She put her head next to Alex and whispered in his ear. "There are no trees here...and no water. Where's my ocean? There are only a few little plants out there...and they are all dead. What kind of place is this? There's nothing here but dirt and dead plants. How do people live here?"

Alex kissed her cheek and answered, "We're in the desert, Honey. There is no ocean here. We're a long way from your ocean."

"Is Sam going to take us back home?"

"I don't know." Alex answered. "But...if he doesn't, I'll make sure we get back."

With that reassurance, Breeze relaxed into his arms.

Not paying any more attention to her surroundings, she was almost asleep when she heard Sam's husky voice booming with excitement. "WE'RE HERE! WE'RE HERE! BEEN A LONG TIME SINCE I'VE BEEN HERE! Last time I was here, I boxed in the arena on the other side of town. Great match! Won that one in two rounds…Decided to quit while I was ahead and turned to wrestling." He stopped the taxi, and they got out in front of a fancy building with stained glass windows and lots of flowers growing outside. Sam turned to Olympia, put his arm around her and asked. "This OK for you, Sweets? I know the people that own this place. Real pretty inside. Great place for a wedding…ah…for TWO weddings." He grinned, looked at Alex and added, "You two ARE going to tie the knot, aren't you?"

Alex smiled and took Breeze's hand. "Hope so!" he answered.

Inside the door was a wonderland of tropical plants, a waterfall, and a small shallow pool that everyone had thrown coins in. Under the waterfall was a statue of a mermaid holding flowers.

Breeze couldn't believe her eyes when she saw the statue. "That looks like my friend, Willow. We kind of grew up together but I don't see her and her brother much anymore. Nice to see water again," she added. Out of the corner of her eye, she noticed several boxes standing along the wall. Humans were sitting in front of them pushing buttons to make pretty pictures appear. "Can I do that?" she asked. "I'd like to see what comes up when I do that."

While Sam was making arrangements for their weddings, Alex gave Breeze several one dollar bills, showed her how to put one of them in a little slot and push the button; then he just stood back to watch. Breeze put her arms around him, pressed her body close against him, gave him a big hug, and then squealed loudly, "OOOOOOO…CAN'T WAIT TO SEE WHAT

COMES UP FOR ME!" She asked the lady who was sitting beside her if she liked the pictures that came up for her.

The lady didn't say much...She just said, "Honey! I've been sitting here at this machine for over an hour, and the right pictures haven't come up for me yet."

Breeze put in one of her dollar bills. Immediately lots of pictures started going around and round. Bells started ringing inside the machine. The pictures began spinning faster and faster and the bells seemed to ring louder and louder. This went on for several minutes. Finally it all stopped. All the other people that were sitting in front of their 'boxes' had their heads turned and were now staring at Breeze. One guy was actually angry! Said he'd been sitting at that machine all morning and just got tired of it, said he was the one who should have won the money. He actually got up out of his seat, stood up, walked over to stand behind Breeze, and asked if she would give him the piece of paper that came out of the machine because it was really his since he'd been sitting there all morning.

Breeze held her hand out to him with the piece of paper in it and was about to hand it to him...not knowing what it was...when Sam walked up and snatched it. "Breeze!" He smiled. Do you know what you've done just now?"

"I KNOW WHAT SHE'S DONE!" The man interrupted in an angry, loud voice. "SHE STOLE MY MACHINE! THAT'S WHAT SHE'S JUST DONE! WHY...I'VE BEEN PUTTING MONEY IN THAT MACHINE ALL MORNING LONG! SHE HAD NO RIGHT—"

Sam walked over to the man, stood about a foot away from him…towered over him because of his size, and looked down at him. He looked right into the man's eyes and calmly said, "Mister, I suggest…if you want to continue having a good day…you leave…Right now!"

The man took one look at Sam, and left the building!

Sam handed Breeze back her piece of paper and led her down a long hall and into another room. This room was also beautiful but had no pool of water in it…just some highly decorated fancy tables with bench type chairs that would seat two. The little benches had two big wooden hearts carved into the middle of the back. One table had a giant clamshell full of punch sitting in the middle of it and little clam-shaped cups sitting beside it. There was another table with a fancy brown cake in the middle of it. The cake was just loaded with lots of decorations, including a couple of little humans standing on top. Each of the other tables also had tantalizing assortments of food on them..

A man entered wearing what looked like a penguin suit, pointed to Breeze and Alex, and asked, "You two want to be first?"

Alex took Breeze's hand and led her under a pretty, rose-covered lattice arch.

The man standing there asked Breeze if she wanted to 'cash in her ticket' first. Breeze thought it was expected of her to give the piece of paper up in order for them to get married…so she handed it to him. She was upset that she had to do this…but Alex was worth it. Because of all that had happened, however, she wasn't really listening to the words the man was saying. The more

Breeze...the Mermaid

she thought about it, the more she didn't like the fact that she had to give up that piece of paper. She could see no reason for it. Alex would have been hers anyway. It was her machine that piece of paper came out of, and she was entitled to it. When the words came up...*Do you take this man to be your lawfully wedded husband*, she stomped her foot on the floor and answered, "OF COURSE I DO! WHY DO YOU THINK I'M HERE? NOW, MISTER! WHAT HAVE YOU DONE WITH MY PIECE OF PAPER?"

Alex knew where the paper went...knew it was being cashed in for the money she won...so...to keep things calm and not cause a scene he swept her up in his arms and said, "I love you, Breeze," and gave her the biggest kiss ever. Then he added, "They're bringing you lots of pieces of paper back. Right now...I just want to hold you."

With that kiss...Breeze forgot all about her little piece of paper.

"Love you, Breeze," Alex said again as he picked her up and carried her to one of the bench type chairs in front of the giant clam punch bowl. "Always will!"

Alex was right about the 'lots of pieces of paper.' As soon as they sat down a lady came up to Breeze and started counting out one-hundred-dollar bills, laying them one by one on their table. When she left, Breeze turned to Alex and said, "I don't have any place to keep all these." She scooped them up and handed them to Alex. "Here! YOU take them! Maybe you can find something to do with them. I think I want to see what's in this big clamshell."

"Breeze! Honey!" Alex split the money into two piles and stuffed one of them into the front pocket of his pants. "I want you to learn some important things about living with us humans." He kissed her on her cheek as he put his arm around her. "How would you like to learn a little about money while we're waiting?"

"OK! But first, I want to see what they put in that clamshell. Want some?" She stood up and moved to the side of the table facing him. Instead of using the ladle that was in the shell to dip the contents out with, she pulled it out and laid it on the table. Then she attempted to pick up the bowl and try to pour some of its contents into one of the little clam-shaped cups. Well, the bowl was about three feet across and had a scalloped edge. It was too big and too heavy for her. Before Alex could stop her, it slipped out of her hands and fell onto the cup she was trying to pour the liquid into.

Alex was quick to move out of the way…but not quick enough. All the punch, and there must have been several gallons of it, flew all over him, all over the hundred dollar bills and his wallet that he had laid on the table, all over the table, and all over the little love seats sitting around it. There was also a very large puddle on the floor that was quickly growing larger. There Alex stood, in the middle of the puddle…with dark red cherry punch splattered all over him.

Sam and Olympia walked into the scene about then. Sam took one look, pointed his finger at Alex, and started laughing. He was laughing so hard he didn't bother to look down. The next thing he knew, he was on the floor keeping company with the punch.

Breeze...the Mermaid

"Hmmm! Not bad for a memorable wedding day!" Olympia snickered as she put her hand over her mouth. "Let's see...Breeze won a lot of money that has just been christened with red punch. Alex, well..." She bent over and laughed. "Alex! You look..." More laughs! "...like you tried to WEAR that punch instead of drink it!...AND YOU!" She put her hand down to Sam to help him up. "My blushing groom!" She giggled some more. "Think I'll walk you out to the swimming pool."

Sam stood up...almost falling again because of the slippery floor...took one look at Breeze and said, "How'd you to that, Breeze? There were FIVE gallons of punch in that bowl. How could you possibly have spilled all of it?"

Breeze gave him a sheepish smile and simply said, "I tried to pour it into those cute little clam cups...but it was too heavy for me. Um...SORRY!"

By the time they got all the money picked up, the janitor showed up to try clean up the mess. He started with the table...which was a mistake. Within a few seconds, he too had slipped onto the floor. There he sat...in the middle of the puddle of punch waving his cleaning cloth around in the air dripping the red punch all over his lap. "FIFTEEN YEARS!" he yelled. "FIFTEEN YEARS, I'VE BEEN TAKING CARE OF THIS PLACE! FIFTEEN YEARS! I HAVE NEVER! EVER SEEN SUCH A MESS! How did you do this?" He tried to get up but had slick soled shoes on, so he fell back into the punch puddle...splattering red punch all over the front of Olympia.

Now, the only one that didn't have punch on them was—you guessed it!—Breeze....And she roared with laughter when she saw Olympia covered with red punch spots.

By now, Sam was laughing too. "Olympia! My sweet! How nice of you to join us." He put his arms around her and pressed close against her, transferring more puch onto her as he gave her a big, strong hug. "May as well join the crowd...my pretty little bride."

Sam laughed some more as he put one hand on the table, making sure he had a firm grip, then he reached out his hand to help the janitor up. Trying his best not to laugh, he added, "We'll leave this punch mess to you! Sorry about that! It was an accident!" He took one more look around and burst out laughing again.

The whole punch-covered bunch of them was laughing as they left the room. "Hey, Breeze!" Sam snickered. "You caused this mess! Won all the money! How'd you escape the punch?"

Alex could stand no more. "She didn't!" He said, smiling. He stepped over to Breeze...put his arms around her, and gave her a big, long, close hug. Alex had a sly grin on his face as he pulled back slightly to make sure the punch transferred from his clothes to hers.... Then he kissed her tenderly. "Sorry, my love! I just had to do that! You just looked too pretty and clean!"

Turning to Sam, he asked, "Where are our rooms, Sam? Think we'd like to get cleaned up."

On the way to their rooms, they walked past a glassed-in room that had an indoor swimming pool. Several people were sitting in lounge chairs and a few were in the pool. Breeze didn't wait for an invitation. She just darted into the room, kicked off her shoes, and dove into the pool...clothes and all. A small, bright red circle was left on top of the water from the punch Alex's hug left on her clothes, and it lost no time spreading across the pool.

The people in the pool scurried to get out. The people that were seated by the pool were startled. A few of them stood up pointing their finger, and a couple of the women started yelling and screaming. One man had seen the red all over Breeze's clothes before she dove in, saw the red tinge on top of the water, and left the room to get the manager.

Olympia knew there'd soon be trouble so she took it upon herself to get Breeze out of the pool. By this time, everyone was alerted, and when they saw Olympia by the edge of the pool, also covered with red punch, they tried to reach out for her. Olympia was too fast for them. Instead of getting Breeze out of the pool, she decided *What the heck*, and just dove into the pool to be with Breeze.

Sam and Alex saw what was happening, took one look at each other, exchanged grins, and said, "Let's go!" Then they burst into the room to rescue their brides.

About that same time the man who had left the pool showed up with the manager. The manager took one look in the pool and saw the two women in there with their dresses on. He noticed the red tinge on top of the water and commanded them to leave the pool area at once. Then he turned around and noticed Sam and Alex, who were standing behind him…with their clothes still dripping with red punch. He opened his eyes wide when he saw their punch-splattered clothes, put his hand over his mouth, and burst into laughter. "Is that from the mess…" More laughter! "…THAT'S

BEING CLEANED UP IN THE OTHER ROOM? IS THAT YOUR MESS?" He looked at Sam and Alex again, scanned them from head to toe, and couldn't contain himself. He just stood there laughing. Finally he spoke. "You two had better get out of here!" More laughter! "Take your women with you!" More laughter! By this time, everyone in the pool area was laughing.

Now, Sam wasn't much for being laughed at. He took off his shirt, threw it on the floor, put his hands on his hips, and said, "Listen, Mister! If your punch bowl had been a decent size…its contents wouldn't have wound up on the floor! We just got married in there…. And this is no way to treat newlywed guests….Do you think?"

Alex had walked over to the pool to help Breeze out. Breeze had other ideas! The water felt so good, and she wanted company. She had already slipped her dress off, and it was lying on the bottom of the pool. Alex took one look at her in her bra and underwear and asked in an almost whispering voice, "Honey, would you please get your dress from the bottom of the pool? We need to go to our room."

Breeze answered with a big smile. "Um-Hum." She dove down to recover the dress. After putting it on the side of the pool, she put one foot and one hand on the ladder, and reached out toward Alex with her free hand so he could help her out.

Breeze took hold of Alex's hand, braced her feet against the side of the pool, gave a great big smile, and said, "WATER'S GREAT! COME ON IN!" Now, Alex was pretty much saturated with punch so when he hit the water its bright red color spread rapidly throughout.

As he came up gasping for breath, Breeze put her arms around him and gave him a big kiss…causing them both to sink to the bottom.

Fearing for their lives, the manager hurried over to the edge of the pool to see if he could help.

"AW!…WHAT THE HECK!" exclaimed Sam as he quickly slipped off his shoes. "CAN'T THINK OF A BETTER THING TO DO…ON MY WEDDING DAY! OH…YEAH!" he yelled, as he rushed forward with his arms stretched straight out to each side. Sam had long arms and, as he leaped into the pool, the unsuspecting manager was taken right in there with him. As Sam came up for air, he started laughing. He took one look at the manager, who was still sputtering from his surprise dip in the water and said, "Sorry about that!" Still laughing he added, "You'll have to admit. The water does feel good!"

Olympia came up behind Sam about that time, turned him around, spoke softly in his ear, and said, "About time you came in here to rescue me, you big lug!" She put her arms around him and planted a long, sensuous kiss on his lips…then added. "You sure know how to give a girl a wonderful wedding, Sam."

Sam returned the kiss and said, "Pretty little mermaid…I'd do anything for you! Then he turned to Alex. "You two going to stay here with us for a while?"

Alex looked at Breeze, smiled and said. "Think not, Sam." He put his arm around Breeze and kissed her cheek. "Think we're just going home. Going to find us a home…Going to brave it and meet her father…See if he will give us his blessing. Maybe if he saw that my intentions were sincere he—"

Olympia cut him off sharply. "YOU DON'T KNOW WHAT YOU SPEAK OF, ALEX!" WHY DO YOU THINK HE SENT ME AWAY TO LIVE BY MYSELF IN THE FIRST PLACE? I'LL TELL YOU WHY…BECAUSE I MARRIED A HUMAN…HAD CHILDREN BY THAT HUMAN…LIVED IN A HUMAN'S HOUSE! DO YOU THINK I CARE? NO! I DON'T. I'LL HAVE MY LIFE…with Sam here." She gave Sam a kiss on the cheek. "…and I'll be happy. My children come to visit me. Neptune doesn't know who they are because I allowed them to live with other mermaids. Breeze here knows. She knows…and she chose you, Alex. Be proud of the fact that she has her own mind. Just want you to know what you're getting yourself into if you think Neptune will accept you as her man."

"She's right!" Breeze added, "He almost banned me because I went to visit Olympia. I have no doubt that I'll be banned from them all now."

Alex felt bad. "Breeze, I—"

Breeze didn't let him finish his sentence. She cupped his face with her hands and gave him a big kiss. "Don't you feel bad! I chose to be with you because I love you…and, if that's what it takes, then that's what it takes! Don't think for a minute you're causing any trouble for me that wasn't already there. Neptune can get pretty mean with his forcefulness but…whatever you want to do…I'm with you, Alex."

She turned to Olympia and added. "Don't you think it's time you told me who my brother and sister are?"

Olympia smiled. "You promise not to tell anyone? I'm not even sure you should tell your brother and sister. It may jeopardize what they're doing."

"I promise! I promise! I won't tell anyone!"

"OK then!" She took a deep breath and looked at Alex. "YOU have to promise too since you two are going to be together from now on."

Alex smiled and looked her right in the eye. "I promise, Olympia. Your secret's safe with me."

Olympia looked first at Alex then at Breeze...then at Sam. "OK! Nautilus and Willow are your brother and sister."

"OH! OH!" Breeze's eyes got really big and her mouth opened wide. "Olympia, I've played with them all my life!"

"I know that. That's why I never told you. Neptune doesn't know they're my children, and he should never know. I don't trust his ways, Breeze. Please! Please! Keep our little secret."

Olympia turned to Alex. "You didn't know what you were getting into...did you? Thought only you humans had problems like this...didn't you?"

Alex smiled and hugged Breeze tight. "That's not good that you have to hide like that....But I'll protect your secret...protect you too...protect Breeze too and..." He looked at Sam...."Yeah! Big guy, even you. Just realized, Sam YOU'RE MY...FATHER-IN-LAW! What do you think of that?"

Sam's eyes got really big, and he smiled at Alex. "Guess so! Never thought about that! Since Olympia is Breeze's mother....That does make you my..." He put his hand to his head. "Oh! NO! All of a sudden...I have a family. Whatever am I going to do?"

Chapter 26

Alex used some of Breeze's winnings for plane fare back home. Breeze didn't seem to be frightened on the large jetliner. She just laid her head on Alex shoulders and slept most of the way. The big, comfortable airplane only went so far though. They had to wait for several hours in a big airport for another plane. When finally it did arrive, a major storm had arisen, making the rest of their trip a very bumpy ride.

Breeze wanted off that little airplane so bad she didn't even wait for the stewardess to make her announcement. As soon as she heard the wheels touch the ground, her seat belt flew off and she was out of her seat and at the door. If Alex hadn't been there to stop her she would probably have been out the door before the airplane stopped. As it was, the stewardess tried to get Breeze back into her seat, but she refused.

To their surprise, they were met at the airport by Sam and Olympia. Sam reached out his hand toward Alex and smiled. "Bumpy ride, eh? Didn't think I was going to let you meet Breeze's father all by yourself…

did you?" He had a big smile on his face as he added, "I remember his statement to us on the beach….Actually, that statement was directed TO ME on the beach. Now, whether he likes it or not…we're ALL part of his family. Let's go meet him right now! Where does he keep himself?"

"Not so fast, Sam." Alex said. "I want to make sure we have a nice place to stay here before we get into that. If it comes to words, I really don't want my Breeze to get hurt by them."

"You don't have to worry about finding a place to stay right away." Sam smiled. "My little sweetie here has that great old ship. We can just all stay there for a while…Give you time to find a place that's decent. It's in the general area and you won't be rushing around that way. More time to…enjoy each other's company. What do you think?"

Breeze smiled, looked at Alex, and said, "It doesn't matter to me. Whatever you want, Alex. As long as we're together, I'm happy…It doesn't matter to me."

Alex felt three sets of eyes on him waiting for a decision. "Oh! OK! Olympia…guess we'll stay with you for a little while."

"Well, come on, then." Olympia smiled. "Let's dump these clothes at the dance studio and go to my place."

As they entered the doors, Alex asked. "Don't these people care that you…just walk in…and don't walk back out again?

Olympia smiled. "The owners knew my husband, Jim. I'm welcome here anytime…and so is anyone I bring with me. No one really watches when I come and go."

They left their clothes in the dressing room; made sure the latch was tight on the trap door, conjured up their tails and swam off.

Sam seemed to get all excited when he got his tail. As they swam, he practiced smacking things with it. He'd dart ahead, little bits at a time just, so he had time to smack whatever happened to be there. He made the mistake of smacking a big electric eel that sent him tumbling onto the ocean bottom…and let out a yell so loud that Neptune could probably have heard it no matter where he was.

On the way to Olympia's old ship, Alex had a queasy feeling in his stomach….He thought it might have been something he ate. It wasn't! It was a premonition! There was Neptune blocking the front door of the ship with his hands on his hips and a scowl in his eye. He yelled out in a loud, angry, commanding voice, "CAME BACK…DID YOU? BROUGHT THOSE HUMANS… DID YOU? TOLD YOU…NOT TO BOTHER TO COME HOME IF YOU DECIDED TO HANG WITH HUMANS. TOLD YOU…YOU'LL HAVE NO PART OF ME IF…"

Sam immediately swam in front of everyone…ready for battle.

Olympia quickly swam in front of Sam…and right up in front of Neptune. "NEPTUNE, YOU'VE ALREADY BANNED ME FROM BEING WITH THE REST OF MY PEOPLE. THIS IS MY PLACE… AND RIGHT NOW…YOU'RE NOT INVITED! I don't see Oceana anywhere. You came to PICK A

FIGHT...DIDN'T YOU?" She started to turn to leave, and then turned back around with her hands on her hips. "FOR YOUR INFORMATION...SAM HERE...IS MY HUSBAND...AND WE'LL STAY HERE IF WE PLEASE. ALL MY THINGS ARE IN THAT SHIP AND I'M NOT ABOUT TO JUST LEAVE BECAUSE YOU ARE JEALOUS."

That last statement set off Neptune's fuse. "JEALOUS!" He yelled. "WOMAN! YOU DON'T KNOW WHAT YOU'RE TALKING ABOUT!" He puffed himself up...like he usually did when he is trying to make a point. "LISTEN TO THIS ONE... MISS X! LISTEN WELL...AND REMEMBER... IF I DID IT ONCE...I CAN DO IT AGAIN." He waited a short time, breathing hard...looking directly into everyone's eyes...and a sly grin came upon his face. "YOU'LL NOT GO AGAINST MY WORDS!...YOU DID BEFORE!...LONG TIME AGO!...AND YOU LOST! WHO DO YOU THINK WAS DRIVING THAT CAR THAT SMACKED INTO YOUR PRECIOUS JIM? IT WAS ME! THAT'S WHO! HAD TO TEACH YOU A LESSON! TOLD YOU NOT TO MESS WITH HUMANS." He looked at Sam...then at Alex. "NEITHER OF YOU ARE EXEMPT! YOU CAN NOW GO THROUGH THE REST OF YOUR LIVES WONDERING WHO WILL BE NEXT... WONDERING JUST HOW AND WHERE YOU'LL MEET THE END OF YOUR LIVES...BUT YOU WILL! I'LL SEE TO THAT! I DID IT TO JIM...AND I'LL DO IT TO YOU!"

Alex started to move forward, but Sam gave him a hard shove backwards. "THOSE ARE FIGHTING

WORDS, NEPTUNE!" he said. "YOU'LL NOT THREATEN ME! YOU'LL NOT THREATEN ANYONE WITH ME! YOU DON'T KNOW WHO YOU'RE MESSING WITH, BUSTER" Sam moved right in...right up to Neptune's face. He pointed first to Breeze then to Olympia. "THERE IS YOUR DAUGHTER! WONDERFUL GIRL! THERE IS OLYMPIA! MY WOMAN NOW...AND BREEZE'S MOTHER...AND YOU WILL LEAVE THEM... AND ALL OF US...ALONE! I CAME HERE TO BE FRIENDLY...BUT FIGHTING IS MY MIDDLE NAME." He balled up his fist. "READY?"

Neptune underestimated Sam, thought he wasn't used to the sea, fighting under water, or using his tail. Neptune slashed out at him as hard as he could with his tail. This did not catch Sam unawares like he thought.

Sam was ready! Instead of hitting Neptune with his fists, like it at first appeared he would...he took advantage of Neptune's being off-balance. He pushed himself off the ocean floor with one swift swish of his tail, lowered his head, and used his whole body as a battering ram to plow into Neptune's stomach area. This threw Neptune backwards and off balance and Sam used that to his advantage also...landing both fists into his face.

Olympia was awestruck. Never had she seen anyone stand up to Neptune. She had heard his harsh words... bragging about what happened to Jim. Anger boiled up inside her, and she could not contain herself. Neptune had broken his own rules...and she just had to do something about it. While Sam and Neptune were fighting, she snuck off and summoned the sharks that always policed her place....She told them what had happened and brought them back to where the fight was still going on. "NOW!" she commanded. "YOU'LL END THIS FIGHT RIGHT NOW!... NEPTUNE!...YOU ARE NOT WELCOME HERE ANY MORE!... STOP THE FIGHTING...RIGHT NOW! MY SHARKS WILL LISTEN TO ME. I'VE LIVED WITH THEM LONG ENOUGH!...YOU SAW TO THAT, BIG BOY!"

Sam kept up his guard but pulled back a bit.

Neptune knew Olympia well enough to know she meant business, and he was no match for a bunch of big-mouthed sharks...So he too stayed his hand. He had second thoughts about his angry words and inside wished he hadn't let slip out about what he did to Jim... but he said no more about it.

Olympia continued..."NOW!... NOW THAT I HAVE YOUR UNDIVIDED ATTENTION!... NEPTUNE, Alex, here wanted to meet you on good grounds.... Wanted to be your friend...Wanted to take Breeze for his own with your blessing. Think you've proved your intentions of being a father-in-law to him. I think you'd better just go. Now that I know you killed my Jimmy... I NEVER WANT TO SEE YOU AGAIN!... EVER! WHAT DO YOU THINK OF THAT?"

Neptune was outnumbered, and he knew it. He gave one last ultimatum. "OLYMPIA, MY DEAR, YOU ALWAYS WERE A GOOD ADVERSARY! I KNOW YOU HAVE TWO CHILDREN FROM THAT...THAT HUMAN, JIM...FLOATING AROUND HERE SOMEWHERE. YOU'D BETTER HOPE I DON'T FIND THEM!" With that, he turned on his tail and added, "SAM, DON'T THINK YOU AND I ARE

FINISHED YET! ANOTHER DAY!" He shook his fist as he turned and left. Then added..."ALEX!...THAT GOES FOR YOU TOO...SONNY BOY! STAY OUT OF MY WAY!"

Olympia put her arm around Sam. "You OK, Sam? No one has ever stood up to Neptune before. Do you know who he is? What he can do?"

"Yes, my sweet little mermaid. I know only too well who he is...and what he is...but I'll never allow him to hurt you again...not as long as I'm alive."

Neptune went straight back to Oceana...but not to stay. "Oceana!" he said with a stern voice. "I'm going to have to leave for a while. We won't be visiting Olympia any more...And she's NEVER allowed to come here." He puffed himself up as big as he could and added, "SHE WENT AND MARRIED A HUMAN. WHAT'S WORSE IS...BREEZE HAS DONE THE SAME THING. NOW... I'M GIVING YOU AN ORDER!... Oceana, YOU ARE NEVER TO SEE EITHER OLYMPIA...OR BREEZE AGAIN!" He glared at her. "IS THAT CLEAR? NEVER!" He turned on his tail, smiled slyly, and said, "NOW, I'M LEAVING FOR A WHILE...GOING TO TAKE CARE OF A FEW THINGS. YOU REMEMBER WHAT I'VE JUST TOLD YOU! DON'T GO THERE... IF YOU KNOW WHAT'S GOOD FOR YOU. YOU HEAR ME?"

Oceana heard all right. She wasn't happy about it either. Unlike Olympia, however. She said nothing. She just smiled. Olympia had been her friend for a lot of years. She raised Olympia's daughter, Breeze...and she loved Breeze dearly. Now...just because they got married to humans, she was restricted from seeing them. Suddenly, she was tired of being passive little Oceana. This time…she was going to follow Neptune to see what he was up to. She'd never had an order like this one and was not going to just wag her mermaid tail and take it.

Neptune went in the opposite direction than she expected. He didn't go towards Olympia's ship. He didn't go towards town or any of the places she knew he frequented. All the rest of the day and part of the next she followed him. At night, she moved up and stayed as close to him as she could to keep him in sight. By morning, he was traveling again and they were in a territory she'd never seen. Suddenly, it dawned on her where he was going. He was going to the Tridon! OH!…NO!

Breeze...the Mermaid

Chapter 27

Now, the Tridon was a wicked sea creature that could destroy both men and ships, a monstrous creature from the deep that Neptune had at his beck and calling to do the dirty work of killing men and destroying ships when he, himself did not want to dirty his hands. Unlike Mermen and Mermaids with their human-like upper features and their tail concealing human legs that could only be conjured up with the proper knowledge…the Tridon was of human form with a scaley body and fins that resemble that of a fish and a monstrous, ugly head with bulging eyes and hornes on top and was rendered in such a grotesque form that anyone looking upon this hideous sight for an extended period of time would be overcome by fear so intense that it could drive most men mad. Many fishermen have already been overcome with such fear that to this day, they are nothing more than mere vegetables with no meaning in life and no recollection of who they were. The Tridon is capable of doing deeds unthought of by men.

Oceana was beside herself with worry for her friends. From the way Neptune acted when he was with her, she was pretty sure he was going to get the Tridon and turn it loose on Olympia, the ship she lived in, the sharks because they threatened to attack him, Breeze, and the two humans they loved. The thought struck her like a bolt of lightening. If Neptune continued, this would mean the end of her beautiful daughter Breeze... the end for Olympia and for the humans as well.

She had to somehow get the courage to face Neptune and stop this madness. *What's the difference?* she thought. *What's the difference that they married humans?* Humans had never done anything wrong to her. The only other human she had really ever known was Jim, and he never did any harm to anything or anyone either. Actually he was very kind and helpful. For a long time she followed, wondering just how she would approach him. They were getting nearer to the Tridon's home. She had to confront him...now! Either that or rush back to warn her friends. No! That would take too long. She chose to confront Neptune...and it needed to be done NOW!

She increased her speed and swam right up behind him...was about to reach out and grab him to stop him so she could say something when a big, heavy steel net dropped down, almost hitting her, and fell over Neptune. Olympia quickly pulled back. She could see him fighting the net. With her mouth wide open in disbelief, she watched him struggle as they hauled him on board a big fishing boat and out of sight. Looking up at the ship more closely, she remembered the description that had been given. From all his boastings, she recognized it as the very same ship that had all the dolphins and whales penned up in little pools on the shoreline waiting for capture and slaughter.

Fear boiled up inside her as she pondered what to do. She knew Neptune was in trouble. At that moment; the only people she could turn to for help were the very people Neptune wanted to have killed. Dolphins and other sea creatures would be of no help. The Tridon!... Yes! She'd go there. Then she thought for a moment. The Tridon! That was another day or so away! BAD IDEA! She also remembered....It only obeyed Neptune, and Neptune was captured...and taken prisoner somewhere on that fishing boat. Now Olympia wished she had learned how to get legs when she had the chance. She could go into that ship and find him. She wished she had been more aggressive in her life and learned more about things Neptune did and tried to teach her. She had to go to Olympia...and hope she could get help. No telling what would happen to him while she was gone...but she had to try. Even that thought was a scary one. Olympia was a good day and a half's swim away, and she was already tired from following Neptune. He traveled a lot faster than she was used to, and all the way following him she was barely able to keep up.

Breeze always hitched rides on dolphins. Maybe she could do the same...but there were none around. With a fear in her heart for Neptune she turned and headed back toward Olympia and...hopefully some help.

Neptune couldn't believe some human was clever enough to actually capture him....But there he was, hanging in a net made of chains in a little bit of water... chains he couldn't break or get out of. They'd dropped him down hard, still in the net, into a hold partially filled with water. Now, there they all were, standing around on the deck looking down at him...pointing their fingers, laughing, and making ugly remarks.

Neptune roared with anger...but it did no good. He was not in the sea where the sound would carry. He was in the ship's hold...with water shallow enough for a human to wade in. It was the same hold those humans were going to use for the dolphins he caused them not to catch. He heard them bickering back and forth about what to do with him.

One human bent over, looked down into the hold, and said, "I think we ought to just kill him and get it over with. We can sell the body for a fortune. No one has seen a merman before. Whatever we do...we don't need to let him out of that net. I've got a feeling...if he's let out of that net...even if we shut him in the hold...he'll escape!"

That man was right, and Neptune hoped they would do just that...take the net away...but they didn't. They all agreed that he should remain in the chain net. Another fisherman was adamant that he should be kept healthy...

sold to a zoo or an experimental place for testing. One thought he needed to be tortured for making them lose all those dolphins and whales. Still another thought he might have special powers and wanted the hold shut up so he couldn't be seen and couldn't see or do anything.

They were all in the process of getting drunk. As the sun went down and they finished their bottles of booze…one after the other, they threw those bottles at Neptune…most of them hitting him because he had no defense. The drunker they got, the more things were thrown into that hold…hitting Neptune…shoes, drinking mugs, metal plates and saucers, anything they could get their hands on with some weight that that they could throw with a force. One guy even threw his air tanks and diving gear in there. Their loud, obscene remarks went on into the night until; one by one…they got so drunk they all passed out.

All was quiet as the sun came up. The cover was never put on the hold, and now what little water was in it was not only tainted with booze but heavily scattered with broken glass, trash, and various floating objects. Neptune couldn't move around very much because of the net….So there he was, in the middle of a fish hold, in the chain net…helpless. Looking up towards the deck, he couldn't see any movement…and he certainly didn't hear anything. He did see an occasional arm or leg hang over the edge but no one seemed to be close enough to it to fall in. Time seemed to move slowly. The sun rose higher, and he was getting more and more uncomfortable in that little bit of water. Some of the broken glass had found its way into his skin, making small, irritating cuts. Still, there was no sound from the humans on the deck.

Several hours later…towards evening when he could no longer see the sun, Neptune heard movement and voices. "SHUT THAT HOLD UP!" someone shouted. "JUST IGNORE WHAT'S DOWN THERE. THINK ABOUT ALL THE MONEY WE ALL LOST BECAUSE OF THAT…THAT…"

A very sloppy looking fisherman appeared and stood with his hands on his hips looking down at his captive prize. "THOUGHT YOU WERE PRETTY SMART… DID YOU? NOW HOW SMART ARE YOU?" He spat into the hold, pulled the cover over it, and left Neptune in the dark. "TIME TO GET UP, MATES! NEED TO GET THINGS TOGETHER! WE NEED TO BE SAILING OUT OF HERE. I'm thinking about selling that…that MONSTER in the hold…to the zoo or to science…whichever will bring the most money. Have to make some of the money back he cost us." Again, loud laughter filtered its way into the hold.

That statement got Neptune worried. He was going to call out, but after thinking about what went on last night, he thought better about it and said nothing. With that net still around him, there was no way to escape. For the first time in his life…he was trapped…and he hated it. Now he was in total darkness, and hearing their voices getting louder and louder told him they were getting drunk again. This time, no one bothered to look into where he was or throw anything at him. The chain netting was beginning to get heavy and was very irritating to his skin. He was getting weary because of little rest and no food. Time wore on, and soon the laughter began to cease. He knew now he was in serious trouble.

All this time, Oceana had been pushing with all her might to make it back to Olympia's. She tried several times to communicate with different batches of dolphins… with no luck. She had never really befriended them and now…when she needed their help so desperately they paid no attention to her. This caused her to push herself way beyond what she should have.

Two full, tiresome days after the shock of Neptune being captured and hauled onto the fishing boat, Oceana finally arrived at Olympia's door…totally exhausted. It took the last little bit of energy she had just to open the door…but no one was there. A feeling of total emptiness and despair took over as her limp body sank to the floor. There was no place else to go, and even if there had been, she was too weak to move anymore. How could they not be there? She needed them so badly! Neptune needed their help so badly…if he was still alive.

Chapter 28

As soon as Neptune left Olympia's…because of his angry words and harsh behavior, Sam suggested they all just be gone for a few days to allow him to cool off…so that's what they did.

Breeze was anxious to show Alex all her favorite places, but Alex had other ideas. "Sam!" he said. "Tell me what you think of this…"

Stopping his sentence, he turned to Breeze. "Sweetheart…I know Neptune is your father and all… but I don't feel at ease with him…I don't trust what he may do. I heard what he did to Olympia's late husband Jim, and I want to make real sure that doesn't happen to any of us. I love you…but I don't want to lose you because of his temper."

Breeze put her arm around Alex. "I understand. I don't want to lose you either. What do you want to do?"

Turning back to Sam, he continued, "Sam, I think we need to plan some sort of safety net in case Neptune does come back and follows through with all his angry threats."

Olympia took a deep breath. "You don't know what you suggest, Alex. Neptune is not just an ordinary being. He is king of his domain. Has the last say on everything in it. Everything in the ocean…every fish…every living sea creature…is under his command and lives according to his order. He has made the rules, and it is all at his command. Then, there is the Tridon. This great sea creature is also at his command, will obey no one but Neptune…and the Tridon can wipe out whole ships, men and all. This creature has such a grotesque form that anyone looking upon it for an extended period of time is overcome by fear so intense that it can drive them insane…leaving them with no meaning in life and no recollection of who they are. It is capable of doing deeds unthought of by humans or mermen. Alex, Neptune IS KING OF THE SEA!"

Sam had heard enough. "I'm with you, Alex. Looks to me like…" He hesitated for a moment, took a deep breath, and continued, "…looks to me like, since you say Neptune is king of the sea, we'll just use his own energy against him. He is NOT king of the land, and Alex and I are land creatures. You, Olympia, and Breeze here are our wives…makes you part of us now. We'll just arrange it to where…as far as Neptune is concerned, we are now ALL land creatures." He gave Olympia a big hug. "Seems to me, since he ran over Jim with a car…he must have violated his own rules. We need to plan for that because it is obvious he doesn't play by his own rules."

Sam could see Olympia was upset with his statement about Jim. The sadness showed on her face. He pulled her close for a big hug. "Sweetums, I'm not out to hurt anyone!...Just don't want anyone of us hurt either...and I aim to stay alive so I can hug you every day and put a smile on that pretty face of yours. Let's all go to town...See what we can see."

Alex smiled and put his hand on Sam's shoulder. "Sam! Remember that old ship we all went through? I saw some kegs of blasting powder in there. You think they'd still be any good?"

Sam pressed his lips together. "Don't know! It's worth a try. If I remember right, they were all sealed. Be a good idea to go by there first."

Turning to Olympia he added, "You suppose we could hide that powder somewhere in or under the dance hall?"

"Of course!" Olympia answered. "But, since it's on the way...because of what's happened. I would like to get Willow and Nautilus and take them with us. I know Neptune doesn't know they're mine...but they'll come to the ship looking for me and I won't be there. If he caught them coming...he'd..."

Sam kissed Olympia on the cheek. "Little Darlin', I think you're right."

He turned and looked at Breeze. "Think you can get them? No one will think anything of it if you just wanted them to keep you company for a while."

Breeze was really excited. "Can I leave now? Where do I bring them? Ah....Is it OK if I tell them—"

"TELL THEM NOTHING!" Sam commanded. "The less they know right now...the better. Don't even tell them where you're going…just meet us under the dance hall. Timing should work out just about right. Think you can do that?"

Giving Alex a quick kiss, she answered, "Of course! All I have to do is find them." With one quick flip of her tail she was gone.

Reaching the old ship, they found several sealed wooden kegs of blasting powder that still looked to be in good condition. At first, Sam was delighted. Then he looked at Alex and Olympia and shook his head. "This is all great! But there's no way we can carry all these."

Olympia pondered the thought for a few minutes then asked, "Just what did you want to do with these?"

Sam put his arm around Olympia. "Sweetums, where do you suppose Neptune is going to come when he chooses to do his dirty work?… YOUR PLACE! That's where. We need to get all this back to that old ship you've been staying in."

"MY SHIP?" She looked at him inquisitively and added, "DO YOU KNOW WHAT YOU'RE SAYING? DO YOU KNOW HOW MUCH STUFF I HAVE IN THERE? DO YOU?"

Noticing how upset she was at the idea, Sam added. "We can go back right now and take the things you want and need out of there, put them in a safe place…. THEN come back for the powder and things we need in town."

Olympia put her head in her hands for a few minutes. She had been forced to live there for a long time…and now Sam was talking about blowing it all up. After taking a deep breath she agreed, and they started back toward the ship.

Only a couple days had gone by, but they knew they needed to hurry. No telling when Neptune would be back or what he'd be back with. Who knows...Maybe even the Tridon.

When they got there, Olympia pulled out several large pieces of old sails and laid them down on the sand outside. It didn't take long for her things to be piled on them. On her last trip inside she brought out a large piece of canvas wrapped around something. I'll just carry this myself, if you don't mind."

"Not as much stuff as I thought." Sam smiled. "We can probably get all this into an apartment on land before night comes."

"Um...Sam!" Olympia said, hoping to change his mind. "There's another old abandoned ship about half day's swim from here. No one goes there because it's so ugly. This stuff has been in the water for a long, long time, and I'm afraid it would all be ruined if we just...all of a sudden took it out and put in an apartment or someplace on land. What I have in my arms would be all right to do that with, but not the rest of my things." She could see Sam was reluctant to go to another ship.

"What if Neptune finds your things there?" Sam asked. "You KNOW he will destroy everything you have!"

"He'll not go there!" Olympia smiled. "Its way out of the way of everything and not on any path anyone takes."

They followed Olympia to an old, half rusted-out submarine that had a hole blown out in one side of it.... And yes! It was ugly! VERY ugly!

Sam decided it was best to stay the night there because the sun was down and it was a very dark night.

Olympia was a bit worried about Breeze bringing Willow and Nautilus to the dance studio without her being there…but she said nothing.

Little did she know Breeze was having trouble finding Willow and Nautilus so she'd decided to stay over night where Neptune and Oceana usually stayed.

In the early morning, Breeze saw them. They were headed towards Olympia's. She stopped them, almost blurted out that Olympia wanted to see them in town… but caught herself. "Hey, guys!" she said, as she smiled and stopped dead in front of their path. "It's been a long time. What do you say we just do something together today?"

"No way!" Nautilus answered. "We used to be great friends…But you haven't been around in so long…NO WAY!"

Willow shook her head in agreement, and they started to leave.

"Wait a minute! Just…WAIT A MINUTE!" Breeze faced them, put one hand on Nautilus and the other on Willow, and said, "I'm going to tell you something right now, something that you're not going to believe…But you'd better…because it's the truth. Olympia—"

They both broke into her sentence in unison, opened their eyes wide with surprise and said, "OLYMPIA! You know OLYMPIA?"

This got their attention. Breeze remembered she wasn't supposed to tell why she wanted them to go with

Breeze...the Mermaid

her...but at this point it seemed the only way. "If you'll come with me...I'll tell you all."

That was all it took, and they were off towards town.

Sam was ready to go early the next morning. "Think the best thing to do is go back and get the powder...plant it around and in that ship of yours, Olympia...THEN go on into town. Save a lot of time that way." He looked at the bundle she was carrying. "Can't you just leave that here? It's going to be hard enough getting all the powder where we want it without you carrying...THAT!"

For a long time, Olympia searched the old sub for just the right place. Finally finding one, she said, "OK! I'm ready now!"

On the way back to get the blasting powder, Olympia led them away from where they were supposed to be going, right into the path of several huge sharks. This scared Alex, and he became angry that she'd done this... said he didn't want to travel with something that was going to eat him. Olympia explained, "These sharks have huge mouths. Each one can carry a keg of the powder...save us a lot of trouble.

Sam opened his eyes wide at that statement. "HUH!...And just what's going to happen when one of them decided to close their jaws? BOOM!"

Olympia caressed his face, gave him a big kiss, and said. "I know my sharks...Lived with them for a lot of years. Trust me!" After she spent a few moments alone with them, they followed her the rest of the way to the ship.

Sam and Alex busied themselves putting one keg after the other into the sharks' mouths. They took one under each arm themselves and headed to Olympia's ship.

The kegs were quickly and carefully hidden around and in the ship. Olympia thanked the sharks for their help and dismissed them...Then they headed towards town. They had no way of knowing that Oceana was on her way to Olympia's and would be lying there, exhausted, in that ship within the next couple hours.

Breeze, along with Willow and Nautilus, had barely made it to the dance hall when Olympia, Alex and Sam showed up.

Nautilus was a bit angry when he approached Olympia. He got right in her face and asked, "All these years! ALL THESE YEARS! We didn't know Breeze was our sister. HOW COULD YOU? WHY DIDN'T YOU TELL US? I think you've been very unfair!"

Olympia put her arms around him and answered, "Son, if I had told you...you might not be here right now...with us..." There was a long pause. "I don't know how to tell you this..." She paused again and looked at Breeze.

"Breeze! Since you took it upon yourself to tell them about you being their sister...did you tell them the rest? Just what all DID you tell them?"

Breeze looked first at Willow, then at Nautilus, then right into Olympia's eyes. "At first they didn't want to come with me so...I told them you wanted to see them. As soon as your name was mentioned...I had to tell them I was their sister...that Neptune was my father...But that's ALL I told them."

Olympia took a deep breath and continued, "You both know your father, Jim, got killed by someone driving a car, don't you?"

They nodded their heads. "Yes!"

"The driver of the car was Neptune...And he hit your father on purpose."

They were both stunned, and it showed on their faces.

"Now!" Olympia continued. "He is angry because I married Sam, and Breeze has married Alex...angry because they are both humans. He and Sam got into a fight because Sam stood up for us all. I summoned the sharks to stop it. Neptune was out numbered...left in a rage...And now...all our lives are in danger. This is why we are not at my ship. This is why you were sent for...So you would not go to my place and find nothing there when you came to visit me. Sam wants us all to be a family...together... and that's what I want too...and I'm hoping that's what you'll want too."

They both threw their arms around Olympia. Willow spoke. "I've always wanted this. I never really fully understood why you gave us to someone else to be raised...Thought it was just because you were sad and alone."

"No, my dear! That was not the case. I would have liked nothing better than to have kept you with me...all of you. Neptune took Breeze because she was his. I was afraid for your lives, so that's why you weren't with me. That's why I asked you to come to me secretly, without anyone knowing...because I feared for your lives. Now, Neptune WILL come back to that ship...with his anger and whatever or whoever he brings along...probably the Tridon! We will be ready for them. I want us all to be a happy family...not living in fear of who we can see, where we can go, or who we happen to want to be with...human or merman."

Nautilus was angry! He turned to Sam and asked, "Sam, you actually stood up to Neptune? WOW! NO ONE DOES THAT! When are we going to fight?"

Sam put his hand on Nautilus shoulder. "We're not, son! Not if I can help it. Let's just say...we're ready for him if he comes again in anger. I appreciate your bravery...But you've still got some growing to do that I'd like to be part of...OK? Now, let's get inside and get some street clothes on." He looked at Willow and Nautilus, thought for a minute and asked, "You two do know how to get legs...don't you?"

They both smiled. Willow answered, "Of course we do, silly! WE'RE HALF HUMAN!"

"Good!" Sam added, "Then...let's get this done! Get what we need and head back to that old ship of Olympia's."

Sam seemed to know what was needed, so they didn't spend much time in town. They did take a few minutes to drop their clothes off back at the dance studio. Olympia had to take time to introduce everyone because they had to walk right through a dance class session.

Once through the trap door and under the building, Sam passed out little bundles to everyone. They all quickly conjured up their tails and left. Olympia was adamant about warning all the sharks and sea creatures that lived around her place...said it was only decent that they not get killed or injured while this was taking place.

Sam said there'd be plenty of time for that AFTER everything was set correctly.

Chapter 29

When they reached the ship, Sam and Alex took the little packages and started to make their rounds to take care of each keg and made sure everything was set just right. They didn't even get the first keg taken care of when Breeze rushed out the door yelling, "YOU'VE GOT TO COME IN HERE!…NOW!…OCEANA IS HERE!…LYING ON THE FLOOR!…RIGHT IN FRONT OF THE DOOR!…HURRY!"

They dropped what they were doing and rushed to the door. There was Oceana, lying limp on the floor. Olympia was in the process of picking her up to hold her in her arms. "What happened?" Olympia asked. "What are you doing here? I thought Neptune said you couldn't come here any more. WHAT HAPPENED TO YOU? YOU LOOK AWFUL!"

Oceana grabbed Olympia's hair with her hand and tried to pull herself up. "We've got to go to him! Got to go now! They'll kill him!"

Breeze put her hand on Oceana's forehead. "What are you talking about? Are you sick?"

"NO!...NO!" Oceana took a minute to catch her breath. "I'm not sick...I...I...YOU'VE GOT TO HELP HIM! YOU'VE JUST GOT TO! OLYMPIA, THEY'LL KILL HIM!" She pulled hard on Olympia's hair. "PLEASE!"

Sam came up close. "Did I hear right...Someone's going to be killed? Who? Let's hear the whole story. What's happened to you? You look worn out, Oceana. Slow down and tell us...real slow. What's wrong?"

Oceana began to cry. "I know what he said...I know what he was going to do...but....He's been taken captive, and they'll kill him."

"OCEANA!" Olympia looked her sternly in the eye. "Crying is not going to help. Now, if you don't tell us...right now...we're going on about our business. You can rest up a bit and tell us later."

"OH! NO! I have to tell you now! Neptune...I know what he said. I know...But...I love him, and now he's been captured by the fishermen that captured all the dolphins and whales...and they're going to kill him. I just know it. You've just got to help."

Sam straightened up and asked, "Why? Give me one good reason why we should go save help someone that's out to kill us? Don't think so, Oceana! We've just been to town...set this old ship up to protect ourselves from that...that...Oceana, HOW COULD YOU LOVE SOMETHING THAT THREATENS TO KILL HIS OWN...BANS YOU FROM SEEING YOUR FRIENDS...RAN OVER OLYMPIA'S MAN? DON'T THINK SO! OCEANA, I think what's happening to Neptune will just save US all a lot of trouble."

Oceana began crying uncontrollably. Other than that, there was complete silence for a long time. Finally Olympia put her arms around Sam and spoke. "Sam!... Alex!... I know how you both feel. I know how I feel... but...not trying to save Neptune wouldn't make things right. It would make us know...for the rest of our lives... that we could've done something and didn't. Believe it or not, Neptune has a good side...A very good side. Do you know why those fishermen want to kill him?" She bit her lip...looked at everyone and continued, "They captured him because Breeze told him someone was capturing all the dolphins and whales to make money off them, putting them for sale and putting them on exhibit...or being killed. He took Breeze and me and several others, and he went to their rescue. Most all of them were saved.

"Those fishermen lost a lot of money. They also lost their pride because their mission was not carried out. I know what he did to Jim, and it breaks my heart, but I think we should do what we can to rescue him."

Sam took a deep breath. "Sweetums, if that's what you want...then that's what I'll do. "You with me, Alex?"

Alex turned to Breeze. "That what you want, too?"

Breeze looked around. "Yes...BUT...I'M GOING WITH YOU. I'M NOT STAYING HERE. I CAN HELP TOO, YOU KNOW." She turned to Oceana. "Oceana, where is he?"

"About two days from here. I tried to get those dolphins of yours to give me a ride, but they paid no attention to me. I guess I deserved that because I've never paid any attention to them. I know where he is, but I don't think I have the strength to lead you there."

"The dolphins will give you a ride if I ask them to." Breeze smiled. "Let's go!"

"Exactly where is Neptune being held, Oceana?" Sam asked. "Is he on land or on a ship?"

"On a ship! On that same...I just know it's the same ship that was going to take all the dolphins and whales. I was mad because of what he said to everyone and decided I would no longer just sit back and let things go by...So, I followed him. He was going to the Tridon, Breeze! He was going to get the Tridon. He didn't know I was following. I had just finished deciding I would try to talk to him....Swam up real close to him when a big, heavy chain net was dropped over him. It almost hit me. He was carried up high in the air and then put into that fishing boat that was going to haul off all the dolphins and whales."

"That's enough!" Sam said. "Let's go! Think I'm going to need some help with this one. Nautilus, think you and Willow can go back and get some help? We'll need several large whales also. When we get there, we need to attract their attention, and I can't think of a better way than to have the ship headed out to sea when it's supposed to be anchored."

"I CAN DO ALL OF THAT!" Nautilus said excitedly. "I HELPED NEPTUNE SAVE ALL THOSE DOLPHINS AND....AND THE WHALES TOO!" He had a grin on his face that reached from one ear to the other as he spoke. "YOU'LL SEE! I CAN BE THE BEST HELPER YOU'VE EVER HAD!" Turning to Willow, he added, "WILLOW, GO HOME AND

GET EVERYONE THAT HELPED WITH THE DOLPHINS' RESCUE AND GET THEM FAST! I'll go get the whales. Oh! How about some octopuses so those stinking fisherman can't see what we're doing?"

Sam laughed and gave him a pat on the back. "Yeah, son! I can see you and I are going to get along just fine. Do you know where we're all going to meet?"

"Well...NO!"

"Where DO we meet you? I don't know where we're going either," Willow asked.

"Just hurry and go. Bring all the...ah...everyone," Sam stuttered with his answer. He was not used to working with mermen, whales, dolphins, and sharks. "Well—"

Breeze cut in. "I know where we can meet...By the giant clams...Near where we live. Oh! By the way, Alex, Sam! Please stay away from those clams! They'll have you for dinner!" She laughed and went about helping to get things together.

Breeze yelled out after them as they were leaving, "We'll be passing by there real soon and will need everything together by then."

"Alex!" Sam exclaimed. "Looks like we're going to have to undo that keg of blasting powder we set up.... Glad we didn't get all of them hooked up. Olympia, I think we'll need your sharks to come along with us too. Just bring them along and we'll load a keg in each of their mouths as they pass by. Alex and I will pick up the rest of the gear. If it took Oceana two days to get there, we'll have to make it in half that time...sooner if we can."

"Oceana, Are you strong enough to ride one of those dolphins?"

"Yes!" she answered. "Yes, I am…Even if you have to tie me on. That's it! That's exactly what I want you to do! Tie me on! That's what I'll have to do. I'll lead you to where that fishing boat is. Just tie me on! We've got to hurry!"

Breeze did just that…tied her onto a fast dolphin… Then she asked the other dolphins to tag along for support in case they were needed for something.

"WHAT A CREW!" Alex exclaimed as they drew near to the giant clams.

Sam looked around at his newly recruited ARMY and laughed. Just stayed in one spot…waved his tail back and forth, and laughed. "Gang!" He laughed some more. "This may be the end of me! Who knows!"

For a few minutes, Sam didn't move. He just shook his head. Then he swam around his 'crew' and looked at Olympia tied onto a dolphin. He shook his head some more when he looked at all the sharks with deadly blasting powder in their big toothy jaws. *Oh!* He thought. *What a mess if one of them decides to bite down.* He looked at the mermen Willow had selected… then cast his eyes on the sidelines were the large whales were towering over everyone. Sam's eyes got as big as saucers as he swam up close to them. He felt dwarfed by their huge size. Just beyond and hiding behind the whales were half a dozen octopuses. Sam just couldn't help it. He shook his head back and forth. "You're right, Alex! This may be the end of us all." He couldn't contain himself any longer. He shook his head back and forth and roared with laughter. "If only the guys on the circuit could see me now! Then he added, "They ought to get THIS in the newspapers! EVERYONE READY? LET'S MARCH…AH…SWIM!…AH…

"HECK! LET'S JUST GET OUT OF HERE!"

Following Oceana, Sam and Alex were in the lead. Sam just couldn't help himself. "Son!" he said to Alex. "I've been at war. I've been in lots of battles. I've almost lost my life a few times." He almost spat the words out as he looked back. "This is worse than NOAH! We're supposed to fight? With…THIS?" More laughter! "Just LOOK at them, Alex! I'm supposed to be the leader here. Leader of…WHAT?"

Olympia swam up and put her arm around him. "Sam! You really don't know what you have here. Those whales don't think we need the blasting powder. They're wanting to ram the ship from all sides right now and sink it…Said it would be much more fun. The octopuses agreed…Said they would like to really murky up the water after the whales got finished."

"SHUT UP! OLYMPIA!" Sam laughed some more as he reached out and grabbed her. Giving her a big kiss, he added, "Maybe I'll just lag behind and watch the fun. For the life of me…I don't see how we're going to pull this off."

Olympia rubbed close to him and smiled as she swam off. "You're just not used to our water-ways. I'll help here! I'm good at this kind of stuff!"

"Oh, no you don't! When we catch site of that… that fishing boat…you, Breeze, Oceana, and Willow are lagging behind." He puffed himself up, much as Neptune would have done if he were in this situation. "This is MEN'S work! NOT…Ah…" Looking around

Breeze...the Mermaid

he added. "Well!...This just ISN'T FEMALE WORK!"

Sam swam out ahead and started muttering to himself. "Can't believe this whole thing! Here I am! Big...Strong Samson! Prize wrestler! Champion boxer! Winner of grand awards! Going to SAVE some creep I don't even know...after he threatened my life. MERMEN! Whoever heard of a MERMAN WARRIOR? Sharks! Sharks that can kill with one bite...carrying explosives in their teeth...And octopuses! My! My! Oh My!"

"HEY, GANG!" he yelled as he turned around. "WHAT DO YOU THINK THIS IS HERE...A PICNIC? LET'S GET A MOVE ON! PICK UP THE PACE! YOU ALL THINK WE'RE GOING TO A SLUMBER PARTY? WE HAVE A BATTLE TO WAGE HERE! PICK UP YOUR TIME!" Sam looked at Oceana up there, tied onto a dolphin, shook his head, and added, "JUST SEE IF YOU CAN KEEP UP WITH ME AND...OCEANA!"

"You tied on there OK, Oceana?"

"Yes...And I wish we'd go faster. If anything happens to Neptune...I..."

"Don't you worry, Oceana. In spite of it all...we're going to save him! Come on! Let's show them some speed!"

The moon came up bright and full even before the sun was all the way down, so Sam decided to keep moving as long as they could see.

"THERE IT IS! THERE IT IS!" Oceana yelled.

In the dim moonlight they could see the outline of a large fishing boat...all lit up.

"TIME TO STOP FOR A REST! A TIRED ARMY IS WORSE THEN NO ARMY AT ALL!" Sam was shouting instructions again. "GET SOME SLEEP…OR WHATEVER YOU DO. WHEN THE SUN STARTS TO COME UP…WE'LL MAKE OUR MOVE."

Oceana was upset. "But…WE'RE HERE!… HE'S THERE!… CAN'T WE…JUST DO IT NOW?"

"No, we're going to rest. I want everyone at their best. Oh, boy!" he muttered as he gazed upon the fishing boat. "This boat is bigger than I thought."

"Alex! You OK to swim around this boat with me… Scope the surroundings?"

"Sure! Let's go!"

Chapter 30

Breeze never was never one to take orders very well… never had been. She was a bit upset about Sam's statement. "Breeze, Oceana, and Willow are lagging behind." She'd never been the 'lagging behind' type, and she wasn't about to start now. Nudging Willow, she whispered, "Willow, I'm not staying here! Someone needs to know what I'm doing…and I'm trusting you to keep my secret."

"WHAT?" Willow yelled.

Breeze put her hand over Willow's mouth. "SSSh! They'll all hear you!"

"What are you doing? There's nowhere to go and nothing to do way out here!" she whispered back.

"I'm going on that ship!"

"YOU'RE WHAT?"

"I said, sssh! You bring attention to us, and someone will stop me. I'm going to get one of those whales to help me, and I'm going on that ship. My father is on there…and when this ruckus Sam has planned starts up…he may get hurt. I'm going to sneak on there and rescue him. Then, we'll just jump off the ship. I know this type of fishermen. Right now, they're probably all drunk and passed out on the deck."

"You can't do that! You'll get caught, Breeze! I can't let you do that!"

"Willow, YOU can't stop me! Don't try to stop me! Trust me! I know what I'm doing!"

"Oh, no!" Willow sighed as she watched Breeze swim up to one of the big whales. Next thing she knew…there was Breeze, with land legs, standing on the whale's back with her hands on her hips and her hair blowing in the wind…headed towards the fishing boat. Her insides sank. She just knew that would be the last time she ever saw Breeze.

The whale swam as near to the boat as it could and slowed down next to a fishing net that was draping over the side. Breeze grabbed onto the net and started climbing…climbed all the way up the side of the boat till she could see over the edge. She was right! There they all were…all drunk! "Hmm!" she mumbled to herself. "This is going to be easier than I thought."

Quietly she tiptoed across the ship, right by the passed out fishermen. She saw the chain hoist that Oceana mentioned. It was hanging over one of their fish holding tanks. Being very careful where she stepped so as not to make any noise…she made her way over to that tank. Daylight was on its way, but it still was not light enough. She could barely see inside. Nothing but a little water, lots of broken bottles, and someone's diving tanks. She looked in the other holding tanks. Nothing! No Neptune!

Now, she was getting worried. What had they done with her father? She cautiously went down the steps into the lower levels. No Neptune! Now she was really upset and getting angry. What had they done with her father? After searching the whole ship from stem to stern, she realized he was no longer there.

On her way up the steps she was met by one of the drunken fishermen. He stopped dead in his tracks... Surprised to see such a beautiful young thing with no clothes on standing there on the steps in front of him. Breeze took advantage of that shock and pushed him off the steps. He went tumbling onto the floor beneath. She didn't wait to see if he would come after her or not...just ran to the edge of the deck and dove off; gaining her tail back while she was still in the air.

Breeze couldn't have timed her dive more perfectly. She landed in the water right in front of Sam and Alex and surprised the heck out of them! "HE'S NOT THERE!" she yelled. "HE'S NOT THERE!"

Alex took her in his arms. "HONEY! WHAT ARE YOU DOING HERE? WHAT DID YOU JUST DO? WERE YOU JUST ON THAT BOAT?"

"YES! Yes, I was!"

Sam looked at Breeze and shook his head. "Guess I was wrong about you. Should never have told you to 'lag behind'...should've had you help scope the ship with us."

"Sorry, Sam! I'm not very good at being left behind. Alex can tell you that." She looked at them one at a time. "Listen, guys! Neptune is NOT on that ship! I don't know what they've done with him...but he's just not there. I looked all over the ship." She thought for a minute. "Think the ship needs to be blown up anyway. There's nothing but scum on board, and as long as they're alive we're all in trouble. I had to push one guy down the steps in order to get off that ship."

"YOU DID WHAT?" Alex asked. "LISTEN, LITTLE WIFE! I know you don't like to take orders… but I want you to stop taking chances! I don't want to lose you!" He gathered her in his arms for a big hug.

"What I'm worried about…" Breeze continued, "…is…WHAT DID THEY DO WITH MY FATHER?"

Sam looked at his…ARMY and scratched his head. "Tell me again why they wanted Neptune and what they did that was so bad. I hate to be judge and jury here. I want everyone's opinion."

Before a word could be said, a loud blast was heard. Water sprayed high up above the other side of the ship, and all the fishermen on the ship started running around and yelling. Olympia counted her sharks. "ONE OF MY SHARKS IS MISSING! DID ANYONE TELL IT TO DO THAT?"

No one said a word. They just looked at the other sharks still holding the barrels of blasting powder in their mouths.

Sam took a deep breath. "Guess I have my answer! OK! Here we go!" He turned to Olympia. "My dear, I really don't know how to talk to…to sharks! Could you…"

Olympia smiled. "Be glad to, my dear. What do you want them to do?"

"Well, I was going to secretly place the charges in just the right places BEFORE those fishermen knew what we were doing. Not going to be so easy now I'm afraid."

"LOOK! LOOK AT THE SHIP!" It was Breeze yelling with glee. "WE DON'T HAVE TO USE THE REST OF THE BLASTING POWDER! THAT SHIP'S SINKING FROM WHAT THAT POOR SHARK DID...JUST LOOK!"

Sure enough! The boat was sinking all right...going down smoothly and evenly...just like something was slowly sucking it under the water. The fishermen began lowering their smaller boats, but as soon as each boat was set into the water it was sucked under...in a strange way...just like the big fishing boat was doing...slowly just sinking with no leaks and no water coming inside. When the water reached the top of the sides of the little boats, it just overflowed and they went under.

"I've never seen such a thing!" Alex exclaimed. He stared in disbelief at the disaster happening in front of him. "Did you see that? DID YOU SEE THAT? ARE YOU ALL WATCHING? THOSE BOATS ARE SINKING! They're being pulled under by something... SUCKED UNDER!"

By now, the deck of the boat was only a couple feet above the water. It was obvious the fishermen were stunned...not believing their eyes. Here was the ship slowly sinking...about one hundred feet away from where the 'army' was secretly watching.

"I'm not going to allow even one of those guys to get away!" Alex exclaimed. "Not one!"

"Don't think you'll have to worry about that." Sam added, "I've never seen anything like this. I know that one little blast didn't do all this! Couldn't have!"

Oceana untied herself and slipped off the dolphin. "I'm OK now!" she said. "Wonder what's happening to it all? And…WHERE'S MY NEPTUNE? If that ship goes down, we may never find him." She started crying again.

Breeze put her arms around Oceana. "He was not on the ship, Oceana…and I don't think there's a one of those guys that would tell us where he is or what they've done with him. You'll have to be strong. YOU have to be strong! We may never see Neptune again. I'll always be here for you Oceana."

When she heard that statement, Oceana totally lost control and let loose with loud, screeching cries of sorrow. Olympia and Willow took her way back behind everyone.

They all stared in awe as the water began slowly seeping over the edge of the fishing boat's deck. It was obvious the fishermen were scared out of their wits. Most of them just stood there dumbfounded. One by one they jumped into the water, only to be sucked under and never seen again.

"I've never seen or heard of anything like this before!" Sam commented. "Seen ships sink…Seen airplanes sink…Never seen anything like this!" He scratched his head again as he continued staring at the fast sinking fishing boat.

Now…the deck's floor was completely under water. Only the captain's cabin and some other taller objects were still visible. Some of the fishermen started climbing the rigging. A couple of them managed to get on top of the little cabin with the steering wheel in it. Others were just standing there on the deck…in the water...as if in a trance, yelling and cursing at the water. They'd all watched what happened to their pals who'd stepped overboard and knew this was to be their end. It was written in their faces. One by one they did jump into the water...and were...just like their friends before them...immediately sucked into the depths of the ocean. Finally, only the rigging was left. There were a couple fishermen on it and each of them were sucked down with the ship. It went down without even so much as a ripple or a gurgle...like it had never been there.

For a long time Breeze, Alex, Sam, Nautilus, and all the others were left staring in the direction of where the fishing boat had been...and were soon joined by Olympia and Willow. "Oceana would rather be by herself right now," Olympia said, in a sad voice. "She's lost what means the most to her and just wants to be alone."

Finally it was Sam that broke the silence. "I don't know what to do about finding Neptune. Something tells me he's not dead! I just can't picture him dead!" He put his arms around Olympia. "Sweetums, I really hate to lose all this blasting powder but somehow, I just don't feel it would be a good idea to take it all the way back to your place!"

Before the request could be made for the sharks to dispose their kegs of blasting powder, loud squalling sounds came to their ears and almost hurricane-force winds began blowing the waters ahead of them... blowing the ocean water high to each side as if to open a path. Suddenly appearing in that path was Neptune, riding on a giant sea horse with some sort of staff or spear in his hand...held high above his head. "COME TO SAVE ME, DID YOU? ME! NEPTUNE! KING OF THE SEA! RULER OF ALL THE OCEANS!" He dismounted in front of them and conjured back his tail. With a fierce voice he bellowed out his statement. "SAM!... ALEX!... JUST WHAT DO YOU THINK

YOU'RE DOING HERE?" He puffed himself up as big as he could. "WHAT DID I TELL YOU LAST TIME I SAW THE TWO OF YOU?" Glaring at Sam, he added, "TOLD YOU, SAM!... THAT YOU HAVEN'T SEEN THE LAST OF ME!... AND HERE I AM! WHAT DO YOU THINK OF THAT, SAM?"

Sam was not the type of person that is easily intimidated. "NEPTUNE! YOU BET I REMEMBER YOUR PARTING WORDS! REMEMBER THEM REAL WELL!" Being the type of person he was, Sam added, "What DO you think I'm doing here, Neptune? What do you think ALL of us are doing here?" He thought for a minute, and then asked, "How did YOU know we came to save you? You weren't on the ship. Breeze snuck off and checked. YOU were not there!"

Neptune laughed. "OF COURSE I WASN'T THERE! PLAYED DEAD! THAT'S WHAT I DID! PLAYED DEAD SO THEY'D TAKE ME OUT OF THAT HOLD...SO I WOULDN'T STINK. NOW, THAT'S where they made their little mistake! Soon as they took that chain cage off me...I was gone and out of sight." He smiled. "Brought the Tridon back with me. Yes, I did! Sam!... Alex!... you ever SEE a Tridon? Ever meet up with a Tridon? What do you think took that ship...and all those men under the water the way it did? Ever see anything like that? Course not!" He leaned over them both. "THE TRIDON! THAT'S WHO! ALWAYS AT MY COMMAND! WILL HEAR NO ONE ELSE BUT ME! I'M KING OF THE SEA AND RULER OF THE OCEANS!" He bent lower...looking at both Sam and Alex. "Where do you think that leaves the both OF YOU?"

Sam straightened up to his full height and made himself as big as he could. Then he looked Neptune right in the eye. "RIGHT HERE, NEPTUNE! RIGHT HERE NEXT TO YOU! GLAD YOU'RE OK! NOW ALEX AND I WON'T HAVE TO WASTE ANY MORE ENERGY TRYING TO SAVE YOU!"

Neptune glared down at the two of them for being so bold as to stand there facing him...looked toward the back of the 'army' they had brought, and noticed Oceana. "OCEANA!... My little jewel of the sea! GET OVER HERE! THINK YOU AND I MAY JUST WANT TO CHECK OUT THE DEPTHS OF THIS PART OF THE OCEAN...AFTER I TAKE CARE OF SOME...UNFINISHED BUSINESS!" He motioned for the big sea horse to leave....And it did.

Oceana was instantly by his side. "Just a minute... Oceana! Not so fast! I have to deal with Sam...and Alex first. Swim aside while I take care of this...unfinished business!

"Now! NOW!... LISTEN UP, EVERYONE! NOW THAT I'VE GATHERED YOU ALL HERE...THERE'S SOMETHING I NEED TO DO...AND SAY...AND I WANT YOU ALL AS MY WITNESSES!" He looked first at Sam, then at Alex. "NEVER HAS ANYONE COME RIGHT UP TO MY FACE AND STOOD UP TO ME BEFORE!... NEVER!" With a voice so loud it could probably knock down a mountain, Neptune yelled, "TRIDON!... HEAR ME! FROM THIS DAY FORTH...THESE TWO MERMEN...ER...MEN ARE MY RIGHT HAND...AND MY LEFT HAND! IF THEY NEED YOU...YOU ARE TO BE AT THEIR COMMAND! YOU DID A GOOD JOB TODAY...

BUT I AM IN NO FURTHER NEED OF YOU RIGHT NOW. YOU MAY GO!"

The Tridon had kept himself unseen, as he usually does, lingering down deep in the ocean. Upon hearing Neptune's command a huge ripple appeared on the ocean surface and like a breeze through the window... he was gone!

"I AM NOT FINISHED SPEAKING!" Neptune continued. "I MADE THE LAW...AND I BROKE MY OWN LAW. SO...I AM GOING TO CORRECT THAT...AND MAKE A NEW LAW. BREEZE! COME OVER HERE! You come over here too, Olympia. I especially want you both to hear this. I COMMITTED THE MURDER OF A HUMAN ON LAND...A LONG TIME AGO. THIS WILL NEVER HAPPEN AGAIN. THIS WAS BECAUSE OF MY OWN SELFISHNESS. Olympia! I know you have two children by that human. They are welcome! You are welcome! All are welcome in my kingdom as long as rules are obeyed and there is no contention. SAM! ALEX! If you choose to do so...you are my right hand and left hand in my kingdom. None other has ever had such bravery as to stand up to me! Have me threaten to do them harm...and STILL come to rescue me. OH! ONE LAST COMMAND!" He looked first at Alex...then at Sam. "Would you two mind telling those sharks to deposit the explosives gently on the ocean floor...before they blow us all up?"

THE END...

Sylvia Fraley

About the Author

Born in Detroit, Michigan, Sylvia had moved twenty-one times by the time she graduated high school … not to mention the dozens of times afterwards. Her journeys took her not only to places of interest and excitement but also to those that required endurance and strength.

Mixing with the various cultures created a hands on knowledge that she incorporates into her books. To her credits, Sylvia has written fashion articles for the Los Angeles Times as well as script runs for fashion shows.

Fraley has created lay-outs for various advertising agencies and numerous free-lance projects. Making her home in the Ozarks by a very large lake, Sylvia enjoys outdoor activities as well as traveling and, of course, writing books that are, like the life she has led, filled with exciting events and unexpected endings.

Born during the Year of the Monkey in Utah, Ronald 'Buddy' WalksHorse was an 'August Child'. Growing up facing the Nuclear Threat, education came second to the daily drill of "Stop, Drop and Cover" in the event that The Bomb was dropped. This constant living on the edge installed a need for survival that has carried him throughout his life.

Ron is a caring and laid back type of person. He is Lakota Sioux Navy Vietnam Veteran, A.I.M.Member (Knee of '73 Veteran), Traditional American Indian Dancer and Professional Firefighter. He enjoys writing, painting and Western history and has degrees in Archeology and Art. Ron is of Welsh/Irish and Oglala Sioux Indian decent.

Ron has also been involved in the motion picture business since he was a small boy working on many productions on location in Utah with his grandfather and three uncles. His private venture "Dazend Movie Props-

Saving Our Movie History" searches out old wardrobe and props that are thrown out or simply discarded by the major studios, then cleans and restores these items to be displayed free of charge to the public at various film festivals, Western events and other gatherings.

Many Hollywood stars, upon hearing of this project have graciously donated items for the public to see. Ron also lectures on Motion Picture History dealing with the early westerns at various high schools, universities and other learning institutions.

Printed in the United States
120978LV00001B/43/P